When Mallo[ry]
her voice w[as]
"Are we saf[e]

Finn watched her, a strange feeling filling his chest. His voice was husky when he answered her. "Yes. We're safe until morning."

"Okay, then…" she whispered. Then, without looking at him, she lay down, pulling the sleeping bag over her. Turning on her side, she tucked her hands under her face and stared at the fire. Finn had to fight the urge to cross the room and tuck the sleeping bag around her, to brush that wealth of hair back from her face.

Fragile. She looked so fragile. And alone. And if there was anything he understood, it was how it felt to be alone. His jaw tightening, he forced himself to turn away.

It was going to be a long night.

He jammed on his Stetson and headed for the door.

A *damned* long night.

Dear Reader,

The year is almost over, but the excitement continues here at Intimate Moments. Reader favorite Ruth Langan launches a new miniseries, THE LASSITER LAW, with *By Honor Bound*. Law enforcement is the Lassiter family legacy—and love is their future. Be there to see it all happen.

Our FIRSTBORN SONS continuity is almost at an end. This month's installment is *Born in Secret*, by Kylie Brant. Next month Alexandra Sellers finishes up this six-book series, which leads right into ROMANCING THE CROWN, our new twelve-book Intimate Moments continuity continuing the saga of the Montebellan royal family. THE PROTECTORS, by Beverly Barton, is one of our most popular ongoing miniseries, so don't miss this seasonal offering, *Jack's Christmas Mission*. Judith Duncan takes you back to the WIDE OPEN SPACES of Alberta, Canada, for *The Renegade and the Heiress,* a romantic wilderness adventure you won't soon forget. Finish up the month with *Once Forbidden...* by Carla Cassidy, the latest in her miniseries THE DELANEY HEIRS, and *That Kind of Girl,* the second novel by exciting new talent Kim McKade.

And in case you'd like a sneak preview of next month, our Christmas gifts to you include the above-mentioned conclusion to FIRSTBORN SONS, *Born Royal,* as well as *Brand-New Heartache,* award-winning Maggie Shayne's latest of THE OKLAHOMA ALL-GIRL BRANDS. See you then!

Yours,

Leslie J. Wainger
Executive Senior Editor

Please address questions and book requests to:
Silhouette Reader Service
U.S.: 3010 Walden Ave., P.O. Box 1325, Buffalo, NY 14269
Canadian: P.O. Box 609, Fort Erie, Ont. L2A 5X3

The Renegade and the Heiress

JUDITH DUNCAN

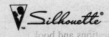
Silhouette®

INTIMATE MOMENTS™

Published by Silhouette Books

America's Publisher of Contemporary Romance

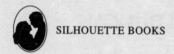

SILHOUETTE BOOKS

ISBN 0-373-27184-0

THE RENEGADE AND THE HEIRESS

Visit Silhouette at www.eHarlequin.com

Printed in U.S.A.

Books by Judith Duncan

Silhouette Intimate Moments

A Risk Worth Taking #400
Better Than Before #421
*Beyond All Reason #536
*That Same Old Feeling #577
*The Return of Eden McCall #651
Driven to Distraction #704
Murphy's Child #946
Marriage of Agreement #975
*If Wishes Were Horses... #1072
*The Renegade and the Heiress #1114

Silhouette Books

To Mother with Love 1993
"A Special Request"

*Wide Open Spaces

JUDITH DUNCAN

is married and lives, along with her husband, in Calgary, Alberta, Canada. A staunch supporter of anyone wishing to become a published writer, she has lectured extensively in Canada and the United States. Currently she is involved with the Alberta Romance Writers Association, an organization she helped found.

To Marlene Dunn and Donna Levia

You are both worthy of rubies and pearls,
but you know you can't depend on me for anything.
So here are a million thanks instead.
I couldn't have done it without you.

Prologue

The mellow earth tones of a fading Alberta autumn lay over the rolling hills, the burnt umbers and rusts of prairie grasses like vibrant brush strokes on a canvas. A few brightly colored leaves still clung to wild berry bushes and copses of aspen, the splotches of yellow and red bright against the stark canopy of naked branches. And off on the western horizon, the jagged gray fortresses of the Rocky Mountains rose up, their high peaks now capped with snow, the base skirted with dense coniferous forests. All of it blended together in a palette of color, the distant panorama framed by the bright blue sky.

It had been a long, perfect Indian summer, and even down the streets of Bolton, the speckled colors of fall still lay draped over the trees and shrubs, the remaining leaves clinging tenuously to the branches, waiting for a hard wind to strip them away and send them tumbling to the ground.

Old Joe Jones thought of himself as something of a poet, and as he drove down the narrow tree-lined street, he figured the big old elm trees looked like grand ladies, dressed in their golden finery. And even though it was nearly the end of October, the lawns still showed signs of green, like faded, worn velvet, but a hard frost had turned the flowers into black rotting skeletons.

Fall was a particular favorite time of year for him. He liked the autumn colors, he liked the way the mountains were so sharp and clear on the western horizon, and he liked the way the street was matted with a carpet of gold and orange leaves. And he especially liked the smell of burning leaves that wafted in from somewhere nearby.

That thick carpet of fallen leaves crunched under the tires of his battered pickup truck as he edged over to the sidewalk, taking care not to speed. He got a speeding ticket once forty-five years ago, and he didn't want another.

Joe passed by the cemetery on the other side of the street, the landscaped grounds surrounded by a wrought-iron fence and a hedge that turned all shades of red this time of year. The hedge was a beauty, but Old Joe figured that building the new senior citizens' lodge right across the street from the graveyard was not very considered thinking. Although he had to admit it was a mighty pretty spot, that cemetery. All them big trees and evergreens, and those real pretty shrubs, especially in the spring. And flowers. In the summer, it was like a picture out of a magazine, with rows and rows of bright flowers. But the frost had gotten them too, and the caretaker had already dug them out. It was still mighty pretty, though, and it made a man's heart lighter, looking at all that beauty.

Slowing down even more, he pulled up in front of the senior citizens' lodge, parking close to the curb. He had to get at just the right spot because he was picking up George Walters. George had one of them three-legged canes that kept getting caught in the cracks, and the old guy was nearly eighty-five. Joe himself was seventy-eight, but even though he was a whole lot younger than George, he didn't have the strength to get the retired farmer back up if he went down. Mostly because his pal was as round and as solid as one of them big market hogs George used to raise.

Today, he and George were going to the seniors' drop-in center for the shuffleboard tournament. George hadn't farmed in these parts, but his daughter lived in Bolton and George had moved into the lodge nearly a year ago. So he and Joe had become pals. And although he might be a bit unsteady on his feet, George could still lick the pants off anybody playing shuffleboard. That was why Joe liked him for a partner—they could clean the clocks of those yappy Campbell sisters without even breaking a sweat.

The other man was already waiting at the curb, leaning on his three-legged cane, a new John Deere cap on his head, his brown jacket zipped right up to the neck. Joe leaned across and opened the passenger door. "Howdy, George. All ready for this here big tournament?"

The other took his time climbing in, his joints stiff with arthritis. "Sure am."

Joe glanced across the street and saw a familiar vehicle turn into the driveway for the cemetery, then pass between the two stone cairns that supported the wrought-iron gates. George slammed the door, pointing a bony figure at the big black SUV. "See that fella over there at least once a month—big man. Ran into him once when I was out walking. Must stand six-three—black hair and eyes like a hawk. A fine-looking fella—but he has a nasty scar on his face. Solemn type, if you know what I mean."

His weathered face turning serious, Old Joe grasped the wheel and spoke, his tone almost reverent. "That's Finn Donovan."

George's voice had a wheezy, waspy tone to it. "And who is Finn Donovan?"

Joe gave him a disgusted look. "You've lived here nearly a year and you don't know who Finn Donovan is?"

George looked offended and was about to respond, but Old Joe didn't give him a chance. He saw himself as something of a storyteller as well as a poet, and he took the opportunity to show his stuff. "Finn Donovan is a legend in these here parts. And that there legend is as tall and as broad as he is."

Seeing he had George's full attention, Old Joe put his battered pickup in gear and eased away from the curb. "Although I don't expect there's anyone who could say they know him—or would consider him a friend. But if there's ever any kind of trouble in them mountains or in the backcountry—you know, like a plane crash or some of them hikers go missing, or if someone gets hurt real bad—Finn Donovan is the first person they call in. He has a way with danger."

George thumped his cane on the floor, his gnarled hand gripping the handle as he glared at Old Joe, sounding cantankerous. "Then how come you know so much about him?"

Feeling smug, Old Joe nodded. "Well, you see, I work for him—do all kinds of odd chores. Treats me real good. He even gave me a place to live—there was a little house on his property he didn't use no more. He's one of them outfitters—you know, a big game guide. And I'll tell you this. He's the best durned tracker around. And he knows every crack and cranny in that there backcountry. That there terrain is so treacherous only a handful ever venture into it."

Old Joe checked the intersection, then slowly turned onto the next street, checking his rearview mirror to make sure no one was coming up behind him. These young fools nowadays drove too fast. Repositioning his hands on the wheel, he continued his story. "Some say it's because he's one quarter Indian that he can find his way through them gorges and canyons and all that forest. Others who've traveled with him swear he's part shadow and part mountain goat, and has a compass for a brain. Others say he's so durned good at it because there's a darkness in him—that he's afeard of nothing."

George looked at Joe, interest glinting in his eyes. "Sounds like you know all about him."

Carefully skirting a pothole, Old Joe shook his head. "Nope. Can't say that I do. Figure no one knows a whole lot about Finn, and that's the way he likes it. I know he grew up in the backcountry. Raised by an uncle who had a string of packhorses—Frank used to hire himself out as a guide to them trophy hunters. But even back then, Finn kept to himself. His teachers said he was as smart as a whip."

Resting both his hands on the top of his cane, George stared out the window, a frown appearing on his face. "You know. Now that you mention it, I recollect my daughter telling me about this outfitter who ended up in jail. Is that the same fella?"

Joe slowed for the school zone, pressing on the brakes when he reached the posted sign, the bright autumn sunlight splintering through the crack in his windshield. He didn't want another damned ticket. No siree. His pace slowed to well below the limit, he answered. "Yep. That's the one. It's common knowledge that he killed a man—must have been fifteen or sixteen years ago. Some say it was self-defense, others say it was done in a hard, cold rage. Didn't know him all that well myself back then, but there was common agreement that Roddy Bracken had it coming."

Old Joe turned onto the street where the drop-in center was located, passed the fire hydrant, then eased into the parallel parking spot under the big old poplar tree. Putting on the emergency brake, he switched off the ignition, watching as the Campbell sisters made their way up the steps of the building. Durned old biddies. Always stirring up trouble.

George spoke up, that same wheezy, waspy tone in his voice. "So are you going to tell me the rest of this here story or not?"

Old Joe looked at him, puffing out his chest. He liked nothing better than telling stories, and he was pretty durned good at it. And although he'd never say so, he liked gossip as well as the next one.

"Well," he said, leaning back in the seat, "as the story goes, there'd always been bad blood between Finn and Roddy. Even as youngsters they had it in for one another. But as soon as Finn was old enough, he lit out."

He paused, trying to recollect, drawing on his trusty memory. "Seems to me he ended up working in some kind of construction—some big overseas project where the big money was. Anyhow, every once in a while, he'd turn up here, and he'd do a little guiding for his uncle." He leaned forward and took the keys out of the ignition and dropped them in his shirt pocket, then looked at his companion. "But it wasn't until he came back for good, with enough money to buy a place and set himself up as a guide that the bad blood between them two got stirred up again."

George took a bag of peppermints out of his pocket and offered Old Joe one, then nodded his head, prodding his friend to continue. Old Joe did. "Sally Logan was the kindergarten teacher—one of them sweet girls who had a kind word for everybody. She grew up here in Bolton—only child of Irene and Marvin Logan—and there wasn't a soul who didn't like her. Anyhow, Roddy had been after her for years, but she wouldn't give him the time of day. Then Finn showed up back in town, and she fell head over heels, and married him instead.''

Old Joe dragged his thumb across his mouth, his expression altering. ''Everyone knew that Roddy had started packing a whole new grudge against Finn once that happened, but no one could have figured on the outcome.''

George thumped his cane on the floor. ''Now don't leave me hanging here. What happened?''

Joe sighed, staring out the window, then shook his head, recollecting. ''Roddy came from big money, and he was spoilt rotten—had a cocky attitude. But that attitude turned mean and ugly after Sally married Finn. And one weekend…''

Old Joe hesitated, sobered by the awful recollection. It had been bad. Real bad. Knowing his friend was waiting for the rest, he drew in a deep breath and squared his shoulders. ''One weekend Finn had taken a group of rich Americans into the mountains on a fishing trip. Roddy got all fueled up on booze and drugs, and he showed up at Finn's little house in town, and he raped that pretty young wife of his. When Finn got back and found out what had happened, he got Sally settled in the hospital, then he went after Roddy. I hear fury was like a wild thing in him. Some of them that was there testified that Roddy pulled a knife first and slashed Finn's face. Then after there were some whisperings that Finn landed the first punch.''

Shaking his head, Old Joe rubbed his thumb against the worn spot on the steering wheel, sobered by the recollections. ''But as to what really happened, no one ever really said. One thing for sure—Finn killed him. Broke his neck and tossed him halfway across the street afore anyone could stop him.''

Old Joe paused and stared off into space, recalling the dark history. Finally he took a breath and spoke. "It caused a real ruckus in the community. No one had much use for Roddy. And Sally—well, Sally was like one of them angels you see on the top of a Christmas tree—something pure and innocent about her." Old Joe shook his head, thinking back. "There was general agreement that Roddy had it coming for what he did, but folks were still pretty uneasy around Finn. There was something about him—something what made folks walk soft around him."

George stuck another peppermint in his mouth, his expression considering, then he spoke. "Well, if it was self-defense, how come he got sent to prison?"

Old Joe gave a small shrug. "Don't really know. Some said it was the Bracken money that put Finn behind bars—some figured it was because Finn showed no remorse. But whatever the reason, Finn did eight years for manslaughter."

George nodded. "A terrible thing. Terrible. Did his wife wait for him?"

Feeling a heavy weight in his chest, Joe rubbed his calloused hand around the steering wheel. His voice was very gruff when he spoke. "Well, she did and she didn't. Finn's appeal was denied, and he was hauled off to a maximum-security prison. Then about a month after he was put away, that girl was killed when her car went over an embankment. No one really knew if it was an accident, or if she just couldn't face life without him—or if maybe she blamed herself for what happened to him. But the truth was, she was behind the wheel when it went over the edge, and they said she was going a fair clip." Old Joe shook his head, recalling the funeral. Things like that weren't supposed to happen in a place like Bolton. That sort of darkness wasn't supposed to touch a small town, but it had. And the ripples were felt far and wide—maybe folks still felt the effects.

As much for himself as for George, he felt compelled to finish the story. "Old man Bracken eventually drank himself to death and Sally's folks moved to the coast. And just when most everyone had put it behind them, Finn got out of jail." What happened after that, Old Joe had seen with his own eyes, how folks couldn't quite look Finn Donovan in the eye. Maybe out of shame for what happened. Maybe out of guilt because no one had reined Roddy in before. Or maybe, Old Joe figured, because no one could face the man. But the truth was that folks gave Finn Donovan a wide berth after he came home. Maybe because of the ugly scar across his face or the cold, flat look in his eyes.

Resting his weight on his cane, George spoke. "You have to wonder why he came back here, after all that happened."

Joe shrugged. "I expect because he had roots here. When he first came back, I used to hear things from his uncle. Like how he'd bought a big chunk of property just off the main road to Kananaskis Country. I heard he was building a log cabin on the place, and then somebody told me he was restoring the old log cabins that were already there. Then the fella at the lumberyard blabbed it around that he had put a new roof on the old log barn." Joe took off his cap and combed his fingers through his thinning hair, then replaced his cap. "Yep, when he first came back, there were all kinds of rumors going around. There was one that when he was in jail, that he'd invested the money he got from the sale of their little house. Some folks say he made a killing on some gold shares. Then it got out that he bought a string of horses from the McCall brothers and he was back in business. But to be real honest, I don't think anyone really knew for sure what he was up to. After his uncle died, the talk slowed to a trickle.'' He looked out the window, watching a cat stalking something in the long grass beside the drop-in center. ''But we'd hear about him from time to time—when something happened in the back-country, and he'd be brought in to help out.''

He met his old friend's gaze. ''I started working for him about five years ago—must be five years—I know he was thirty-seven when he hired me. And all I can tell you is that Finn Donovan doesn't show his cards to anyone. Folks still speculate, but the facts are a muddle,'' he said. Then drawing on his skill as a poet, he added, ''It's all twisted by time an' tainted by fiction. But he's pulled a lot of people out of that backcountry. And his reputation as a tracker is part of that there legend. And it's kept alive by the retelling.''

But there were some things Old Joe didn't tell his shuffleboard partner. He didn't tell him that he had the feeling that Finn Donovan knew he cast a long shadow in the ranching community, and that was one of the reasons he kept to himself. Old Joe knew that sometimes in the winter, when the nights were dark and cold, Finn Donovan would take off for warmer climes. And, Old Joe suspected, warm bodies. He figured that it had taken his boss a lot of years to disconnect from the past. And that he wanted to keep it that way. As Old Joe saw it, Finn Donovan lived from season to season.

The cemetery stretched across a rise of land, opening it up to a view of the mountains, the trees along the drive still golden with the last of the autumn foliage. Finn Donovan settled his black low-crowned Stetson on his head as he got out of his SUV, then reached across and retrieved a spray of perfect pink roses off the passenger seat. Slamming the door behind him, he walked between the rows of headstones, the flowers clutched in one hand, his expression somber as he thought about this pilgrimage. He wondered where the last year had gone.

The scent of autumn hung in the crisp clean air, underscored by the faint smell of burning leaves and the sweet fragrance of the roses. Reaching the small white marble headstone tucked in between two lilac bushes, he crouched down, brushing away the fallen leaves.

Sally Lynn Donovan, beloved wife and daughter.

Experiencing the familiar hollowness in his chest, Finn took off his hat and carefully placed the spray against the white marble. She would have been thirty-seven today. He couldn't imagine her at thirty-seven. She had been so young when she died—only twenty-two—and she had remained young and full of life in his mind. But after fifteen years, he could no longer recall her image, and that made the empty feeling in his chest expand. His sweet, sweet Sally. It had been so long ago, it was almost as if that part of his life had never happened.

Getting to his feet, he repositioned his hat on his head and stared at the grave for another moment. Then he turned and started back toward his truck, the fallen leaves crunching beneath his feet. He looked toward the western horizon, checking to see if there was a weather system moving in against the Rocky Mountains. He wanted good weather. First thing tomorrow, he was heading out into those mountains to restock and repair the line shacks he used as base camps on his most frequently used routes. It was a trip he made every fall. Sometimes he wondered why he did it. Other times, he knew exactly why.

Chapter 1

The weather did hold, and Wednesday morning dawned bright and clear. There was still a touch of frost hanging in the air as Finn reined his big buckskin gelding around and headed up the trail behind the barn. His dog Rooney nosed through the underbrush, his head down tracking some scent. The packhorse, all loaded down with supplies, plodded along behind him.

If he had special-ordered it, Finn couldn't have asked for a better day to head out. Not a cloud in the sky, the air crisp and clean, aspens still cloaked in gold, the rugged countryside so beautiful it made his chest hurt. Dried fallen leaves crunched beneath Gus's freshly shod hooves as they passed through a thick stand of poplar, their passage startling a huge raven off the trail ahead. It was the kind of day where a man should be able to fill his lungs and savor being alive. But for some reason, the brightness of the day left Finn feeling even more empty than usual. For more years than he cared to remember, he'd been making this trip. And over the years, it had turned into a kind of spiritual pilgrimage—a time to think, a time to assess and evaluate, a time to try and locate some small kernel of peace within himself. But finding even a trace of that inner contentment was becoming harder and harder to do. He wasn't even sure what he hoped to find in himself anymore.

Guiding Gus around a shale face, Finn hardened his jaw and studied the jagged gray barrier rising up in his path. Maybe he was just like those mountains. So damned hardened and dead inside, there was nothing left.

It was a long, empty ride. By the third day out, the skies had turned dark and somber, and the wind kept changing direction. A sure sign that something ugly was building in the mountains. Finn had spent the first night and the entire second day at the first line shack, making repairs to the roof, stocking the shelves with nonperishables and chopping a supply of wood. It was a little after noon when he headed out, and by the time he reached the old tree shattered by lightning, a weather front had moved in. The sky had gotten heavier and more ominous, and the dense, heavy clouds huddled low, with the wind beginning to shift and moan.

It was midafternoon when the first snowflakes started to spiral down, and Finn shifted in the saddle, the thick flakes catching in his eyelashes and graying the landscape. Squinting against the falling snow, he flipped up the collar of his fleece-lined coat, then turned to check on Trouper. The packhorse followed without a lead, and the piebald was plodding along behind, his gait slightly off from a crooked shoulder. The corner of Finn's mouth lifted just a little. Trouper was probably the most miserable piece of horseflesh he'd ever laid eyes on—thick neck, huge head with mulelike ears, hooves the size of dinner plates, and a thin, stubby tail.

But in spite of all his bad conformation, Finn wouldn't have traded him for a sack of gold. Trouper was the best packhorse, bar none, that he had in his stable. He was as surefooted as a goat, had better mountain sense than most humans, and was as wily as a coyote. If Finn ever needed to get out of a bad situation, all he had to do was turn the horse around, smack him on the rump and let the big piebald lead him home.

A smile still tugging at his mouth, Finn straightened in the saddle, angling his head against the falling snow, using the wide brim of his Stetson to keep the snow out of his eyes. He checked the underbrush, then whistled for Rooney. The dog appeared on the trail in front of him, tail wagging, his eyes bright. Rooney was mostly German shepherd, with a few other strains mixed in, and the dog loved these outings. Finn figured that between Trouper and Rooney, he had every contingency pretty much covered.

Finn guided the buckskin around a thick knot of twisted roots, the gust of cold air funneling down around him. Pulling his collar higher, he wondered why in hell he continued to do this—to make this ride every fall. He was getting too old for this crap. And on top of his current disinclination, he did not like the low, ominous sound of the wind.

The buckskin had to lunge up the last steep leg of the trail, and when they broke into a small clearing, Finn reined up, squinting against the whiteness as he studied the sky. The rugged landscape was nearly obscured by the falling snow, the outcroppings of granite and the trunks of trees like ghost shadows in the gloomy whiteness. An eerie silence had settled like a thick blanket, muffling even the sounds of the horse's breathing. He didn't like the feel of it, and he didn't like the way the wind kept shifting. Nor did he like the way the snow was coming down. Unless he missed his guess, there was a helluva storm brewing, and it was the kind of warning anyone who knew these mountains would never ignore. Especially when the second line shack was still a good day's ride away.

His mount tossed his head and pulled on the reins, then dropped his head and began grazing on thin clumps of grass now coated with white. Within seconds, the gelding's black mane was thickly dusted with the big wet flakes.

Allowing the horse his head, Finn rested his arms on the saddle horn and stared off into the distance, his expression fixed with consideration. He didn't like the look of it. Didn't like the feel of it. And it wasn't as if he had to complete the trip—and he sure as hell didn't relish getting caught out here in an early blizzard. This trip was mostly for his own peace of mind.

He studied the scene for a moment longer, then made up his mind. The smart thing to do was turn around and head home. His decision made, he reined his mount around, giving a spoken command to the packhorse.

Their tracks were already covered by the time he crossed the narrow draw, and Finn settled in for a long, miserable ride, the dampness like a cold, wet blanket around him.

The snow continued to fall as Finn backtracked, the sky growing heavier and heavier. He tipped his hat lower on his head, then pulled the collar tighter around his neck and snapped it closed as he guided Gus onto the old goat trail which traversed a rocky ridge. Below was the fast moving river, the water cold and gray and dangerous. It felt as if the temperature had dropped ten degrees, and Finn hunched in the warmth of his coat.

Rooney appeared from the underbrush, his brown-and-black coat dusted with white, his tail arched over his back. He sniffed along the trail, then started across the ridge, his head low, tracking some critter as he trotted ahead of Finn. Suddenly the dog stopped and cocked his ears, turning his head into the wind, his body going perfectly still. Rooney held that pose for a split second; then he dropped his head and emitted a low growl. Finn watched the dog, his expression tightening.

Rooney was as much a legend as his master—a natural tracker and as close to human as any dog could get. He had been on more rescue missions than Finn could count, and just two months before, he'd successfully tracked a kid lost in the bush. He was no ordinary dog. And when he went on alert like that, Finn paid attention.

Finn rode along the ledge to where Rooney was standing, then reined up, turning his mount for a clear view. His expression fixed, he let his gaze slowly drift over the scene below him. Squinting against the relentlessly falling snow, he scanned the scene again, his attention arrested by a shadow of movement on the far side of the river. His muscles tensing, he shifted his head slightly, allowing his peripheral vision to catch the movement again, then he focused on the spot. No doubt about it—someone was there, a barely visible figure stumbling through the heavy veil of falling snow.

A cold prickle feathered along the back of his neck, and Finn narrowed his eyes. Not only should there not be anyone in that area, something was also definitely wrong. Yanking off his doeskin gloves, Finn twisted in the saddle, flipped open one saddlebag and took out the case holding his binoculars. He yanked the powerful binoculars free, then lifted them to his eyes, swearing when he couldn't locate his target through the heavily falling snow. Finally he got a fix, and he went dead still.

The stumbling figure was a woman, dressed only in a dark green sweater and slacks, with something black wrapped around her head. And the reason she was having so much trouble keeping her feet under her was because it appeared that her hands were tied together in front of her. And even at this distance, Finn could recognize fear. Jamming the binoculars back in the case, he wheeled his mount around, his voice sharp as he gave a hand signal indicating the distant figure. "Rooney. Go. Go find." He wheeled Gus around again, giving Trouper the command to stay, then he spurred the gelding toward the narrow twisting trail that led down from the ridge, his expression grim, an ugly feeling unfolding in his gut.

It was pretty damned obvious she was on the run from something or somebody—and that was bad enough. But it was going to take him at least half an hour to get to her— half an hour through falling snow and dropping temperatures, and terrain that was so dangerous it was an accident just waiting to happen. But there was no shortcut. He had to get down from the damned ridge, then fight his way through the dense bush to the old wash below and find a reasonably safe, shallow place to ford the cold, churning river.

A series of barks signaled Rooney's movements, and Finn settled his weight in the saddle, his face even grimmer. Out of habit he loosened the rifle in the scabbard, a hard knot in his belly as he urged his horse downward, ducking to miss some low-hanging branches. It was going to be one hell of a ride. He just hoped he got her before whoever was after her did.

Pushing his mount and his horsemanship to the limit, Finn battled his way through the rough terrain, one forbidding thought replaying in his brain. If she were to lose her bearings and stumble down the steep bank and into the river, she wouldn't stand a chance in hell. And he wouldn't stand a chance in hell of getting her out.

Every minute seemed like an hour, and by the time he finally found a safe, shallow place to ford the churning, glacier-fed river, a good thirty minutes had passed. And by the time Gus scrambled up the bank, the snow was falling so heavily, Finn could barely make out anything.

Breaking through a thick stand of trees on the periphery of the natural meadow, Finn squinted into the blur of white, his heart missing two solid beats when he spotted her on the ground, Rooney whining and nuzzling her head.

Dread shooting through him, Finn pushed his mount into a gallop. Reaching her, he reined up, and he was out of the saddle before the gelding stopped moving. She was lying there, so still. So very still.

Dropping to his knees beside her, he stripped off his gloves, his frozen breath hanging in the air as he pressed his fingers against the carotid artery in her neck. He found a pulse, and a feeling of relief pumped through his chest. She had a pulse. And he could see her breath in the cold air. That at least gave him something to work with.

Rooney whined and nuzzled her again, and Finn pushed the dog away, his voice gruff when he spoke. "Down, boy. Give me some room here."

The figure on the ground stirred, and with a massive effort pushed herself up, the fingers on one bound hand closing around a grapefruit-sized rock on the ground. Realizing she had every intention of slugging him, Finn grasped her bound wrists, humor lifting one corner of his mouth. If she had enough juice left to slug him, she was in better shape than he expected. Muttering something, she tried to jerk free from his hold. As she gave a savage twist, the black garment on her head—the thing that looked like a black hangman's hood—slipped over her eyes, partially blinding her.

Grasping her wrists in one hand, Finn tightened his hold, not about to take any chances with the rock. "Easy, now. Easy," he murmured quietly, then reached out and pulled the head cover off, releasing a cascade of long, wild red hair.

Still trying to fight her way free, she gave her arms another hefty jerk, grinding out the kind of cusswords he rarely used. Half amused by her tenacity, but with one eye still on the rock she had clutched between her hands, he grasped her arms, holding her immobile. Okay. So he'd give her a minute, until she realized he was not a threat; then he would try to talk some sense into her.

Dragging herself to her knees, she shook the curly mop of hair out of her eyes, then lifted her head and glared at him. She might as well have hit him with the rock. Finn stared at her, his pulse coming to a complete stop. He felt as if an avalanche had broken loose in his chest. With the snow falling around her like something mystical—and that cascade of fantastic hair—it was as if she were right out of some childhood fable. Snowflakes caught in her bright copper hair like perfect jewels, and the sensation in Finn's chest expanded. She was almost too much to comprehend. With her face sprinkled with freckles, and with her flashing eyes the exact color of spring moss—she reminded him of the wild Celtic warriors that were part of his Irish heritage. It was, he thought dazedly, as if a piece of ancient history had suddenly landed right in his lap.

For an instant, it was almost as if she were transfixed—like a deer caught in headlights, the undercurrent of terror paralyzing her. Then fire and fight appeared in those wide eyes, and she tried to twist free again.

Finn tightened his hold and spoke again, his voice low and gruff. "It's okay. It's okay—I'm not going to hurt you."

As if finally realizing it was a total stranger who was holding her, she let go of the rock, then covered her face with her bound hands, a violent reaction shuddering through her. "Oh, God. Oh, God," she whispered brokenly over and over again, her body folding into itself, as if all her strength was gone.

It was as if her words broke Finn's own trance, and he hauled in a deep breath. Roughly snapped back to reality, he quickly brushed the snow off her hair, not wanting it to melt and leave her head wet. His expression tightened. There was something wrong—very wrong—with her eyes. They were dilated, almost as if she'd been hit on the head— or heavily drugged. Recognizing the sluggishness of her movements as the onset of hypothermia, he finished brushing the snow off her, then pulled her against him, trying to shelter her with his body. Pressing her head against his shoulder, he wrapped his arms around her. "It's okay," he whispered, his voice husky. "It's okay. I've got you."

A sob broke from her and she huddled into him, and Finn tightened his hold, trying to fold her in his own warmth. As if handling a terrified animal, he rubbed her back. His tone quiet and calm, he spoke again. "The name's Finn Donovan." Very carefully he turned her so he could get at her bound hands. "And I'm going to check you over to make sure you're not hurt anywhere. Then I'm going to get the knife off my belt, and I'm going to cut the bindings on your wrists, okay?" The only response he got was another ragged intake of air, and he pressed her head more firmly against him, giving her a little shake. "Okay? I don't want you to be scared. I'm just going to check you over, then I'm going to cut you loose."

He knew it was a rotten thing to do, to leave her hands tied, but he didn't want to give her a chance with that damned rock again. Keeping his touch slow and light, he checked her head, looking for any bumps that might explain the glazed look in her eyes. All he found was a couple of lacerations on the back of her head and some scrapes. And the only other injuries were some deep scratches on her hands. Reaching back under his coat to retrieve the knife in the leather sheath strapped to his belt, he spoke again, using the same tone he used on a spooked horse. "I'm not going to hurt you, honey. I just need to use it to cut the bindings, okay?"

As if the last of her strength had just deserted her, she shuddered and went slack in his arms. "Okay," she answered weakly, her voice soft and thick.

Bringing the knife from under his coat, Finn cut the thick layers of silver duct tape binding her wrists. A strange feeling rose up in his belly when he pulled the tape away, and discovered that whoever had bound her had been in such a hurry, they had taped tightly over her watch, and her skin was purple and bruised from the pressure. His expression hardened by unexpected anger, he replaced the knife in the sheath, snapping the cover closed. Then he awkwardly removed his thick coat, trying to keep one arm around her.

With the sheepskin lining still warm from his body heat, he wrapped it around her, tucking the collar tightly around her neck. Then as if dressing a rag doll, he stuffed her arms into the sleeves. He was a big man, and the coat enveloped her, the sleeves long enough to cover her hands.

It was as if his tucking the coat around her broke through her shock, and she finally realized she was truly safe. Grasping the down-filled vest he had on underneath his coat, she curled into his arms. "Oh, God, oh God," she sobbed over and over again.

For some reason, her hanging on to him made Finn's heart hurt. Tight-faced with concern, he buttoned up the coat, tucking the folds snugly around her, then he spoke, stroking more snow from her hair. "I don't know what's going on," he said, his tone husky, "but whatever it is, I think we'd better get you out of here."

Making sure the coat was tucked firmly around her, he scooped her up, then got to his feet. The moment he straightened with her, she wrapped her arms around his neck and hung on, another sob breaking loose. It was as if the exposure to warmth set something off in her, and she started to shiver violently. A strange sensation climbing up his chest, Finn turned and started toward Gus, immediately recognizing two things. One: she was not a tiny little thing. And two: they were in a very bad situation. If he'd had any doubts before, he was now damned sure she was running from someone, and that alone was bad enough, especially when the clearing was so exposed. But the worst part was that they didn't have many hours of daylight left. And it was clear that she was definitely in no shape to spend a night, as had been his original plan, in a makeshift shelter. Which meant at least a three-hour ride back to the first line shack.

As if aware of what was going on in Finn's head, Rooney remained on guard. The dog stood behind Finn and stared off across the clearing, his ears pricked, his attention fixed, as if watching for someone to appear. Knowing the dog would give him advance warning, Finn concentrated on the redhead. A funny feeling unfolded in his chest as he shifted his hold, and she immediately tightened hers. He gave himself a few seconds for the sensation to settle; then he tucked his head against hers and spoke, his throat tight. "Do you think you could stand up if you held on to old Gus here? I need to get some extra gear out of the saddlebags for you."

She didn't respond for a second; then she gave a single nod, but she didn't loosen her grip. The corner of Finn's mouth lifted just a little. He gave her a little squeeze and spoke again, his voice gruff. "You're going to have to let go of me, honey. I don't think this will work if you keep holding on.''

A weak, muffled response came from the vicinity of his neck. ''Don't call me honey.''

Finn's expression relaxed into a wry smile. At least she had some fight left in her. That had to be a good sign. Making sure she was sheltered by the horse, he carefully set her down, the wind whipping her long hair across his face. It felt like strands of silk, and another avalanche took off in his chest. He had forgotten how silky a woman's hair could feel.

Avoiding her gaze, he took her hand and tucked it under the cinch so she had something warm and solid to hang on to. Then he went around to the other side of the horse and took two pairs of heavy wool socks, a black wool cap and a heavy scarf out of the saddlebag. The snow was coming down so heavily that he could barely see the trees at the far side of the clearing, and his expression sobered as he latched the buckles back up on the saddlebag. Now the heavy snowfall was a blessing. As long as it continued, that snow was going to provide excellent cover.

The extra clothing in his hand, he rounded the horse again. She was standing with one hand grasping the saddle horn, and she was weaving around like a Saturday night drunk, trying to get one foot into the stirrup. Experiencing a small flicker of amusement, Finn stuffed the gear in his pocket. Then he reached out and steadied her. At least she was aimed in the right direction.

Knowing there was only one way to do this, he stepped beside her, caught her leg and hoisted her up. She grasped the saddle horn and steadied herself, her eyes closed and her face very white, her whole body wracked with shivers.

Shutting down his expression, Finn yanked the socks out of his pockets. Her shoes were very fine leather, and know-

ing that wet leather was a better insulator than no leather
at all, he pulled both pairs of socks over her shoes. The
long cuffs of the socks stretched almost to her knees. He
finished pulling on the last sock, and he was pulling up the
cuff when she whispered, her voice thick. "Thank you."

One hand still resting on her leg, he glanced up at her.
She was hanging on to the saddle with both hands, and it
was clear that she was fighting with all she had to remain
conscious. His gaze narrowing, he took another hard look
at her eyes, and Finn experienced a cold feeling deep in
his belly. He was no doctor, but he was willing to bet his
best horse that she was fighting the effects of heavy-duty
drugs. Which put her in even more danger. He experienced
another cold sensation. They were both sitting ducks out
here in the middle of the clearing.

Catching a glimmer of fear in her expression, he forced
a half smile onto his face. "You're welcome." He undid
the wool army blanket from the back of his saddle, and
tucked it under her arms. Then grasping the reins and horn
in one hand, he put his foot in the stirrup and swung up
behind her. Gus tossed his head and did a side step in
response to their combined weight, and Finn corrected him
with a small jerk of the rein and a sharp command to whoa.

Bracing her weight against him, Finn pulled the wool
cap over her head, then wound the scarf over the top of
that. Shifting her legs so she was sitting sidesaddle, he
wrapped the blanket around her, covering her from head to
foot.

It was as if his covering her up allowed her to let go,
and he felt her sag against him, her head lolling against his
shoulder. He would have thought she was out cold, but she
grasped the back of his belt, as if she needed something to
hang on to.

His face hardening, he shifted her slightly so he could

support her weight with one arm, then lifted the reins and clucked to Gus. An ominous feeling—one that slid like cold fingers down the back of his neck—made his jaw harden even more. He felt as if he had a gun pointed at his back. A long time ago, he had learned to respect his gut feelings—and his gut was telling him to get the hell out of that meadow and across the river, where they would be less exposed.

Giving Rooney a quiet command to heel, Finn rode through the clearing, the falling snow sticking to the trunks of the aspens and coating the rocky outcroppings. Visibility was maybe two hundred feet and getting worse by the minute. It was a damned good thing he knew this area. With conditions the way they were, it would be very easy to lose his bearings. And getting lost was the last thing they needed.

The wind gusted, sending the snow swirling in front of him, and Finn squinted against it, the landmarks nearly impossible to see in the near-whiteout conditions. But he wasn't going to complain about that. If landmarks were invisible, so were they. And right now invisibility afforded them the best protection of all.

Another gust of wind flurried around them, pulling some of her hair loose and feathering it across Finn's mouth. Tightening his arm around her, he transferred the reins to that hand, then tucked the blanket more snugly around her head. She muttered something and stirred and Finn pressed her head more firmly against him and spoke, his voice low and gruff. "It's okay. I've got you." He tucked a loose flap of blanket under her head, then spoke again. "It's going to get a little rough here. We have to ford the river, and the banks on either side are pretty steep. So just hang on, okay?"

He felt her hand shift on his belt. "Okay," she whispered, and Finn could feel her tighten her grip and fight to remain conscious, but the fight only lasted seconds, and she went slack in his hold. Locking his jaw against her vulnerability, he scanned the rough terrain through the falling snow, trying to spot the huge boulder that marked the location where he'd forded the river. Now all he had to do was get her from this side of the river to the other, keeping her dry in the process, and they'd be relatively safe.

With the ford hidden under boiling white water, the river provided a formidable natural barrier. No one in his right mind would even consider crossing it. No one, except Finn.

They made it across safely, although Finn got a shot of adrenaline when Gus stumbled once in midstream, and it was all Finn could do to hold on to her. And there was another tense moment going up the other bank, the falling snow, the steepness of the riverbank and the extra weight testing the horse's strength and agility to the limit.

But once in the impenetrable cover of the trees, Finn relaxed a bit, knowing their tracks would be obliterated within minutes. And with the river between them and whoever she was running from, he felt reasonably sure they were safe—at least for the time being.

Finn whistled for the packhorse, hoping that it wouldn't take the animal too long to find him. Finn had been well schooled in the unpredictable treachery of the mountains—especially this time of year—and he always carried spare gear. As far as his own welfare was concerned, he could manage with what he had on. He had dressed for the weather—thermal underwear, heavy wool shirt and an insulated vest, his felt Stetson. But he was going to have to get more clothes on her—and something hot into her, or she could end up in big trouble.

Rooney appeared through the trees, shaking water from his thick coat, his ears pricked. Finn's expression eased a little. The dog was totally pleased with himself, and it almost looked as if he were grinning. The weight in his arms pulled on his shoulder, and Finn focused on his passenger. Shifting her weight so she was more balanced in the saddle, Finn tucked the blanket tighter around her. Now all he had to do was get her back to the line shack.

They had just rounded the bend in the trail when there was a sound of something moving through the bush, then a few seconds later Trouper appeared on the trail behind them. Finn experienced another flicker of humor. It was as if the damned horse knew exactly where they were headed.

The heavy canopy of trees provided some shelter from the falling snow, and now distanced from the sound of the river, it was as if the whole world was enveloped in a peculiar stillness.

Gus stumbled on some loose shale, the sharp movement jarring his passenger to consciousness. She began to struggle weakly, and it dawned on Finn that the snug folds of the blanket wouldn't feel a whole lot different from the black hood. Telling Gus to whoa, Finn spoke, his voice calm and quiet. "Hey. It's okay. I've got you. Everything is okay." Shifting his hold, he peeled the blanket away, his insides giving a funny twist when she opened her eyes and stared at him, confusion transfixing her. Needing to reassure her, he managed a lopsided smile. "How are you doing in there?"

She stared at him a second, then as if realizing who he was, she closed her eyes. Then she swallowed hard and looked up at him, her eyes still glazed, her pupils dilated. "I'm fine. But I'm really thirsty," she whispered.

He gave her another half smile. "Tell you what. There's a place just up ahead that's really sheltered. We'll pull up there, and I'll build a fire, then make you something hot to drink."

Her eyes widened and she tried to struggle free, panic claiming her. "No!" she muttered, trying to break loose. "No."

Gus started to toss his head and sidestep, and Finn gave him a sharp command, aware that if she really started to fight him, they could both end up on the ground. And right now, that was the last place he wanted to be. Letting go of the reins, he locked his arms around her, holding her immobile. "Easy," he said, his voice husky. "Easy. It's okay."

She gripped his arm and hauled in a deep, uneven breath, then opened her eyes again. Staring at him, her gaze dark with fear, she tried to sit up, the black wool hat accentuating her fair skin. "No." She swallowed and abruptly closed her eyes again, as if suddenly very dizzy. Her face noticeably paler, she swallowed again and looked up at him. "No. We can't. If we—if we stop—" She forced in another deep breath and spoke again, her voice shaking. "If we stop, they'll find us."

Snow slid from one of the heavy spruce boughs overhanging the trail, plopping on the ground in front of them, and Gus tossed his head, his bridle jingling.

His expression very thoughtful, Finn stared down at the woman, studying her pale face, considering the pros and cons. Common sense told him to stop, caution warned him to move on. The hat covered her head down to her ears, but her thick, red hair hung past her shoulders, its copper color bright against the dull gray of the blanket. His expression sober, Finn again considered his charge. Then he spoke, his voice quiet. "We still have a good two-hour ride to shelter. And I think it would be a good idea if I got something hot into you."

Her movements very sluggish and her eyes shut, she

twisted her head. "No. Please," she beseeched. "If they find you—if they find you with me—they'll kill you too."

His expression fixed, Finn studied her, processing what she had said. He didn't like the sound of that—not one bit. And if that really was the case, he needed to get her as far away as possible from that small meadow. He had a spare mackinaw and a survival blanket packed in the gear on the packhorse, and he debated about getting them. Then he decided against it. With her all wrapped around him, she was plenty warm enough. And she had stopped shivering. Besides, she was so far out of it, he wasn't sure he'd be able to get her back on the horse if she slid off.

Turning her head so her face was against his neck, she let go a soft sigh and went slack again. Affected by that small show of trust, Finn carefully tucked the blanket around her, then made his decision. He never dismissed anyone's fear, and hers was very real. But the fact that she didn't seem to be suffering any serious effects from exposure was the deciding factor. And if they moved out now, they would be at the line shack before darkness settled in.

Satisfied that she was well enough insulated to contain her own body heat, he adjusted his position on the back of the horse. Hoping that Gus was up to carrying double through the rough terrain ahead of them, he picked up the reins and urged his mount forward. Now that she had voiced her fear, there were a dozen questions he wanted answers to. But those questions would have to wait. If he was going to get from Point A to Point B in this kind of country, while trying to hold on to a woman who was half out of it, he'd need to have his wits about him. With the snow coming down the way it was, making it even more treacherous underfoot, he couldn't afford to let his mind wander for even a moment, or they could both end up dead.

And he wasn't about to let that happen.

Chapter 2

It took just a little over three hours to get from Point A to Point B. A heavy twilight had settled in by the time Finn reached the narrow, twisting trail leading up to the cabin. The snow had stopped an hour earlier, and it had turned very still, with just a breath of air moving through the dense spruce and pine. It was so still that the branches remained heavily laden, the caps of snow still clinging to even the most fragile branches. The smell of pine hung in the cold, still air, and even in the fading light, Finn could see the tiny prints of blue jays in the unspoiled blanket of snow.

The snow was so thick, so undisturbed, it was as if a white cover had been draped over the entire landscape, the whiteness now tinged with the purple and blue shadows of the encroaching night. It was going to be one of those pitch-black nights, where the heavy cloud cover blocked out even a trace of starlight, and that suited Finn just fine. That kind of darkness would serve them well.

He wasn't too sure what was really going on with the

woman sagging heavily in his arms. After periodically coming to, then trying to fight her way out of the constraints of the blankets, she had finally gone quiet. And thank God for that. A couple of times she had put up such a struggle that he'd nearly lost her, and he was feeling the strain in his entire body.

But she had barely moved in the past hour, and the only thing that assured Finn she was still alive was the rise and fall of her chest. He couldn't tell if she'd just given in to whatever was in her system, or if she was genuinely asleep. But one thing for sure was that she was getting damned heavy. His left arm, the one that was bearing most of her weight, felt as if it was being slowly extracted from the socket, and his hand had been numb for at least forty minutes. And on top of all that, he was beginning to feel the cold. He had maybe a hundred yards to go—that was all.

As he guided Gus through the shallow stream adjacent to the cabin, he caught something on the air—something faint—something almost indistinguishable. Reining his mount to a full stop, he went still and turned his head, his expression intent as he listened. His tracker's senses finely tuned, he was finally able to extract a distant sound from the chilled silence. He shifted his head slightly, his expression tightening. A small plane—he narrowed his eyes and stopped breathing, listening intently—no, there were two, the sound far-off and barely discernible. But there were definitely two distinct sounds. And even with the distance distorting the faint stutters, he knew exactly where the planes were. They were flying over the narrow valley where he had found her—his wildcat in the snow.

Two planes indicated a search, which also indicated a downed plane. But until he got some answers from her, he refused to speculate.

Glad for the cover of both the trees and nightfall, Finn twisted around to make sure Trouper was right behind him, then he shifted around and nudged Gus into a walk. He glanced over toward the underbrush and spoke, his tone clipped with command. "Rooney, heel." The dog immediately obeyed, trotting along the path at Gus's shoulder, his ears suddenly pricked.

Shifting his weight to ease the cramp in his back, Finn glanced down at his cargo, the heavy dusk crowding in and obscuring the remaining light. So. Someone had called out a search party to look for her. He didn't like the feeling twisting in his belly. He didn't like it at all.

His expression set, Finn guided his mount through a narrow archway of trees, taking care not to disturb the snow clumped on the low-hanging branches. At least for tonight he could keep her out of harm's way. He'd worry about tomorrow later.

The dark hulking shape of the cabin appeared in the dusk, the tin roof capped with snow, a drift crouching against the single step. Finn walked Gus right up to the low overhang that sheltered the plank door, the weight of his burden pulling painfully at his shoulder. Dropping the reins to ground-tie the horse, he stiffly dismounted, using his good arm to hold her in the saddle. He was so damned sore and stiff, he felt as if he'd been thrown and trampled. He waited until his circulation was restored and the cramps in his legs eased; then he gave her a small tug, and she slid into his arms like a sack of oats. Now all he had to do was pack her inside.

It was pitch black in the cabin, and damned cold. In fact, it felt colder inside than out. He had boarded up the windows that morning, and it was as black as a cave inside, and he had to wait a moment for his eyes to adjust. Using what little illumination that came from outside, he crossed the small space and carefully laid her on one of the bare wooden bunks, her still form swaddled in the coat and blanket. The inside of the small cabin was planked with rough-hewn fir, the wood weathered and dark, aged by years of exposure. Extra supplies hung suspended in dark, green heavy plastic containers from the open pole rafters, the shapes bulky and irregular in the deepening twilight.

Stripping off his gloves, he went to the shelf by the door and found the stash of candles and matches in an old syrup can. He lit one and let liquid paraffin form, then dripped some of the melted wax onto the lid, the faint, wavering light swallowed by the heavy shadows and the dark weathered planking.

Fixing four candles in place, he set the makeshift candleholder on the battered wooden table, then turned back and latched the door, shutting out the cold and the fading dusk. Glancing at the form on the bunk to make sure she was still asleep, he gathered some kindling from the wood box and placed it in the old potbellied stove, then struck another match and put it to the tinder, assessing their situation as he waited for the bark to catch and flare. With the windows boarded up, there would be no light visible from outside, and with the cabin hidden beneath the heavy canopy of trees, it would be practically invisible from the air. But the most critical factor was that the falling snow had covered their tracks, making their trail invisible. And invisibility was exactly what they needed. At least until he knew what in hell was going on.

Leaving the door of the stove open to provide more light, he disconnected from those thoughts, making himself focus on the tasks at hand. The first thing on his list was to make sure he had a good fire going, then he'd have to go down to the creek for water. And after that, he was going to have to fix something to eat. One way or another, he was going to have to get some nourishment into her. Giving her one final glance, he headed for the door.

It was nearly dark by the time he returned from the creek. The horses were standing slack-hipped by the cabin, and he retrieved his saddlebags and draped them over one shoulder, then pulled the rifle from the scabbard on his saddle. He had no intention of leaving anything to chance.

Stamping the snow off his boots, he pushed the door open and entered the cabin, his expression altering when he saw that his houseguest was struggling to sit up. Still clearly dazed and unsteady, she dragged the scarf and hat off her head, then tried to thrash her way out of her blanket cocoon, her movements oddly uncoordinated. Finn kicked the door shut with his heel, the cold air from outside mixing with the scent of burning spruce pitch. He propped the rifle by the door and dropped the saddlebags beside it, then turned and set the pail by the stove. Not wanting to rush her, he removed his gloves and stuck them in the pocket of his vest, then crossed to her. Deliberately avoiding eye contact, he peeled away the blanket so she could get her arms free.

He felt her gaze on him; then she spoke, her voice very unsteady. "I can't remember your name."

He looked down at her, keeping his expression impassive as he answered her question. "Finn Donovan."

She stared up at him, her eyes wide with uncertainty; then she spoke again, her voice stronger, more assertive. "How come…how come you found me…what were you doing out there?"

Carefully, he draped her scarf over the head rail of the bunk, then met her gaze. "I'm an outfitter, and I take most of my clients out in this area. This is my line shack, and I was out securing my campsites for the winter. And I didn't find you. My dog did."

As if struggling to assimilate that information, she stared at him, the flicker from the fire glinting in the wild tumble of her hair. She stared at him a moment longer, then she tipped her head back and closed her eyes, and he saw the muscles in her throat contract. Finally she straightened her head and looked at him, an odd stricken look on her face. She swallowed again and spoke, a tinge of tightly contained panic in her voice. "Where am I?"

Tossing his gloves on the table, Finn answered her, knowing there was a helluva lot more to the question than those three words. He met her gaze, his own level. "You're in southwestern Alberta in the Rocky Mountains, just inside the Canadian border."

A shiver ran through her and she folded one arm across her middle, then covered her eyes. Even from eight feet away, Finn could feel the rigid tension in her. He continued to watch her, waiting for her to say something. When she didn't, he turned away and went back to the stove, annoyed with himself. One thing he knew how to do was mind his own business.

Sharply aware of both her presence and her silence, Finn dumped water from the pail into two smaller pots—one to heat up a couple of vacuum-packed stews he'd had in his saddlebags, the other for tea. As he set the pail on the floor, he heard the distant drone of a plane, only this time it was much closer. His expression altered. With darkness settled and in this kind of rough terrain, he knew they would have to call off the search soon. If it was a search. And he'd bet his boots it was.

The pots of water heating, he glanced over at her, the inadequate light casting that side of the cabin in deep shadows. She was sitting with her back against the wall, her hands slack in her lap, her head turned to one side, and it appeared that she had fallen asleep again. He knew he was speculating, and speculation was always dangerous, but it had to be drugs that had knocked her out like that. It was the only explanation.

With a dozen questions running through his mind, Finn picked up the rifle and went back outside and tended to the horses. It had started to snow again, the whiteness giving off an eerie light, and Finn checked the sky above the cabin to see if the rising smoke was detectable. Satisfied that they were safe, at least for the night, he lugged the tack, spare gear and extra supplies into the cabin, again propping his rifle by the door. He checked the sleeping woman, then fed Rooney his kibbles, the firelight from the open door on the stove flickering and dancing on the rough-hewn walls. He thought again about the planes he had heard, wondering who had called them out.

The cabin now warm, he stripped off his vest and set about fixing the meager meal, which consisted of opening the heated vacuum packs and dumping the contents back in the pot. Recalling that she had said she was thirsty when they were still on the trail, he stuck a spoon in his shirt pocket, then scooped a tin cup into the ice-cold water in the pail. With the pot in his other hand, he crossed to the bunk. Soundlessly he set the cup on the wooden slats and crouched down, studying the woman on the bunk.

The flickering flames in the stove cast her face in a soft light, banishing most of the shadows. She was sitting in the same position, with her head turned against the wall and her mouth slightly opened, presenting him with her unobstructed profile. Delicate features, full mouth, an aristocratic nose and long, long lashes. His expression sober, Finn assessed what he saw. All the evidence added up to money. The sweater she was wearing was cashmere, the studs in her ears were unquestionably diamonds, and just visible below the cuff of his sheepskin coat was the platinum wristwatch. And even if it weren't for all those obvious and visible markers, he would have suspected it anyway. He had dealt with enough high rollers in his business to recognize the signs. There was just that air about her, a nuance that reeked of priceless things. And even he could tell that her thick curly hair hadn't been styled in some discount cut-and-hack shop.

A flicker of light caught in her magnificent hair, and a funny, full feeling climbed up Finn's chest. Suddenly he felt very alone and solitary. Dragging his gaze away from her face, he wearily rolled his shoulders, his attention snagging on her left hand, which was lying motionless in her lap. No rings—no huge diamond solitaire, no wide platinum band, not even a telltale mark.

Realizing his thoughts were heading down a trail that didn't go anywhere, Finn gave his head a disgusted shake. He had no time for mental slips like that. Right now he had a job to do, and that was getting some hot food into her.

Schooling his expression, he grasped her shoulder and gave her a gentle shake, then spoke, his tone gruff. "You're going to have to open those eyes, Red. Supper is ready."

As if taking a massive effort on her part, she opened her eyes and turned her head, her gaze still slightly unfocused. She licked her lips, then spoke, her voice sounding rusty and a tiny bit belligerent. "Don't call me Red, either."

One corner of Finn's mouth lifted as he met her gaze, his amusement surfacing. This one had a bit of scrap in her; that was for sure. He handed her the tin mug, and she closed her eyes and drank the water as if parched with thirst; then she looked at him, her expression softening as she handed him the cup. "Thank you," she whispered, a husky quality in her voice.

Finn set the mug on the floor, then raised the pot he was

holding. "This restaurant isn't exactly in the best part of town, and it's damned short of amenities, so I'm afraid you're going to have to eat out of the pot."

She stared at him a moment; then she smiled, her eyes lighting up. She grasped the pot and took the spoon he offered. She met his gaze, her voice soft and husky when she responded. "With all those candles, it looks pretty darned first class to me." The firelight glimmered in her eyes and she smiled at him again. "But right now I couldn't care less about ambiance. I'm so hungry I could eat this bunk."

Finn gave her a lopsided grin and tapped the pot. "Well, have at it. It's not prime rib, but it goes down okay."

She took a mouthful and closed her eyes, reveling in the taste. "God, nothing has ever tasted this good." She savored it a split second longer; then she practically attacked the stew, her hunger obvious, her hair like fire around her face. Crouched on the floor, Finn watched her, amusement altering his expression. He'd bet his bottom dollar that right now, she'd give a starving wolf a run for his money.

Picking up the tin mug, he got to his feet and crossed to the stove. Fishing two tea bags out of another can, he tossed them into the boiling water, then set the pot aside, giving it a chance to steep. A burst of fragrance was released from the perforated bags, the smell kicking off his own appetite. Right now, *he* could give a starving wolf some competition.

Using a glove as a pot holder, he filled her mug and a second one, then carried both over to the bunk, setting hers on the bare slats. Lifting his mug, he took a sip, watching her eat, wondering how long she'd gone without food. The way she was going after that stew, it had to be quite a while.

As if feeling his gaze on her, she looked up, her expression going very still when she saw he had only a mug in his hand. Then she abruptly clapped her hand over her face, obviously realizing the pot held shared portions. "Lord, I'm such a dummy." Dropping her hand, she looked up at him, and even in the inadequate light, he could tell that she was blushing. "I'm not normally such a pig," she said, extending the pot to him and looking sheepish. Then she gave him a warped smile. "I get a little territorial about food."

Folding his arms, Finn leaned back against the corner of the roughed-in closet. Watching her over the rim, he took another sip, then offered a warped smile of his own. He indicated the nearly empty pot with his mug. "Go ahead and finish it off. There's more where that came from."

As if assessing him, she stared at him a moment, then gave him another sheepish grin. "If you were a gentleman, you'd turn your back on my gluttony. I tend to shovel when I'm this hungry."

Amusement pulling at his mouth, Finn watched her a second longer, then went over to the stove, picked up the poker and stoked the fire. "By all means, shovel away." Aware of the scrape of the spoon in the pot, he took the package of trail mix out of his saddlebag. Hooking the leg of a battered chair with his foot, he dragged it over to the stove, then sat down. He stretched out and propped his feet on the fender, watching the flames dance as he ate a handful of the trail mix. It was a miracle he'd found her. In all those thousands and thousands of acres of pure wilderness, it was a damned miracle. If he believed in it, he would have said it was fate.

"The china aside, dinner was excellent. Do I get to tip the waiter?"

His feet still propped on the fender, his cup of tea clasped in his hand, Finn turned his head and looked at her. The food and hot tea had had the desired effect. The sluggishness had disappeared and her eyes were absolutely clear. Sprawling in the old willow chair, he crossed his arms and considered her. With the effects of whatever was in her system obviously worn off, it was time to do a little tracking.

His gaze fixed on her, he took another sip of tea. Then he lowered the tin mug and cradled it in his hands, his eyes still riveted on her. Finally he spoke, his tone even. "I think it's about time you gave me some answers, Red. Like who you are and what in hell you're doing here."

As if someone had just pulled the plug on her newly restored vitality, she carefully set her mug down on the wooden bunk and as if suddenly cold, she pulled the blanket up around her shoulders. Avoiding his gaze, she took off the extra socks he had put on her, her expression drawn, the flickering light from the candles casting her face in a patina of soft light.

There was a brief silence; then she finally spoke, her tone almost too quiet. "My name is Mallory O'Brien." She hesitated a moment, then let out a sigh and tipped her head back against the wall and stared at the ceiling, her expression stark. "And to be absolutely honest, I don't have a clue what's going on."

Finn didn't say anything as he continued to watch her. He sensed she was gearing up to go on with her story, and he simply waited her out. Finally she dropped her head and met his gaze. She stared at him a moment, then began toying with the corner of the blanket. Her voice was devoid of emotion when she spoke. "None of it makes any sense. I live in Chicago. I was driving back to my apartment early last night, and I stopped for a red light. Two men wearing black ski masks yanked me out of my car. It happened so fast it was over before I had a chance to react. They forced me down on the floor of a van and blindfolded me, then injected me with something. And the next thing I remember is being moved—like on a stretcher—with my hands bound, and I was outside. I was lifted into something and given another injection.'' She lifted her head and looked at him, her face ashen, her expression stiff. ''Everything after that is a blank, until I came to in the passenger compartment of a crashed plane.''

His face impassive, Finn dropped his feet to the floor and swiveled his chair to face her. The mug still clasped in his hands, he leaned forward and rested his forearms on his thighs, fixing his gaze on her. ''What happened?''

She held his gaze for a moment, her face like wax, then she took a deep uneven breath, rubbing her thumb against the tin mug. ''I must have been jarred awake by the impact from the crash. I didn't know where I was, and it was so cold.''

She took another deep uneven breath and continued, her voice just barely above a whisper. ''I managed to push the hood up so I could see, and I was working on the bindings around my ankles when I heard movement in the cockpit.'' She closed her eyes and swallowed hard, and Finn could sense the spurt of terror in her. She swallowed again and visibly pulled herself together. ''I knew my only option was to get away while I had the chance. I managed to rip the rest of the tape off my ankles, and I crawled through the rupture in the side of the plane. I knew if I didn't escape then, I wouldn't escape at all. So I just started running.''

She paused again and finally met his gaze, not a speck of color left in her face. ''You know the rest.''

He watched her, reading her expression. ''What kind of plane was it? Big or small?''

She cupped her hands tightly around her mug, a stricken look on her face. ''Small. Single engine, maybe six-passenger.''

His face devoid of any expression, Finn watched her, assessing what she had told him. He was pretty certain she was telling the truth. But he was also damned sure she hadn't told him everything. Considering whether to push the issue or not, he continued to watch her, analyzing all the facts. Deciding that she had been as honest with him as she dared under the circumstances, he straightened. "Would you like more tea?"

As if realizing that he was not going to grill her, she managed an uneven smile, and Finn had the uncomfortable feeling she was on the verge of tears. But she pulled it together, and offered him a slightly embarrassed look. "What I'd really like is directions to the ladies' room."

Leaning back in his chair, he tipped his head to one side and gave her a very wry smile. "Like I said, the amenities leave a lot to be desired. The ladies' room is outside behind the cabin."

She gave him a genuine grin and dragged the blankets away. "And well air-conditioned, no doubt."

He gave her a wry smile back. "That's one way of putting it." He indicated the pile of gear by the door. "I've set out a spare pair of boots—you'd better put them on. The snow will be deep back there."

She stared at him, her eyes wide and steady, then as if giving herself a mental shake, she nodded. She crossed the room, resting one hand on the wall as she slipped out of her shoes and into his boots. It was all Finn could do to keep his butt planted in the chair, resisting the sharp urge to pick up the rifle and follow her outside. With the steady snow and the care he'd taken, there wasn't a chance in hell that anyone could have picked up their trail.

But he wasn't going to take any risks either. He spoke, his voice gruff. "My dog is in the doghouse under the big spruce. Take him with you. His name is Rooney."

She met Finn's gaze, then gave him a half smile and nodded, more than a little amusement in her eyes. "Yes, sir. I will take the dog with me." She hesitated, then looked at him again. "Are you married?"

"No." Not anymore.

"Me either. And I'll still take the dog."

Her show of cheek almost made Finn smile. Almost. And he made himself relax the grip on his mug. With Rooney along, he knew that nothing—not anything or anybody— could get within a quarter mile of them without the dog letting him know.

Finn stared at the door for a good ten seconds after she left, then he downed the remainder of his tea and got up. He took the kerosene lamp off the shelf by the door and lit it, placing it on the battered table. His expression fixed, he extinguished the candles and dropped them back in the can, then picked up the extra sleeping bag off the floor. He had recognized the symptoms of genuine exhaustion in her after she had finished telling him her story. He didn't have a whole lot to offer in the way of creature comforts, but he could fix her a half-decent bed.

Using the spare bedroll from his extra gear, as well as his own, he made a bed for her on the bunk, spreading his top-of-the-line sleeping bag out on top. After the chill she'd had, the last thing she needed was to get cold during the night. And there was a spare sleeping bag stored in one of the big plastic containers tied in the rafters.

The door opened and she reentered, flakes of snow still snagged in her hair. His coat pulled tightly around her, she gave an involuntary shiver as a blast of cold air swept in when she closed the door behind her. She looked much better after the trip outside, invigorated by the cold mountain air. It was almost as if she'd had a shot of pure oxygen.

She stepped out of the boots and put her shoes back on,

then crossed to the stove, warming her hands over it, the illumination from the lamp lighting her profile. Even in the faint light, Finn could see she'd just about run out of steam, and his own expression hardened. It was a wonder she was still alive.

He picked up the poker out of the wood box and opened the door of the stove. "We've got a hard ride ahead of us tomorrow."

She lifted her head and looked at him, the lamplight setting her hair on fire, making her eyes seem dark and bottomless. Finn felt her steady gaze right down to his bones, and he abruptly looked away, a strange flurry in his chest. Her gaze was so penetrating it was as if she could see right through him, and that made him uneasy. No one had seen through Finn Donovan for a very long time.

Careful to avoid looking at her, Finn stoked the fire then closed the door on the stove, sticking the poker in the corner of the wood box. He indicated the bunk, trying to keep his tone easy. "You look like you've run out of energy, Red. It might be a good idea if you called it a night and climbed into bed."

There was a brief pause, then out of the corner of his eye, he saw her look at the bunk. "Hold on," she said, an unexpected, bossy challenge in her voice. "If that's my bed, just what are you going to use?"

Her tone caught him by surprise, and wry humor pulled at his mouth. After she'd tried to slug him with a rock, he might have known he'd get some lip. And his gut told him that he had to win this one, or she'd test him at every step. Erasing all expression from his face, he turned and faced her. He didn't say a word; he just stared at her with that inflexible stare he had learned in prison. She folded her arms and stared right back at him, an ornery set to her jaw.

"I'm not taking your bedroll, Mr. Donovan. I'll sleep in the chair."

He folded his arms and stared back at her. It took about ten seconds of a silent standoff, but she finally let go a long sigh and conceded. "Fine. I'll sleep in the damned bed." She stomped across the room and sat down on the edge of the bunk, then her shoulders sagged and she closed her eyes. It seemed to take all the energy she had as she wearily combed her hands through her hair. She let go another sigh, then looked up at him and tried to smile. "You think I'm acting like a spoiled brat, don't you?"

The corner of Finn's mouth lifted, and he leaned his shoulder against the wall. "Under the circumstances, I think it's allowed."

She tried to smile, but couldn't quite pull it off. Her voice was unsteady when she spoke. "Are we safe until morning?"

He continued to watch her, another strange feeling filling up his chest. His voice was husky when he answered her. "Yes. We're safe until morning."

"Okay then," she whispered, then without looking at him, she kicked off her shoes and slid her feet into the sleeping bag and lay down, pulling the covers over her shoulder. Turning on her side, she tucked her hands under her face and watched the fire flicker through the grate in the stove. Finn had to fight the urge to cross the room and tuck the sleeping bag around her, to brush that wealth of hair back from her face. Fragile. She looked so fragile. And alone. And if there was anything he understood, it was how it felt to be alone. Tightening his jaw, he forced himself to turn away.

It was going to be a long night.

He jammed on his Stetson and picked up his vest, then headed for the door. A damned long night.

By the time he returned from outside, she had fallen asleep, her breathing soft and even, her hands still tucked under her face. It was like before—when it hit him that she was like something out of a fairy tale, something other-worldly. He hardened his jaw and turned away. He had never been given to that kind of whimsy, and he sure in hell wasn't going to start now.

The fire had burned down by the time he decided to retrieve the spare sleeping bag from its container. The containers held the emergency rations he had topped up the day before, and were used as a deterrent against mice and other marauders. His shoulders ached with weariness as he set it on the floor.

The sleeping bag removed, he nudged the chair closer to the stove and opened it up. His body wanted to lie down, but for some reason, he didn't want to use the other bunk. And he knew if he slept on the floor, by morning the cold would have penetrated every muscle in his body. And he'd be stiffer than hell. So the chair was it for the night.

Draping the open sleeping bag across him, he stretched out in the big old willow chair, again propping his feet on the fender of the stove. His expression somber, he crossed his arms and watched her sleep, a strange sensation unfolding inside him. He had no idea why he was so damned certain, but he would bet his life she was all that she seemed to be—honest, direct, untainted—with a survival instinct that no amount of money could buy.

Resting his head against the high back of the chair, he assessed her features. She wasn't what he would consider beautiful, but there was a certain quality to her face that appealed to him. A depth of character, maybe. And, from the angle of her jaw, there was also evidence of a whole lot of Irish bullheadedness.

Finn's expression hardened as he considered her survival. It was probably that strength of will, that bullhead-edness that had kept her alive today. It made his gut knot, thinking what might have happened to her if Rooney hadn't spotted her.

A log fell in the stove, the flare of light burnishing her hair, making it come alive, and Finn locked his jaw together, feeling suddenly hollowed out inside. Dragging his gaze away, he studied the toes of his boots. It was a miracle that he'd found her. Except he didn't believe in miracles. Nor did he believe in second chances. But he did believe in atonement. And maybe she was his. Because somehow or another, he was going to have to keep her safe.

This one, he had to keep safe.

Chapter 3

By morning, the clouds had settled lower, and it had started snowing again, the thick, fresh blanket obliterating the sharp contours. Dawn seeped over the jagged horizon, casting the landscape in a purple hue, the dull light eerie and filled with gray shadows.

The new snow squeaked under Finn's boots as he approached the cabin, his rifle in one hand and a pail of water in the other. It was a drab morning, heavy and overcast and muffled in silence, the clouds so low that they nearly touched the ground. Hoarfrost coated the trees and glittered on the fresh blanket of snow, but in spite of the whiteness, everything was cast in a dreary, monochrome gray.

The brim of his hat shielding his eyes from the denseness of the spiraling flakes, Finn paid attention to his footing as he negotiated the slippery rocks that spanned the shallow stream. Unshaven and hungover from lack of sleep, he considered what he was faced with. Under the circumstances, he couldn't have asked for better conditions. With the heavy skies, he was assured of several more inches of wet snow—enough to cover all their tracks. His only concern was that with this kind of weather moving in, it could get really ugly before the day was over. And if that happened, it would make for very tough going, especially with a greenhorn along. But on the plus side, it also meant that any search aircraft would be kept on the ground, which significantly lowered their risk of detection. Providing it didn't get a whole lot worse than this, and taking into account how much she was going to slow them down, they could still make it from here to his place in nine or ten hours—providing she could take that kind of physical punishment. And it would be punishing. The ride back would be no picnic. Even with the falling snow, he was going to make damned sure their trail was nearly impossible to track. And that would mean some hard riding.

The horses were in the makeshift corral, their haunches turned into the storm, their long winter coats dusted with snow. He had fed them each a flake of hay before he went down to the creek, and he had given Rooney his morning ration of kibbles. But the dog was nowhere to be seen—likely off chasing rabbits. Finn stepped under the overhang of the log cabin, a gust of wind sending a flurry of snow under the eaves. There was a sharpness in the air that hadn't been there before, and Finn compressed his mouth. The bite in the wind was a sure sign it was going to get ugly. He wasn't looking forward to the next few hours, that was for damned sure.

Pressing down the latch, Finn stamped the snow off his boots and opened the door, the flame in the kerosene lamp wavering in the draft. He had left that lamp burning all night. He knew what it was like, to wake up in pitch black, your heart pounding, not knowing where you were.

He closed the door silently behind him, then propped his

rifle against the wall and set the pail by the stove, his gaze shifting to the bunk. She hadn't moved since he'd gone out. With the flap of the sleeping bag pulled over her head, the only indication there was actually a person under the mound of sleeping bags was that he could see the toes of one foot. If she was that huddled in, he doubted she was going to appreciate the chill in the brisk mountain air.

He shucked his coat, then opened the door on the stove and added another log, the crackle and snap of burning resin perforating the silence.

A muffled voice came from the bed. "I'm not going to like getting out of bed, am I?"

Finn closed the stove door and latched it, then set a pan of water on to heat. He glanced back at the bunk, a touch of humor hovering around his mouth. "I think we can safely assume that."

"Damn." She pushed back the flap and struggled up on one elbow, her hair absolutely wild around her, her dark green sweater crushed and wrinkled. She scrubbed her hand across her face, then opened her eyes really wide, as if trying to get them to stay that way. She looked at him, a disgruntled tone in her voice when she spoke. "Don't you ever get cold?"

"No."

She flopped back down and pulled the sleeping bag up over her shoulders, snuggling deep in the warmth. "Great. I had to hook up with an ice man." Then, as if recollection had come back in a rush, she abruptly rolled onto her back and covered her face with her hand, a tremor running through her.

Finn knew from experience that the worst thing he could do was to give her time to reconnect with the horror of what had happened to her. He spoke, his voice clipped. "We've got bad weather moving in. If we're to stay ahead of it, we're going to have to hit the road pretty damned quick.''

He watched her struggle for control, and he saw her physically pull it together. His earlier estimation of her climbed up a notch. She also had one hell of a lot of grit.

Her face fixed like cast wax, she rose up off the bunk, her shoulders square, her chin held high as she slipped her feet into her shoes. ''Excuse me,'' she said, her tone royal. ''I need to make a trip outside.'' Her whole body stiff with indignation, she picked up his coat and put it on, then went to the door. ''If you can give me ten minutes, I'll be ready to go.''

With far more force than necessary, she slammed the door shut behind her, and Finn heard all the snow slide from the tin roof. Then he heard her swear. Great. Now both her shoes and her coat would be wet. Resting his hands on his hips, he let out a sigh and looked at the ceiling. Okay. Maybe he'd been a bit sharp. And she'd been through a hell of a lot. It wouldn't have killed him to be a little nicer. He let out another sigh. It was going to be a damned long day.

She was gone longer than he expected, and he had coffee perking and a pot of instant porridge steaming by the time he heard her at the door, cooing to Rooney. Finn dropped his head, priming himself to be nicer. And in deference to her sensibilities, he had gotten a tin bowl out of the plastic storage container, so she wouldn't have to eat out of the pot again. And he'd even mixed up a small portion of powdered milk.

The door swung open and he looked up, expecting a haughty, royal entry. Framed by the gray light from outside, the snow falling behind her, she huddled in the warmth of his coat, a guilty look on her pale face. I'm sorry,'' she said, her voice uneven and sounding as if she meant it. "I can be a real pain sometimes."

It was the look in her eyes—that solemn, imploring look—that made Finn's pulse stumble, and he found his chest suddenly tight. An odd kind of intimacy crackled between them, suspending time. It was as if this had happened before, as if they had known each other a very long time. The sensation upended his equilibrium, and he curled his hands into fists, his heart suddenly pounding in his chest. It was all he could do to force air into his lungs and dredge up a warped half smile. "Under the circumstances, I think that's allowed."

She stared back at him, time still weirdly suspended, then she turned abruptly and closed the door, and more snow slid off the roof. "No, it's not," she said, her voice even more unsteady. "There is never an excuse for bad manners."

Finn experienced a flash of unexpected insight. And he knew, from that one comment, that Mallory O'Brien had grown up being brutally honest with herself. And probably with anyone she came in contact with. Needing to alter the mood, he spoke, his tone clipped. "Sure there is."

She turned and looked at him, a startled expression in her eyes; then she gave a soft laugh. Finn felt the effects of that chuckle down the entire length of his spine.

Watching him, she folded her arms and tipped her head to one side, amusement still dancing in her eyes. "Really? You might change your mind on that. You don't know the levels of rudeness I can sink to."

He held her gaze a moment, then looked away, finding it far too easy to get lost in her eyes. "Breakfast is ready," he said, his tone gruff. "And there's warm water in the washbasin on the stove. It's about all I can offer."

Her voice was subdued when she answered. "Warm water sounds like heaven.'' Feeling suddenly claustrophobic, Finn did up the bottom two snaps on his vest, then picked up the rifle. ''There's a towel on the washstand, and there's brown sugar and powdered milk on the table, coffee in the pot.'' He settled his hat on his head and reached for the door. ''I'm going to water the horses and get them ready to move out.''

Once outside, he blew out a deep breath, his heart still pounding, his body far too hot. He didn't know what in hell was wrong with him, but it had to stop. He had to stay focused, damn it—her life could depend on it.

Sobered by that thought, Finn watered the horses in the creek, guessing that the temperature had dropped by another few degrees. He led them back to the corral, then brushed the snow off them and rigged up a hackamore for Trouper. The packhorse didn't even have a halter on, and since Finn would be breaking trail with him, he needed some method to guide him. He figured he'd killed maybe twenty minutes, maybe half an hour when he went back to the cabin.

He didn't know what he expected, but it definitely wasn't for the bedrolls to be perfectly rolled and stacked neatly on the floor, the dishes washed and packed in the storage container, the towel neatly folded and laid by the repackaged food she had placed by his saddlebags. From the pricey clothes she had on, from her jewelry, he hadn't expected that kind of capable efficiency. It hit him again that he only knew what she had told him, and that had been damned little. And for some reason, that suddenly irked him.

His face felt wooden when he tipped his head toward the stacked supplies, acknowledging her effort. ''Thanks,'' he said, avoiding her gaze. Crouching down by the gear Trouper had been carrying, he undid one waterproof kit bag and started pulling extra clothes out. ''The wind has picked up and it's going to get damned cold before the day's over. So I want you to put this stuff on. We need to get as many layers on you as possible."

She didn't say anything as she picked up the stack of clothing he'd piled on the floor, a faint scent of soap he had left out for her snagging his senses. He clenched his jaw, giving himself a moment; then he eased out his breath very carefully. Too close. She had gotten far too close.

His shearling coat appeared on the pile of gear as he pulled another item of clothing out of the waterproof kit bag. He handed her back the coat. "You'll need that as well."

"No," she said, her tone quiet—rebelliously quiet. "I won't."

He looked up at her, getting nailed with a hot rush as his gaze slid up her long, long legs, the cashmere sweater clinging to the shape of her breasts. He turned away and closed his eyes, forcing himself to take some even breaths. Hell. He hadn't had this kind of slip in years—and he didn't know why it was happening now. Over the years, he'd learned to shut everything down. Especially that. Sexual encounters had always been on his terms—not something that snuck up on him and nailed him from behind.

He took another deep breath and fixed his gaze on her, giving her a don't-mess-with-me look. "Yes," he said, his tone short and abrupt. "The last thing we need today is you experiencing another bout of hypothermia."

She jammed her hands on her hips, pulling the fabric of her sweater tight. "Oh, of course," she said, her tone snippy as she looked down her nose at him. "And just where would I be if you fell off your horse and froze to death? I'd be dead, that's where I'd be. So it's pure common sense that you wear the coat."

For some reason, Finn wanted to grab her and shake her,

but he ground his teeth together and literally counted to ten. Then he spoke, his own tone measured and quiet. Dangerously quiet. "I have another coat," he said, lifting up the lined mackinaw he had just pulled out of the bag. "You will wear that one."

She gave him one of her heated looks, snatched it out of his hand and tossed it on the bunk. "Fine," she snapped.

Finn started stuffing things back in the kit bag, his annoyance escalating. It was going to be a damned long day if she argued with him over every damned thing. He pulled the flap over the zipper on the bag and snapped it shut, and was just setting the bag to one side when he saw her try to pull one of his polar fleeces over her head. She winced and grabbed her shoulder, her face turning ashen. Without saying anything, Finn got to his feet and crossed the room. Hell. He should have checked her over better—she'd probably got hammered up pretty bad when the plane crashed.

He removed her hand and gently probed the shoulder socket, her skin warm and very soft beneath his touch. "Have you ever dislocated it before?"

She went very still under his touch, and he was sure she quit breathing. "No," she said, her voice uneven. Then her chest rose and she spoke again, her voice a little stronger. "I think I must have jammed it against something in the crash."

Finn's insides started to heat up, and he felt suddenly very shaky. Light-headed and shaky. Exposed and shaky. His first instinct was to back away. Getting a grip, he locked his jaw and carefully checked her collarbone and shoulder. Trying to keep his touch impersonal, he pressed his hand against her shoulder blade, finding the scapula intact. The heat from her body made his fingers tingle, and his pulse turned heavy. Too close. Much too close.

Avoiding her gaze, he took the pullover. "Here. Let me help you with this."

She remained very still as he eased her injured arm into the sleeve, then pulled the neck open so she could slip it on. Recognizing the discomfort her shoulder was giving her, he went to pull the garment down, but she caught him completely off guard when she softly touched the long scar on his face.

Her voice was very soft when she spoke. "How did you get this?"

Still avoiding her gaze, he gave a mirthless smile. "You don't want to know."

She traced the length of it, her touch sending a current through his whole body, and it was all he could do not to snatch her hand away. Nobody had touched that scar since the stitches were taken out. Nobody.

She dropped her hand and stepped away, her tone even softer. "I can do it," she said.

Finn turned away from her, his heart laboring in his chest. She could do it. And he could do himself a big favor and keep away from her. A long way away.

He completed the rest of the preparations, speaking only when he absolutely had to, the tension getting to him. He kept telling himself that once they got moving, it would be okay. It was just the close quarters that were making him so edgy.

With the extra gear he was leaving behind properly stored and the fire extinguished, Finn cast one cursory glance around the cabin, satisfied that it was as it should be; then he pulled the door closed and latched it. His rifle in his hand, he turned toward the horses, experiencing another shot of aggravation. He had told her to get on Gus. He had been specific that she was to ride Gus. With the rough terrain they had to traverse, he wanted her on the horse with the saddle. But no. She was on Trouper, her long legs straddling the big packhorse.

The snow was falling heavily, and her tracks were already nearly covered, the branches of the spruce trees bowed with the weight. She had the black wool cap pulled down low over her forehead, the scarf wound around the upturned collar of his shearling coat, and her hands lost in a spare pair of his gloves. And already her clothing was dusted with snow. She looked at him, her chin stuck out and her eyes glinting with challenge.

The muscles in his jaw working, Finn stared at her. "I want you on the other horse," he ordered.

She stared at him, brazen in her defiance. "No."

He started toward her. "Yes."

As if realizing he intended to haul her off, she backed Trouper away from him. "Oh, for Pete's sake. Don't be so pigheaded, Donovan. I've done three-day eventing, so I'm sure I can manage to stick on this very docile, well-behaved horse for a few hours." When Finn kept coming toward her, she got very conciliatory. "And besides, I'll be much warmer riding bareback." She tried to charm him with a smile. "And you want me to stay warm, right?"

Finn stopped and glared at her, then turned and stomped back to where Gus was rubbing his head against the pole corral. Damn her. She was going to drive him crazy. But three-day eventing was the kind of riding that separated the men from the boys. Accomplished or not, if she didn't measure up in the first hundred yards, she was changing horses if he had to wrestle her to the ground to make her do it. He jammed the rifle in the scabbard, gathered up the reins, then swung into the saddle. If she argued with him every step of the way, he just might not get her back alive. He might strangle her first.

It was one hell of a ride. The wind picked up as they

crested the first rise, the blowing snow cutting visibility down to feet instead of yards. And if that wasn't bad enough, snow cascaded down from the heavily laden fir boughs, dumping snow on them at every turn. The dampness in the air made the cold all the more penetrating, and Finn watched her like a hawk. She never complained once, toughing it out with an endurance that surprised him. And if he had any doubts about her ability on horseback, those disappeared when he watched her maneuver Trouper up the first narrow, rocky incline. It was obvious that she knew what she was doing, and Finn relaxed a bit. Turning up the collar on his mackinaw, he tipped his head into the wind. He would put up with cold miserable weather, the blowing snow and rotten vision. There wasn't a chance in hell that anyone could track them in this weather, and it also meant that air search would be definitely grounded. And every miserable step moved her that much further away from whoever she'd been running from.

It took a little over eight hours to make the torturous ride. And it was torturous. Cold. Wet. Hard going. Dangerous. And they wouldn't have made it in that kind of time if she hadn't been such a damned fine horsewoman. Under any other circumstances, Finn would have holed up somewhere and waited for the storm front to pass. But he'd pushed on, knowing that the snow was the best cover they had.

It was dark by the time they reached his spread, the snow piled up in drifts around the buildings. Winter always came earlier in the high country, and this year it had come even earlier than usual. It wasn't that often that there was this much snow before the end of October.

Reaching the barn, he sidestepped Gus over to the door, then reached down and slid it open, the heavy plank door rolling smoothly on the well-oiled track. Still mounted on

Gus, he ducked down and hit the light switch, and the structure was immediately filled with gloomy light. There were eight box stalls in the structure, and Finn dismounted by the second stall, flipping the reins through the heavy metal ring bolted to the wall. He felt damned near drunk from exhaustion and cold. He waited for Mallory to clear the door; then he pulled it shut behind her, closing out the chilling wind.

Taking Trouper by the hackamore, he led him to the stall next to Gus's. When he glanced up he saw Mallory lying sprawled facedown on the horse's back, her arms and legs hanging down like a rag doll. Her voice was muffled when she spoke, doing a routine from a familiar car commercial. ''Gee, Dad. When are we going to get to Grandma's house?''

He gave up a small smile. ''So you get that one in Chicago, do you?''

As if she barely had the strength to move, she sat up, pulling off her scarf and hat, setting her hair free. ''We get everything in Chicago. Fire. Flood. Plague. Pestilence.'' Dragging her leg over, she slid off Trouper, her legs nearly buckling beneath her as she hit the plank floor. She caught herself on the door of the box stall, a wry look appearing. ''Oh, you're in great shape, Mallory. One lousy day in the saddle, and you turn to spaghetti.''

Finn pulled the hackamore off Trouper, then dragged open the door to the box stall and slapped the horse's rump, cueing him to move. He had no idea why he wanted to give her a hard time, but he did. ''Shame on you,'' he scolded, looping the hackamore through the bars on the stall.

She lifted her head and stared at him as if he'd done something unexpected, then she grinned, flashing him two perfect dimples and a perfect row of teeth. ''Humor. My God, the man has humor.''

Stretching her arms over her head to try to limber up, she glanced at the heavy plastic feed barrels lined up against the wall. "Is this what you want me to feed them?"

Finn hooked the stirrup over the saddle horn, then began undoing Gus's cinch. "I don't want you to feed them anything. I want you to go to the house and get into a hot shower."

She turned and looked at him, giving him that steady unwavering stare. "I don't think so," she stated evenly. "I'm going to look after my horse."

Finn stared at her, then let out a tired sigh. He didn't have the energy to argue with her. He just didn't. Flipping the cinch over the seat, he dragged the saddle off Gus and headed toward the tack room. Halfway there, it hit him that maybe she didn't want to go anywhere by herself. He resigned himself to a retraction. "You can give them each a scoop out of the blue barrel, and there are some old towels in here if you want to rub him down."

She didn't just want to rub Trouper down. She wanted to prepare him for the show ring. She went to such extremes he wouldn't have been surprised if she started putting show sheen on his hooves.

Shamed into it, he gave Gus a thorough rubbing, then broke off two flakes of hay from the bales stacked at the end of the barn, giving each horse his allotment. Closing Gus's stall, he draped the saddlebags over his shoulder, then snagged her by the collar and steered her toward the door.

"But I never closed Trouper's stall."

Finn pulled open the side door, then flipped off the light, leaving the barn in total darkness. "He's not going anywhere."

The high overhead yard light cast a broad halo of illumination, the falling snow sliding through its brightness, creating a sense of motion. Finn aimed her toward the path, and she tried to turn back, but he continued to march her ahead of him, the snow nearly to her knees. "We're done here, Red. And now we're going to the house. Then I'm going to phone the local RCMP detachment—"

She abruptly stopped in her tracks, then turned to face him, a stunned expression on her face. Thinking it was confusion over the term, he clarified. "RCMP. The Royal Canadian Mounted Police. It's our national police force."

She grabbed his arm, her eyes wide with fear. "No," she said. "No. You can't call them—not yet." She hauled in a deep, steadying breath. "Please don't call them."

Finn frowned and stared at her, her fear apparent. Something was going on here, and he didn't know what. But he knew fear when he saw it. He held her gaze. "Is there anyone you do want to call?"

She shook her head, and he thought maybe she was close to tears. "No. No, not now. Can't we leave it for tonight?" she whispered. Finn considered her, picking up on some very heavy dread. Normally he would have been on the phone immediately, but there was something about the look in her eyes that made him hesitate. And one more night wouldn't make much difference. It wasn't as if there was a rescue crew out there risking their necks trying to find her, not in this weather. He forced a smile and nudged her to get her walking. "Okay. Fine. But we're going to the house. And you're going to have a hot shower, and I'm going to make us something to eat."

At the mention of food, she quit balking and went willingly. "Food," she said with obvious longing. "I'll go anywhere for food." Rooney came bounding around an old wooden granary, his eyes gleaming in the dark. Assured that his human companions were indeed headed toward the house, he lunged ahead of them, rooting through the drifts with his nose.

Finn picked up the sound of a distant motor, and his gut dropped away. Old Joe lived a quarter mile down the road, and when Finn was gone, he checked the stock a couple of times a day. And it would just be his luck for the old guy to show up now, to make sure the automatic watering system in the stalls was working and the heaters were on in the outdoor watering troughs. The last thing Finn wanted was for anyone to stumble onto his redhead, at least not until he got the whole story. And he was going to get the whole story, one way or another.

He turned his head into the wind, his expression relaxing when he heard the sound retreating. At least that was one thing they didn't have to worry about.

The dark outline of the cabin appeared. The log structure squatted in the shelter of a little ravine, nearly hidden from view by trees, its location sheltered from the wind. Silently they plowed their way through the snow, Mallory walking ahead of him. Finn could tell by the sag of her shoulders that she didn't have a whole lot of energy left. And neither did he—he felt as if he had been plowing through snow for days.

They had just reached the flagstone pad leading to the back porch when the wind changed direction and started to gust, whipping her hair across his face. He caught her elbow to steady her, his head slanted against the blowing snow. ''Watch your step. It might be icy.''

They reached the landing and Finn opened the door, the wind nearly ripping it out of his hands. Sheltering her with the bulk of his body, he waited for her to enter, while Rooney scooted in ahead of them.

Out of the wind, he took off his Stetson, then reached past her and pushed open the inside door. Nudging her inside, he flipped on the switch over the boot rack, the brightness of the track lighting making him squint.

Finn closed the door, the cold draft eddying around his legs as he let the saddlebags slide to the hemp matting; then he dropped his hat on the row of hooks over the boot rack. He expected her to do the same, to start stripping off her outerwear, but she hesitated, scanning the interior of the stripped-log structure.

His home was very basic. The kitchen and living room were one large great room, the most dominant feature the huge stone fireplace that actually formed the bearing wall, which bisected the cabin. The walls on either side were lined with bookshelves, while the east wall was mostly windows. Beyond the fireplace and bookshelves, there was a short hall that led to the two bedrooms, with the bathroom at the end. There was a loft over the kitchen and the storage room, the area fenced in by varnished pole railings. In fact, the logs were stripped and varnished throughout, and over the years they had aged to a soft amber color.

There had been two major priorities when he had built the place. One was the view, and the second was big windows. There were times in prison when he had felt as if he was actually suffocating from being trapped in a windowless bunker. And when he got out, he needed to know that the freedom of outdoors was just a pane of glass away. He still felt that way.

Her head tipped to one side, Mallory began to slowly undo her buttons. "This is very nice," she said, sounding as if she meant it. She tapped her toe on the dark pine flooring. "All you need are some of those beautiful Navajo rugs on this floor."

Finn took off his mackinaw and hung it on the hook by his hat, just a little ticked at her forwardness. She'd been in his house maybe thirty seconds, and she was already redecorating—and he liked it just fine the way it was. And besides, the only thing he wanted laid on the floor was his saddle-sore, beat-up body, preferably with a good shot of whiskey in his hand.

As if tuned to what he was thinking, she turned and gave him a grin as she dragged off his sheepskin coat. "I should have known you'd be a minimalist, Donovan. I should have figured that out from your dearth of speech." She draped her coat over his, then looked back at him, a glint of impishness dancing in her eyes. She used her two pointer fingers to lift the corners of his mouth. "And a dearth of mirth as well. Your face won't fall off if you smile once in a while, you know."

He didn't want to do it. He did not. And he tried to hold it back, but a lopsided grin worked itself loose in spite of his efforts. "If I'd been smart, I would have dumped you in one of those big snowdrifts in the pass."

She grinned and patted his cheek, then bent over to pry the boots off over her multilayers of socks. "Ah. Now I get the tough talk. You can't fool me, Donovan. I can see just fine out of both my eyes."

His own rusty chuckle caught him totally by surprise. He hadn't done a whole lot of that over the past few years. And it wasn't as if her situation was any laughing matter. But the amusement lingered, and he turned to look at her, his mouth still wanting to smile.

He caught her watching him with a wide, steady gaze. And as soon as their gazes connected, she smiled the most beautiful, sweet smile. That smile sent such a rush of plain old human warmth through him that Finn didn't know what to do with it. Unnerved by the reaction, he turned and walked into the kitchen area. "Go have a shower," he commanded gruffly. "And I'll rustle us up something to eat."

Out of the corner of his eye, he saw Mallory hesitate,

and he braced himself for another one of her arguments. She continued to watch him for a second longer, then turned toward the bathroom. "Thanks," she said softly, easing the polar fleece off over her head. Remembering her sore shoulder, he made a move to go help her, then used some common sense and kept his distance. In a strictly defensive move, he turned toward the storage room instead. His voice was abrupt when he spoke. "There's a cupboard in the hallway—you'll find clean towels and a pile of sweats. And there's a stash of new toothbrushes in the drawer by the sink. Help yourself."

Feeling oddly out of step with himself, Finn dumped three cans of soup in a pot, then made some man-sized ham sandwiches, his gut in knots. He wasn't used to having women around. Yeah, he'd had women on trail rides, and he'd even had some out big game hunting, but this was different. This made him feel exposed somehow.

He had a fire going in the fireplace by the time he heard the shower shut off. She hadn't taken as long as he had expected, and when she reappeared, she was barefoot with a towel wrapped around her head. She had on a set of his navy sweats, the sleeves shoved up, the waistband down around her hips. Her face was scrubbed clean and shining, but even in his clothes, there was a sense of style about her.

Feeling as if he was fourteen years old instead of forty-two, he motioned to the chair at the end of the table. "Have a seat."

It wasn't until she was seated under the light hanging over the table that he saw how exhausted she was—even her hands were trembling. Sobered by that reality, he set a steaming bowl of soup in front of her, followed by a spoon; then he slid the plate of sandwiches toward her. "Eat up."

Pulling one leg up so she was sitting in a half lotus, she gave him a wan smile. "I don't think I have the energy."

He brought his own bowl to the table and sat down, then reached for a sandwich. "Eat, Red. After the day you've had, you need the calories."

She gave him a long look, then picked up her spoon, her mouth quirking a little. "You never tell a woman she needs more calories, Donovan. Don't you know that?"

Finn almost smiled. He wondered if she ever quit, or ever let anything go. He suspected not. They ate in silence, more questions piling up in Finn's head. He had promised himself he wasn't going to hound her—he'd wait for her to start talking of her own free will. It wasn't really his business anyway. And be damned if he'd start poking around in someone else's business.

"Have you always lived in Chicago?"

There was brief silence; then she answered him, her voice strained. "Yes."

"Were you on your way home from work when they grabbed you?"

"No."

He looked at her. Her face had gone very pale, and he caught the glimmer of panic in her eyes. Disgusted with himself, he held her gaze, forcing an off-center smile. "Okay, then. How old are you? And are those teeth your own?"

The panic disappeared, replaced by a hint of laughter, and she narrowed her eyes at him. "Has anyone told you that you ask rude questions?"

He gave her an amused look, then reached for the last sandwich. "I don't get asked out much."

She grinned, pulling up the other leg so she was sitting cross-legged. "Pull the other one, Donovan." She took the last bite of sandwich, then pushed her empty bowl away.

Sitting back in her chair, she continued to watch him. "Tell you what. I'll give you a personal profile. How's that?"

He stared at her, and for some reason he wanted to push her a little off center. "How personal?"

She laughed, her eyes dancing. "Not that personal." She started ticking things off on her fingers. "I'm five foot nine, and won't tell you how much I weigh, and I'm twenty-eight years old. I love hockey, detest football, and I wear a size eight shoe. I like to watch old movies and I'm an ardent recycler. I read almost anything I can get my hands on, and would rather be skinned alive than go to a tea party. My favorite colors are green and yellow." The gleam in her eyes intensified, and she gave him a steady, pointed stare. "And nobody, nobody, calls me Red."

His elbows hooked on the edge of the table, Finn watched her, amused by her litany, wondering if she had any idea how much of herself she had let show. He held her gaze, allowing himself to smile. "So. Do you drink whiskey?"

She grinned at him. "With a name like Mallory O'Brien, and you ask me if I drink whiskey? I was weaned on whiskey. Neat and straight up."

Finn pushed his chair back, went to the cupboard and took out a full bottle, then reached in another cupboard and got out two glasses. As he fixed drinks Mallory cleared the table, placing the dirty dishes in the sink.

When he turned from the counter, she was sitting on the floor in front of the fireplace, and the towel was draped over the back of the sofa. Her hair like a corona of fire around her, she sat staring into the fire, her arms stacked on her upraised knees. She looked young, pensive and very alone. His own expression somber, Finn flicked off the light in the kitchen, then crossed the room, wondering why she didn't want anyone to know he had found her. He figured she must have a damned good reason—and he always tried to respect another person's fear. He handed her a drink, then kicked the ottoman closer to the big leather chair. Sprawling out in the soft comfort, he propped his feet on the ottoman, then took a swallow, his thoughts preoccupied as he watched the flames flicker and dance. Finally he spoke, his tone very quiet. "You're going to have to tell me sooner or later, Red."

She took a stiff drink, then rolled the remaining amber liquid around in the glass, her profile burnished by firelight. There was a long silence; then she spoke, her tone uneven. "I know."

Finally she looked up at him, her face drawn, a haunted look in her eyes. "Can we leave it until tomorrow?"

He considered her for a moment, then nodded. Not letting anything show on his face, he lifted his chin toward the bedrooms. "Your bedroom is the one on the right. There's an extra blanket in the closet."

She drained her glass, then set it on the table by the sofa. As if her whole body was stiff and sore, she got to her feet, casting him an odd little smile. "Then I think I'll turn in," she said softly.

Finn watched her go to her room, the familiar feeling of aloneness settling on him. He didn't know why, but the room seemed suddenly very cold and empty.

His expression set in rigid lines, Finn unplugged the phone and abruptly got up and went over to the east windows that overlooked the ravine. Bracing one arm on the window frame, he stood staring out, the faint illumination from the distant yard light casting long shadows in the blanket of whiteness.

His mood heavy, he watched the huge snowflakes pile up in the boughs of the fir trees, creating fragile canopies in the undergrowth. He knew he had accepted the little she'd told him at face value, but he believed her. And although he had no way of knowing for certain, he was damned sure the two planes he'd heard were part of an air search. Which meant that someone, somewhere knew the plane had gone down. And who that was, under the circumstances, could be anyone's guess. But if it was a search called out by the authorities, there was a damned good chance he'd get a call. Considering that possibility, he wondered if whoever she'd heard moving in the cockpit was still alive.

Deep in concentration, he rehashed what little he knew, and there was one question he'd give a lot to know the answer to—and that was the final destination of the flight. If they had grabbed her in Chicago, what in hell were they doing flying across the Rocky Mountains?

Yeah, he had accepted a whole lot at face value, all right. And under any other circumstances, he would have made camp, made sure she was safe and warm, then tracked her trail back to the crash site. But he had a sixth sense where danger was concerned—one honed to a razor's edge in prison—and those warning bells had all gone off like a five-alarm fire. She had been in danger—real danger—out there. And it was still there, just waiting to close in.

Realizing that he was starting to jump fences in the dark, Finn downed the remainder of his whiskey, then set the empty glass on the mantel above the fireplace.

All this speculation was getting him nowhere. And he was so damned tired he couldn't think straight. He was going to have a long hot shower, and hope like hell the heat would ease some of the stiffness in his body.

By the time Finn had his shower and entered his bedroom, he was practically staggering with exhaustion. Not wanting to have to deal with any calls concerning a possible search, he also unplugged the phone on his night table.

Feeling as if his body wasn't really his own, he eased himself into bed, nearly groaning aloud with relief as he stretched out. Damn, but it felt good to finally lie down on something soft. After an entire night spent in a bone-breaking chair and over eight hard hours in the saddle, he felt as if he'd been mauled by a grizzly.

Stretching out on his back, he tucked his hands under his head and stared at the ceiling, thinking again about the woman asleep across the hall. There was something about her—something very disconcerting. He was by nature a wary person, and eight years in prison had compounded that wariness to basic mistrust. And there weren't that many people he was at ease with. But for some reason, it was different with her. It was as if the circumstances, as if the danger, had short-circuited his usual wariness and caution. And he wondered if she would be so at ease with him if she knew his history—knew the truth about the scar. That thought set off a heavy feeling inside him, and Finn closed his eyes, swallowing against the sudden thickness in his throat. Feeling suddenly raw, he dragged one arm across his eyes.

The wind moaned around the corner of the house, the sound low and mournful, and Finn locked his jaw against the sound.

Sometimes the emptiness in him was more than he could handle.

And sometimes there was not a damned thing he could do about it.

Chapter 4

The bedroom was cast in midnight darkness as Finn came sharply awake, his heart pounding, his subconscious pricked by something out of the ordinary. The only light in the room was coming from the snow outside, the whiteness creating an eerie, faint illumination that infiltrated his room.

His senses on full alert, Finn remained perfectly still, every muscle primed to make a sudden move. Keeping his breathing slow and even, he carefully turned his head and fixed his attention on the door. Catching the barely perceptible sound of fabric against wood, he redirected his focus, his gaze snagging on a gray shadow huddled against the wall. He let his breath go in a rush.

Bracing himself on one elbow, he wet his lips and spoke, his voice rough with sleep. "What in hell are you doing there? Why aren't you in bed?"

The shadow shifted, and Mallory's head came up. "I

couldn't sleep," she said, as if offended by his bluntness. "I keep hearing noises outside."

Recognizing the undercurrent of fear in her voice, Finn heaved a resigned sigh and spoke again, his tone a little less harsh. "You should be hearing noises—you're on the edge of the wilderness, for God's sake. This place is crawling with wildlife."

She challenged him. "Like what?"

Knowing he wasn't going to get a moment's rest until he answered her, he resigned himself to a detailed answer. "Deer, coyotes, bear, elk—hell, there's even a resident cougar."

He expected some lip; what he got was a soft chuckle. "Great. Are you trying to scare me senseless, or just give me something else to worry about?"

He scrubbed his hand down his face, trying to clear away the last vestiges of sleep; then he let go another sigh. "Whatever." He lay back down, too damned tired to stay propped up. "But there isn't a chance that anything will get near the house, not with Rooney sleeping in the porch. So go back to bed. Nothing is going to get you tonight."

Unwinding from her huddle, Mallory O'Brien rose, and before Finn had a chance to put it together, she moved around to the other side of the bed and crawled up beside him. Finn was so shocked he could only stare at her shadowed form, not quite believing she'd done what she had. Nobody in her right mind would crawl into bed with him. Nobody.

He heard her ease in a shaky breath; then she spoke, her voice very uneven. "Don't get the wrong idea, Donovan," she whispered. "I'm not up to anything. I just cannot stay in that room by myself—not when it's so dark. At least not tonight."

The little quiver in her voice got to him—really got to

him, and Finn continued to stare at her, a strange, fuzzy feeling unfolding in his belly. He'd seen her sheer grit and courage, but it was understandable that her nerve had worn a little thin. He'd always had the utmost respect for anyone who could keep going, no matter what the odds. And he clearly remembered what it was like in prison, when hard, cold reality piled in during the middle of the night.

Feeling as if he had something thick wedged in his chest, he tucked the sheet around his nakedness, then pulled the comforter from underneath her and covered her up. "Here," he said, his own voice low and gruff. "You don't want to get cold."

She whispered something and caught his hand, and he could feel a terrible tension in her. He heard her swallow, her fingers tightening around his, her shaky voice just barely above a whisper. "If it weren't for you, I'd be dead now. God, I'd be so dead."

Vividly recalling the hundreds and hundreds of times he would have sold his soul for a little human warmth, Finn closed his eyes and swallowed hard, his chest suddenly jammed up tight. He laced his fingers through hers, palm against palm, and tightened his hold, the fullness of emotion getting worse. He couldn't remember the last time he'd held a woman's hand.

He heard her breathing falter, as if she were on the verge of tears and didn't want him to know it, and that silent struggle kicked off such a surge of protectiveness in him, he had no choice but to act. Letting go of her hand, he shoved his arm under her neck and gathered her up in a tight embrace. Grasping the back of her neck, his fingers tangling in the long silk of her hair, he drew her head onto his shoulder. Tightening his hold, he began to rub her back.

She made a ragged sound and curled into him, locking

her arm tightly around him. And Finn could feel how hard she was fighting to keep it together.

Needing to lighten her load however he could, he gave her shoulder a little squeeze, then spoke, a touch of amusement in his voice. "Nah. You wouldn't have been so dead, Red. You would have slugged him with a rock, taken his clothes, then hiked out. That's what you would have done."

He was awarded a shaky laugh, and she turned her face against his neck. "I just hate being scared, Finn. Hate it."

It was the first time she'd used his given name, and it gave him a sudden, heavy rush, and he locked his jaw against it. It had been a lifetime since honest human warmth had gone both ways. Experiencing a need to comfort and protect that he hadn't experienced for a very long time, he smoothed down her wild tumble of hair, pressing her head tighter against him. God, but it felt good to hold another human being—just to hold someone to give them warmth and comfort. He had forgotten how good that felt.

Resting his head against hers, he continued to slowly stroke her back, thinking about what to say to her. He knew he couldn't run a bluff by making assurances that everything was going to be all right—she was too savvy to buy that, but he could at least give her tonight.

Easing the cramp in his throat, he spoke, his voice husky. "I can't promise you much, but I can promise you that you're safe for at least tonight."

He felt her let her breath go, and her body softened against his, as if he had given her the exact assurance she needed. Resting her hand on his naked chest, she spoke, a different quality to her voice. "I didn't tell you how much I love your country, Donovan. It's so big and beautiful. I'd never want to leave it if I lived here. It makes you feel really free and unfettered somehow."

Finn found himself swamped with emotion, the kind that

compressed his lungs and made his throat close up. She couldn't have said anything—not anything—that would have connected her more directly to him. This high country was like freedom to him, and it was the only place in the world where he could breathe, where he could survive.

Closing his eyes against an unexpected burn, he let his jaw go slack in an effort to ease the painful cramp in his throat. Then he spoke, his voice still roughened. "I feel the same way."

She shifted her head and pressed even closer, her hand warm and flat against his chest. "I know you do," she whispered. "That's why I could say it to you."

Her trust and closeness warmed him, and not just physically. It was as if her physical warmth and her confiding about freedom had touched something deep, giving him a burst of inner contentment he hadn't experienced for years. Wishing he could tell her what that blind trust meant to him, he clutched the back of her head, fighting the urge to turn to her, fighting the urge to crush her against him. Instead he eased a breath through the awful fullness in his chest and tightened his hold just a little, then turned his head so his mouth was against her forehead. God, maybe he was still human after all.

The last thing he remembered was listening to the sound of her breathing, acutely conscious of how good it felt to hold her, her softness and warmth making his heart labor.

Then the next shard of consciousness was coming awake, her head still on his shoulder, her weight still warm against him. And the clock on his bedside table indicated it was 6:23 a.m. Drugged by the effects of a very deep sleep, Finn shifted his head against hers and let his eyes drift shut again. He couldn't believe he had slept the way he had. He had turned into a very light sleeper in prison, and it was a pattern that had remained. It was as if, even in sleep, he remained on guard. And for him to fall so sound asleep was as foreign to him as waking up with a woman nestled against him. He'd never spent the entire night with any of the women he had associated with over the years. Never really wanted to.

Tightening his arm around her, Finn allowed a small, wry smile, amused that life still offered up a few surprises.

A series of barks snapped him back to reality, and he went absolutely still. Rooney didn't bark like that, not unless someone was approaching the house. Several sharp knocks sounded on the outer door, and Finn stared stiffly into the darkness, assessing the situation. It was about a half hour too early for Old Joe to be looking for a cup of coffee, and too damned early for anything else. He swore under his breath. Sure as hell this had something to do with the plane crash.

Easing his arm out from under her, he slid out of bed and covered her up, then pulled on his jeans, his expression tense. Damn, this was the last thing he needed.

Avoiding the squeak in the floor, he slipped out of the room, closing the door behind him. Able to see by the faint illumination of the yard light, he swept up the extra clothing Mallory had left on the end of the sofa and dumped it in the wood box by the fireplace, then soundlessly closed the lid. Trying to recall any other possible traces of her, he moved across the room.

Fixing his expression, he flicked on the light, then opened the door to the porch, giving Rooney a command to stay.

The frigid air prickled against his bare skin and bit into his bare feet as he opened the outer door, his eyes narrowing when he recognized Constable Arnie Jeffery from the Bolton RCMP detachment. The cop was in full uniform, and Finn could see the white 4X4, the distinctive emblem plastered on the door, sitting just up the hill. Finn had worked with Arnie on two previous searches, and he'd had the constable on two vertical-rescue training exercises. He was as straight as an arrow, and one of the few men Finn trusted on the business end of a rescue line. Which meant if Arnie was here in full uniform, driving the 4X4, this was official business.

Keeping his expression neutral, he opened the door wide in a silent invitation to enter. "Arnie. You're out pretty early."

Pulling off his cap, Arnie stomped the snow off his feet, then entered the porch and followed Finn into the cabin. As Finn closed the door behind the other man, he gave the area another quick check, swearing under his breath when he saw one glass on the table and another on the mantel. Damn it. He'd forgotten about the glasses.

Turning so the constable's line of sight was blocked, Finn folded his arms and rested his weight on one leg, keeping his expression neutral. "So what's up?"

The other man pulled off his regulation gloves, giving Finn an apologetic look. "I'm sorry I had to drag you out of bed at such an ungodly hour. I tried to call you last night, but there was no answer. I gave Old Joe a call this morning, and he said you were home, that he'd checked the barn late last night, and both horses were there."

Finn forced himself to let go of the stiffness in his muscles. "Sorry about that. It was hard going yesterday, so I was pretty beat when I got home. I unplugged the phones when I went to bed."

Arnie Jeffery stuck his gloves in his pocket. "Well, we've got a problem. A light plane went down west of here day before yesterday. We had planes in the air for a bit, but they got grounded because of bad weather. But we did get a fix on the transponder signal." He shook his head, his expression worried. "It's about five klicks from Carlson Falls—right around that little glacial lake where we went fishing a couple of years ago."

Knowing that sometimes the best way to hide trail was to lay a bunch of other tracks over it, Finn shifted his weight, making sure his expression gave nothing away. "I was in that area the past couple of days. Winterizing the line shacks. I figured I heard planes, but never thought anything about it."

Arnie heaved a sigh. "Then you know what it was like out there yesterday. With that kind of weather, and such strong winds, there was no way we could bring in a helicopter." He raked his hand through his trimmed hair, then shook his head. "We've been advised that this weather system is going to settle in for at least three days, so we're going to have to send in a ground search and rescue team." He gave Finn a wry smile. "Which means you, Donovan."

The police officer rubbed his head again, worry lines forming around his mouth. "Unfortunately, we're going to have some private-sector people coming along. The passenger on the plane was the daughter of a very wealthy industrialist in the States—Patrick O'Brien—I don't know if you've heard of him or not."

Thinking about the platinum watch and the diamond earrings, Finn allowed himself a wry smile. "Yeah, I've heard of him." He doubted if there was a person in North America who hadn't heard of Patrick O'Brien.

"Well, from the reports we've had, she was on her way to Alaska—I guess her old man has a hunting lodge up there. It was some private tracking system that notified us that they'd gone missing.

"But there are some other concerns for her safety, mostly because of some kidnap attempts in the past. And I take it those attempts have had some lasting effects on her." Arnie met Finn's gaze, his expression solemn. "The chief of security for O'Brien Industries arrived about an hour ago. And he told me that the daughter is very fragile emotionally and must be handled with enormous care. And that's why they want some of their people along, someone who is familiar to her."

Finn stared at the cop, having to work very hard to keep his expression neutral. If he didn't already have the very wealthy industrialist's daughter stashed in his bedroom, and even if he didn't know she was being transported against her will, it would have still been damned suspicious. The whole setup smelled bad.

The flight path didn't match up, and the fact that it was someone in the private sector that notified the RCMP didn't sit right. Nor did the fact that security people were already on-site. And since when did a U.S. corporation security chief get to call the shots at a crash scene in Canada? Keeping his face expressionless, Finn listened as Arnie continued to talk, his mind working double time.

From the location that Arnie had given him, it was clear that Mallory had covered a fair distance before he found her. Two or three miles at least—which meant it would have probably taken her at least half an hour to travel that far.

His arms still folded against his chest, he assessed his own situation. He was not at all happy about being called out for the search. But there was no obvious reason for him to say no—not a damned one.

But everything depended on Mallory O'Brien. If she still refused to let anyone know that he'd found her, then that put a personal spin on it. It meant he was going to have to leave her alone. And she would be on her own—if she wanted total secrecy, he wouldn't even be able to tell Old Joe. And it would suit him just fine if no one found out she was alive until he had a chance to find out what in hell was going on—and why she was so terrified. Still, he did not like the idea of leaving her alone.

But the tracker in him also saw a possible advantage to being there for the supposed rescue. It was going to tell him a whole lot if he could see for himself how her father's people reacted when they discovered she wasn't at the wreck.

A breath of sound from the hallway caught Finn's attention, and it was all he could do not to turn his head in that direction. As if physically connected, he could feel her there, standing at the bedroom door listening. He hoped she had enough damned sense to stay quiet. Right now, Jeffery didn't have a clue she was there, and Finn wanted to keep it that way. At least until he had a chance to talk to her.

Finn forced himself to maintain a relaxed pose. It was imperative that he didn't drop the ball here. And he didn't want to leave any loose ends that someone might question later—like why he'd cut his trip short, and why he'd come home missing most of his gear.

Nodding his head as if in agreement, he spoke, his voice even. "I'm going to be short equipment. I had to leave quite a bit of mine behind yesterday. My packhorse looked as if he might be coming up lame. And with the weather the way it was, I didn't want to take a chance with him." Which was partly true. Trouper always looked as if he was going lame.

"Don't worry about that. We've got extra." Arnie Jeffery pulled out his gloves, clearly anxious to get this show on the road. "I talked to that new game warden last night, and he figured you'd want to trailer the horses up to that South Point campground."

Finn endorsed the plan with a nod. If the roads were clear enough that they could trailer the horses up to the wilderness campground, it would save at least five hours of search time. Although it would have been shorter to go in the same way he'd brought Mallory out, going that way would be much more difficult. If they had to transport injured survivors, it would be a nightmare. And setting up a base camp at South Point was better for him. While laying a trail to the crash site, he could also construct a trail away from her.

"You'll bring Rooney, right?"

His attention dragged back, Finn considered his response. He had already made up his mind that he was leaving Rooney with Mallory. The dog was the best defense she had. And he did have a sound reason for leaving the dog behind. Keeping his voice easy, he answered. "No. I don't think so. The only way we can reach that site is on horseback, and with this bad weather and the deep snow, it would be too hard going for him. I'll leave him with Old Joe." Finn straightened. "I've got to put together another survival kit for myself. I expect Old Joe is already at the barn. Tell him I'll take Jakes instead of Gus—I worked Gus pretty hard yesterday. And tell him to load the big roan as a packhorse. Joe's done this before—he'll know what gear I'll need."

Arnie Jeffery jammed his hat on his head, then reached for the door. "I'll give him a hand. This search isn't going anywhere until you're ready to roll." He stepped onto the porch. "As soon as we've got the trailer loaded, I'll head back to town. We've told everyone to muster at the fire hall."

The cop disappeared into the darkness, and Finn closed the door behind him, feeling a whole lot edgier than he liked. Everything felt wrong. Remembering what it felt like to wake up with Mallory O'Brien in bed beside him, he amended that thought. Almost everything.

But the reality of her being Patrick O'Brien's daughter

made his insides knot up. He knew pretty much from the moment he laid eyes on her that there was something untouchable about her. But now he knew for sure. That kind of distance couldn't even be measured.

He turned and headed toward the bedroom. And now he was going to have to get her side of it, whether she liked it or not. Geared for a battle of wills, he went down the hallway. But just as he reached his bedroom door, a hand shot out, grasped him by the waistband and hauled him into the room, the power of the jerk nearly dislocating his neck.

He never got a chance to get a single word out.

In one hell of a temper, she faced him, her hands on her hips, fury blazing in her eyes. "That is the biggest crock of lies I've ever heard in my life," she practically shouted, her freckles standing out like a million little beacons. "Fragile. Do I look fragile to you? And I was *not* on my way to my father's hunting lodge. I was being *taken* against my will!"

For some reason, her fury amused him—some women would have been wringing their hands, or sobbing their hearts out. Not Mallory O'Brien. Mallory O'Brien was all geared up to tear a strip off someone.

Resting his hip against the highboy, he folded his arms, barely suppressing a grin as he looked down at her. "No," he said, his tone casual. "I wouldn't say you were fragile. Emotionally or otherwise."

She stopped and stared at him, and he could almost see the fight drain out of her. And he caught a glimpse of fear and uncertainty as she opened her mouth, ready for another tirade of self-defense.

Knowing he didn't have a lot of time to waste, he held up one hand. "Hey," he said, cutting her off. "For what it's worth, I think it's a crock. And I'd sure like to know what the chief of security is doing up here." He hooked one thumb in the front pocket of his jeans, fixing a steady gaze on her. "But right now, I need to know what you want to do, Red. We can go out to the barn and tell Arnie that I found you—"

"No!" Her eyes wide, she grasped his arm. "No," she said, lowering her voice and trying to affect calm. She hugged herself, the light from the doorway glancing across her pale face. "They can't know," she whispered unevenly. "If they find out I'm still alive, others will be put at risk. No one can know, Finn. Especially anyone from O'Brien Industries."

Finn stared at her, something making him edgy. "Why?"

Her face was strained, and she clutched her arms tighter, her eyes fixed on him. He could tell she was debating whether to answer him or not. Finally she spoke, her expression stark, her voice uneven. "The plane that crashed was an O'Brien Industries plane."

A cold feeling slithering through his gut, Finn stared at her. "You're sure?"

She gave him a humorless smile. "Very sure." She rubbed her hands up her arms as if she was cold, then inhaled unevenly. "That's why no one from OI can know I'm alive. Somebody high up has to be involved."

Finn had a dozen questions he wanted answers to, but there simply was not enough time. Holding her gaze, he acquiesced with a tip of his head. "Fine. But I don't have a lot of time to waste here. If I'm not out at that barn in twenty minutes, they're going to come looking for me."

Her lips pale and her eyes wide with the first flicker of panic, she nodded her head, her gaze fixed on his.

He wanted to touch her, but he didn't. But he did manage to soften his tone. "I'm going to have to go on this mission—under the circumstances, I don't have a choice." He straightened, jamming both hands in the back pockets of his jeans. "And if you don't want the authorities to know you're here, we can't afford to stir up even a whiff of suspicion. Which means things are going to have to happen exactly the way they would have if I hadn't found you."

She looked at him, her eyes dark and beseeching. "But they're lying, Finn. *They're lying.*"

Needing to reassure her, needing to simply touch her as a man would a woman, he reached out and tucked her hair behind her ear. "I know that, Red," he answered, smiling into her worried eyes. "I was there, remember?"

Clamping her mouth shut, she nodded, and as if exerting a huge amount of self-discipline, she hugged herself even tighter. "You won't tell them you found me, will you?"

He gazed down into her anxious eyes, and for some reason it was important that she believe him. "No. I won't tell them."

"Promise me, Finn."

He gave her a small smile. "I give you my word."

She took a deep shaky breath, then lifted her chin. "Okay, then."

He could not resist the urge, and he smoothed his thumb across her cheek. "I know you probably aren't too thrilled about staying here by yourself. And I'm not too damned happy about having to leave you." Holding her gaze, he caught the back of her neck and gave her head a little shake. "But right now—at least until we find out what's going on—I think it's our only option. Something really stinks about all this." He hesitated, asking again, knowing she was still hiding something. "Are you sure you don't want to get in touch with your father?"

Her jaw tight, she shook her head, then eased in a deep fortifying breath. She took another deep breath and let it go. "No," she said, her voice controlled. "I want to wait until you get back."

He dropped his hand to her shoulder, giving her a firm squeeze. "Fine. And if you do exactly as I tell you, you're going to be fine. And no one ever need know you're here."

Still watching him, she gave her head a single nod, clearly trying to marshal her resources. He gave her shoulder another squeeze, then turned toward the huge chest of drawers. Running a mental checklist in his head, he started tossing clothing on the bed. "This thing with the plane puts a different spin on things," he said, keeping his tone almost conversational. "Maybe it's a good thing I'm going along. I'll able to watch what's happening. And I might find out a few things—like who is behind this." He glanced at her, and she nodded again, only this time she wasn't quite so stiff.

Not having time to cater to whatever modesty she had, but still needing to find out any information she might have, he turned his back on her and stripped out of his jeans, then began yanking on layers of survival gear. "Okay, Red. I need you to tell me what you know about this security team."

He heard her take a deep breath; then she answered, her voice steady. "If it really is the chief of security who's here, his name is Ed Jackson. My father is big on security, and Jackson is supposed to be very good at his job. I do know that he's into very high-tech surveillance and security systems. And I also know from what my father has said that he used to work in some top-secret capacity for the government. I certainly don't know all the people who work under him, but the ones I've met are all the same." He heard her move toward the bed; then she spoke again, an edge in her tone. "Professionally, he's supposed to be the best. Personally, he makes me want to back away."

Yanking a turtleneck sweater over his head, Finn turned to look at her, his expression altering as he pulled the sweater all the way down. "Then that's good enough for me." He picked up a web belt and began threading it through the loops on his wind pants, also attaching the sheath for his Buck knife. "I know you haven't told me everything," he said, using that same conversational tone. "But right now, I don't have time to deal with that."

Stacking up the clothing on his bed, he continued. "But I'm going to want the whole story when I get back." He turned to face her, assessing her reaction. Hugging herself, she mutely nodded, and Finn headed for the door, his spare clothing in his hands. He heard her follow him. "I'm leaving Rooney with you. Old Joe checks the place morning and night when I'm gone, but he never comes to the house—not unless I ask him to. He'll feed Rooney at the barn, so don't you feed him here. Rooney always hangs around the house when I'm gone, so his being here won't kick off any suspicions."

He lifted the lid on the wood box and took out the polar fleece she'd been wearing, adding it to the rest of the clothes he was carrying. "Do not go outside and stay away from the kitchen windows at night. Those are the only windows that can be seen from the drive. I quite often leave the track lights on in the kitchen when I'm gone, so leave them on all the time. There are more boxes of books in the loft, and the washer and dryer are in the room behind the kitchen. And there's also a good supply of canned food on the shelves and stuff in the freezer. And help yourself to my clothes." He paused, considering telling her about the gun safe in the storeroom, then changed his mind. No one had any reason to check his house, and Ed Jackson would be with him.

He picked up the saddlebags he had dropped by the door,

slapped them on the kitchen table, then started stuffing things inside. Of course she was going to be safe. But in spite of knowing that, he still could not look at her. "You have to do exactly what I say, Red," he said, his tone firm. "Right now, you can't afford to take any chances."

He finally looked up at her, his stomach doing a funny little barrel roll when he found her watching him, her head tipped to one side, not a trace of fear on her face. She met his gaze, offering up a small smile. "I will do *exactly* as you say, Donovan."

He watched her, a tight knot letting go in his belly. Feeling guilty for imposing such heavy restrictions on her, he felt compelled to explain. "We can't have you outside making any fresh prints in the snow," he said, his voice gruff.

She folded her arms in a relaxed stance. "I know."

He held her gaze for a split second, assuring himself that she did know; then he turned and headed for the storage room. "I gotta get my 'go' bag," he mumbled.

When he came back out, carrying the backpack, he found that she had pulled everything out of his saddlebags and was folding it neatly, then just as neatly replacing it. He stared at her. He wasn't going to some resort, for God's sake; he was going into the backcountry. He just about snapped at her, but instead he locked his jaw together. All right. It was no big deal. She just needed something to do.

She indicated the backpack. "Called a 'go' bag because it's always ready to go, right?"

He gave her a narrow, questioning look. "That's right."

She gave him a wry half smile. "I have one of those, too, only I call it my flight bag, as in fleeing."

It was the tone in her voice, almost as if she had resigned herself to her way of life that made him pause. He picked up the three pairs of heavy woolen socks she had also retrieved from the wood box and had rolled together. He stuck them in the side pocket of his pack. He watched her do up the buckles on the saddlebags, then he spoke again, his voice husky. "You're going to be fine here on your own, Red." He forced a smile. "It'll give you a chance to catch up on your reading."

She slid her hands up the sleeves of the sweat suit she was wearing, giving him a small smile back. "I thought I'd weave some nice, pretty baskets while you're gone."

He gave her a lopsided grin, then reached for the shearling coat she'd worn the day before. He shrugged into it, then picked up his Stetson, his heart giving a lurch when she reached up to straighten the collar of his coat. "Go careful, Donovan. I don't want to be stuck in this cabin till spring."

She was so close, he could feel the warmth of her, smell the scent of his shampoo on her hair, and it was all he could do to keep his hands at his sides. She had shown so much courage, and there was such trust in her moss-green eyes, such openness, such confidence in him that he almost felt trapped by it. He stared at her, feelings he didn't know he was capable of building up in his chest. And his own sense of honor kicked in.

It would not be right for him to leave her with any false impressions. He had too much regard for her. And he knew if he were able to keep her alive and deliver her back to her father, her rescue would be front-page news. Then the truth about him would come out. And the one thing he did not want was for her to find out what kind of man he really was from some headline. If she was going to find out, he wanted it to be from him.

He shifted his gaze, his heart suddenly pounding as he geared himself to tell her; then he took a deep breath and lifted his head to look at her. "Don't turn me into some kind of hero, Red,'' he said, his voice very gruff. "I've done things that would scare the hell out of you.''

He expected her to move away. She didn't. "What things?'' she asked softly.

Feeling as if his insides had just dropped out of him, he looked at her, age-old regrets making his voice rough. "I killed a man.''

She continued to watch him, her gaze steady and unblinking. "Why?''

It wasn't what he expected from her. He wanted to hold her gaze, but he couldn't. He stared down at the floor, aligning the sole of his boot with the hemp mat, a band of tension around his chest. He didn't want any exoneration— he just needed to tell her the truth. It was a few moments before he spoke. "He raped my wife—and when I found out what he did to her, I went after him, and I killed him.''

The next question was quiet and soft. "What happened to your wife?''

He lifted his head and stared across the room, old painful memories resurfacing. "She died in a car crash while I was in prison. Some think it was no accident.'' It was as if saying the words released him, and he shifted his head and looked at her, dread sitting like a rock in his chest. He thought she would have turned away. But instead she was watching him, her arms tightly folded, and she had tears in her eyes. But it was the expression on her face that nearly did him in. No fear, no revulsion—just a soul-deep expression of understanding.

Thinking she had misunderstood him, he held her gaze. "Don't get the wrong idea,'' he said, his voice hoarse. "I was guilty as sin.''

"Oh, Finn,'' she whispered, crossing to him, placing her hand against his face and covering his scar.

Feeling as if his soul had been stripped naked, he looked

down on her, swallowing hard against the painful knot in his throat. With infinite tenderness, she caressed his cheek, more tears welling up, making her eyes greener than ever. He felt as if he were drowning in those eyes.

Then she spoke, the tenderness in her touch, the softness in her voice belying the violence of her words. "Any bastard who used that kind of violence against a woman deserves to be dead." As if absolving him of his sins, she cupped his jaw and reached up, brushing her mouth against the scar. The kiss was so soft and gentle, it was like an absolution. "I don't care what you've done," she whispered against his cheek. "I only care about who you are." She caught his hand and squeezed it hard, then looked up at him. "You're a good man, Finn Donovan. And don't you ever forget that."

He stared down at her, a huge surge of emotion washing through him, and he couldn't have spoken if he wanted to. Her eyes glistening with the unshed tears, she reached up and cupped his face again, and something huge and hurting let go in Finn. Closing his eyes, he locked his jaw together and put his arms around her, a second wave of emotion slamming into him as she stepped into his embrace. Feeling as if he was being ripped apart, he grasped the back of her neck and tightened his hold, burying his face in her hair. Fighting to contain the awful pressure in his chest, he clutched her closer. He had never felt so indebted—or so raw. It was almost as if she'd cauterized an old, gaping wound.

Sliding her arms around his waist, she hugged him back. "Please take care," she said, grasping the back of his coat. "And stay safe. I need you to stay safe."

Finn wasn't sure he had the strength to let her go, but he heard the growl of a vehicle in deep snow, and he knew he had to get out of there. Grasping her face with both hands, he made himself take a deep, uneven breath and gently set her aside. His throat still painfully tight, he tried to smile as he carefully tucked her hair behind her ear. "You don't have a whit of common sense or judgment, Red."

She clasped his hand between both of hers, unspoken assurance in her eyes. "I have very good judgment."

He heard the vehicle draw closer and he gave her hand a hard squeeze. "We've got to shut off the other lights, and I've gotta go," he said, his voice still rough with emotion.

She reached up and kissed his cheek again, then stepped away, shoving her arms back up the sleeves of her sweatshirt. She managed a smile. "Watch out for wolves in sheeps' clothing, Donovan."

He flipped the end of her nose, then reached out and shut off the lights, leaving on the track lights in the kitchen. "Remember, stay in the house."

She gave him a more genuine grin. "I'll stay in the house."

It was one of the hardest things Finn had ever done, to pick up the backpack and saddlebags and open the door.

"And stay away from the windows."

She grasped the door to close it after him. "You sound like a mother. I'll stay away from the windows."

He cast her one last glance and opened the outer door, a cold blast of winter stinging his lungs. Never in his life had he experienced such reluctance.

And the only thing that allowed him to leave at all was knowing that she would be there when he got back.

If he got back.

Chapter 5

There were at least two dozen people milling around the cavernous, cinder block ambulance bay at the fire hall. Some of them were on-duty volunteer firemen, a couple were paramedics dressed in their dark blue uniforms, others were wearing winter gear and the bright fluorescent green vests that designated the members of the Bolton Area Search and Rescue Team.

His Stetson pulled low over his eyes, Finn propped his shoulder against the concrete wall and folded his arms, the bright orange fluorescent vest of team leader in one hand. It wasn't the volunteer firemen or paramedics that had his attention. It wasn't even the search and rescue team.

It was the squad of six men dressed in dark green para-military jumpsuits that had Finn's full attention. He watched the proceedings, deliberately removed from the crowd, narrowly assessing the situation. When he had pulled into the parking lot, there had been half a dozen trucks with horse trailers on behind, all those trucks and trailers parked at random in the freshly cleared lot. But when he'd made a wide U-turn so his rig was pointed toward the road, his high beams had cut a bright swath across another vehicle, parked as if it had the unalienable right, on the a͜ ͞n in front of the big fire doors. It was big and ominous, and looked like a modified armored car, painted dark green with the O'Brien Industries logo emblazoned on the side. It was a vehicle with an attitude, obviously flown in for the mission, obviously there to make some sort of power statement. And obviously going to be one huge pain in the ass.

Isolated in the noise of so many voices, Finn shifted his shoulder against the wall, watching the posturing of the six men, dark humor surfacing. After one look at the squad, he knew he had it figured right. They were all going to be pains in the ass. But the one that Finn watched most closely was the man with the big O'Brien Industries flash on his jumpsuit, his nameplate identifying him as Ed Jackson, Chief of Security. Finn disliked Ed Jackson on sight. Arrogant, used to having full control, liked giving orders—in it for all the wrong reasons. He had that cocky swagger of someone who knew he was good at what he did, and wanted everyone around him to know it. It didn't help that Ed Jackson bore a striking resemblance to one of the SOB guards in prison—the one who had beat an inmate blind, then smirked about it afterward, knowing no one could touch him.

Jackson had that same brittle, cold look in his eyes, and Finn figured he could trust him about as far as he could pitch him over a high board fence. Definitely not the man Finn would want spotting his equipment if he were rappelling down a six-hundred-foot cliff.

Finn had already picked up whisperings from the rest of

the team, about how that Jackson guy was acting as if he expected to run the show.

Checking out the rest of the people in the bay, Finn paused, his eyes narrowing even more as his gaze settled on Chase McCall. Finn could tell by the other man's body language that Jackson had also rubbed the rancher the wrong way. Finn didn't know Chase all that well. Bought some horses from him a year ago, had a beer with him a couple of times. But after going on four searches with him, Finn respected the man's judgment. And right now, Chase McCall was watching Ed Jackson as if he was watching a snake. From the cold, tight smile on Chase's face, it was apparent that his read on the situation matched Finn's dead on.

Finn shifted his glance back to Ed Jackson. All he needed was for the chief to give him a good excuse to walk, and he'd be out the door.

His parka undone, Arnie Jeffery addressed the group, his gaze direct. "You folks were contacted because you're all experienced horsemen—" he glanced at the single woman paramedic and grinned at her as he added "—and women. We know the downed plane is in a valley about fifteen kilometers from the South Point campground. We've been told that there were three people on board. And we also know, thanks to some high-tech assistance from O'Brien Industries, that there is at least one survivor, possibly two."

Finn's expression went still, and he glanced around the room, his internal radar on full alert. So. They had already determined that someone was alive. Which meant they had some very serious high-tech capabilities, like forward-looking infrared.

Finn had done a fair amount of reading on various search technology around the globe, and he knew the military was the only source that had that kind of technology at their disposal in Canada. And he doubted if O'Brien Industries had the clout to call in the Canadian military. Which meant the advanced technology had to be in one of the search planes—and it also meant that Ed Jackson had a whole arsenal of goodies at his disposal.

Realizing what Mallory was actually up against made his stomach roll, and he locked his jaw together, a sick feeling rising up in him. He was lucky to have found her before they did. Damned lucky.

"If we get a break in the weather, and there is a small chance we might later today, we'll send in a helicopter. But if we don't get that break, the folks from the weather service say this front could sit here for a couple more days. Which means we could be the only hope for any survivors." Taking a cup of coffee from one of the firefighters, Arnie took a sip, then glanced at Finn. "I see Finn Donovan back there. Finn, have you—"

Finn started to straighten, but Ed Jackson moved to stand slightly in front of Arnie, his hands on his hips. "Thank you, Constable. I'll take it from here." As if briefing a paramilitary group instead of a bunch of volunteers, he began to speak. "My name is Ed Jackson, and I'm the chief of security for O'Brien Industries. I'm sure you all know who Patrick O'Brien is, and as you are already aware, Mr. O'Brien's only daughter, Mallory, was on that plane. I have been assigned the task of locating her, and to make sure she is brought out quickly and safely. I understand that Mr. Donovan has been designated as team leader, but because of what is at stake, I will be directing this search-and-rescue mission."

Finn didn't move a muscle, anger making his jaw tense. The ensuing silence was so immediate, it was as if all the sound had been sucked out of the room. Finn stared at the chief of security, then gave a hard, tight smile and straightened, tossing the team-leader vest on a table. Not a chance. Not a damned chance.

Possibly every single person in North America might know who Patrick O'Brien was and how much money he had, but as far as Finn was concerned, Ed Jackson could go straight to hell. This might be O'Brien's crack security force, but there was no way in hell that he was going to ask this dedicated team of volunteers to put their lives on the line for this know-it-all. No way in hell.

There was the sound of a full cup of coffee hitting the metal garbage can with considerable force. "That's it. I'm cutting loose from this circus," Chase McCall snapped, his tone flat. "There isn't a person in the whole damned country who knows that backcountry better than Finn. And if he isn't calling the shots out there, in that terrain and in this goddamned weather, you can count me out. I've got a wife and kids that are counting on me to get back alive."

Arnie Jeffery spoke over the noise of the crowd. "Just a minute, folks. Just a minute." The constable looked at Jackson, his face flushed with annoyance. "Sorry, Mr. Jackson. I don't know where you got the idea you'd be directing this search. This mission is under my jurisdiction, and until somebody tells me otherwise, I make the decisions. And if you have any problems with that, I suggest you take it up with your employer." He scanned the crowd, his expression still flushed with anger. "And Chase is right. There's too much at stake here." He spotted Finn heading for the door, and he spoke to him directly. "We're going to need you to get us in there, Finn. This ground team is the only chance those folks have."

Ten more steps and Finn would have been out the door. And had he made it out, there would have been no damned way he would have come back in. He wasn't sure he wouldn't have kept on walking anyway, but Chase McCall stepped in front of him. The rancher looked at Finn, wry humor in his eyes. "I don't like the son of a bitch any better than you do," he said, watching Finn. "And I think he bears watching." Then his face sobered and he continued, his gaze steady. "But Arnie is right. You're the only one who can get us in and any survivors out."

The muscles in his jaw flexing, Finn stared at the other man, a cold rage simmering in him. McCall had got that right—he didn't like that arrogant son of a bitch, but there was much more at stake here than the rescue. And she was sitting in his cabin.

The muscles in his jaw working, Finn stared at Chase a moment, and Chase tipped his head, his gaze steady. Finally Finn let his breath go, looked down at the floor and waited for his fury to settle; then he turned and fixed a cold gaze on Ed Jackson. "Anyone on your squad that isn't an experienced horseman is off this search," he snapped, challenging the other man with a cold look.

As if realizing he had crossed a line, Ed Jackson gave Finn a good-old-boy smile. "I agree. Myself and my second in command are both very experienced."

Finn glared at him. "You'd damned well better be. We won't have time to wet-nurse you through this. If you can't keep up, we'll leave you behind. It's that simple." He strode toward the front of the room, tossing his gloves on the table. "I want a complete equipment check before we roll out of here. Keep in mind that with this weather, it's not going to be a simple in-and-out trip—it could take us a couple of days, maybe longer." He glanced at one of the off-duty paramedics who would be going with them. "We can expect to be transporting injured survivors, so I want three of those collapsible rescue toboggans included." Then he looked at Chase McCall. "I need to know how many horses are going in, and every man is to be outfitted with snowshoes.'' He shifted his attention to the game warden who was part of the team. ''And I need a thorough checklist for food rations for both horses and team members.'' He made the muscles in his face relax and he spoke again. ''Double-check everything. We can't afford any mistakes. I want to be at South Point by first light, which means we have to be on the road in less than an hour.''

They were on the road in forty-five minutes, and it took them an hour and a half to get to South Point—half an hour longer than Finn had estimated. It was one hell of a trip. A snowplow had cleared the road, but it was hard going with trailers loaded with horses.

But it wasn't until they were a mile from the campground that it got really ugly. Slippery and dangerous, the blizzard conditions impeded visibility and obscured critical landmarks. And then it started snowing in earnest. It got so bad that at one point, Finn thought he was going to have to abandon the horses and go in on snowshoes. But then they hit a long sheltered valley that, with the eccentricities of mountain weather, had only suffered a light skiff of snow. It was still slow going, though, the cloud cover so low that the mist was less than fifty feet off the ground.

When they left the fire hall, he figured they should be at the crash site by midafternoon. They didn't reach it until just before nightfall. And if it hadn't been for the dark green O'Brien Industries paint job, even with the transponder signal, they might not have found it till daybreak.

When it crashed, the plane had plowed into the throat of a shallow rocky ravine rimmed by a dense stand of trees, the topography and falling snow making it impossible to see. But Finn found a deep gouge on a rocky ledge, pointing him in the right direction, and the blowing wind had swept clean a dark green piece of the wreckage.

With the grimness of night settling in, and his battery-powered searchlight practically useless in the blowing snow, Finn hooked onto a line and climbed down the rocky outcropping.

The twisted fuselage was jammed up against a stand of fir trees, nearly covered with snow, the rupture in the side gaping like a big black wound. Realizing that it was another miracle that she'd survived the crash at all, Finn faltered for a moment, then clamped his mouth in a hard line. He'd worry about that later. Now he had other things to consider.

He flashed his light off and on, signaling the rest of the team that he had reached it. Then he unhooked his harness from the safety line and made his way to the downed plane. Lucky. She had been so damned lucky to walk away.

It was the copilot who was still alive—unconscious but alive—with survival gear and blankets packed around him. It was obvious, by the way the copilot had been taken care of that someone else had survived the crash. Finn knew it wasn't Mallory who had provided basic first aid, so that meant the pilot was still out there somewhere. It gave Finn a cold feeling in his belly knowing that, and he wondered how far he'd gotten.

With a perimeter of battery-powered searchlights set up, it took them two hours to stabilize the injured man and get him out of the wreckage, then another hour to get him out of the ravine. And by then, darkness had settled in and the weather had gotten even worse. The heavy clouds settled right to the ground, the fog so dense that visibility was down to maybe a dozen feet. Finn called the search off for the night, and no one argued. Not even Ed Jackson.

The copilot was in bad shape. Both legs had been shattered, he had a serious head injury and he was in shock. In spite of all that, the paramedic had been able to stabilize him, and he was still unconscious but holding his own. It was going to be a long night.

And it was a long night. Finn checked the weather every ten minutes, able by some miracle to communicate with the base commander at South Point. Now everything depended on the weather. And blizzard conditions were the lesser of two evils. Come daybreak, there might be enough visibility to bring in a helicopter. But this kind of dense, low cloud cover created a whole other hazard. With zero visibility, and with the entire area completely socked in, it was just too dangerous. What they needed was a window of opportunity, like a forty-minute break in the weather. That would give them enough time to bring in a chopper and airlift him out. Everything depended on the weather.

It was just after dawn that the fog started to thin, and Finn used that window of opportunity to go back to the crash site.

The white mist shifted and swirled like a living thing, the slightest motion making it drift, the moisture coating the trees with a thick layer of hoarfrost. It was beautiful, in an eerie sort of way, and the fog closed in behind him as Finn followed the now-beaten trail they had hacked out to the ravine floor. As a result of the rescue mission the night before, the twisted fuselage was now more exposed, the dark green stark against the trampled snow.

There were things that Finn wanted to check out in the wreckage. Like empty syringes. Like a flight plan. And he also wanted to see if he could still pick up any tracks from the missing pilot. Because come full light, he was going to have to track him down. That was one loose end he didn't want left dangling.

He went around to the far side of the plane—the side he'd seen when he first climbed down. Entering the rupture in the side of the plane, Finn flipped on his flashlight, scanning the dark interior. He had checked it briefly last night just to make sure there was no one inside. But now he intended on searching it more carefully.

The fog seeped in through the opening and diffused the beam of light, and Finn moved with great care, not wanting to disturb anything. His insides balled up when he found a thick wad of duct tape caught on the floor under the plush seats. Then the light caught on something shiny, and Finn stepped further back, his stomach doing another barrel roll when he realized it was a small gold pendant, the chain broken.

"Thought you might want to know our boy is awake." Keeping his face expressionless, Finn picked up the locket and dropped it into his pocket, then glanced toward the ragged hole leading outside. Chase McCall was standing there, his hands on either side of the rupture, his gaze fixed on Finn, an intent, thoughtful look on his face. His own expression shuttered, Finn turned to face him, the beam from his flashlight glancing brightly off the fluorescent green of Chase's search-and-rescue vest.

The rancher offered up a wry lopsided grin. "And Jackson is throwing his weight around."

By the time Finn and Chase got back to the camp, Arnie Jeffery was tearing a strip off of Ed Jackson. It was clear that something had happened that had set Arnie off, and it took Finn maybe three seconds to put it together. When the paramedic let the constable know the patient had regained consciousness, Arnie had gone immediately to the tent, intending on questioning the copilot about the others. But Ed Jackson had beaten him to it, posting his man on the outside, barring Arnie's entry.

Shoving his gloves in his pocket, Finn looked at Jackson, his expression fixed. "I thought we made it clear last night who was calling the shots here."

The security chief gave Finn an easy smile, holding up

his hands in deference. "Sorry. I just wanted him to know that we were taking care of things, and he didn't have anything to worry about."

Damn sure the guy was lying through his teeth, Finn looked at Arnie. "Have you talked to him yet?"

The officer gave Jackson a heated look. "Yeah. I got to talk to him. For about a minute, then he passed out."

Knowing he had to play this out, Finn spoke again. "What did you find out?"

The other man heaved a sigh, his exhalation of breath adding another coat of frost on the fur trim of his parka hood. "He said that they discovered Ms. O'Brien missing shortly after the crash, and the pilot went looking for her, and he never came back."

Finn forced his expression to remain passive. "Did you find out what they were wearing?"

The RCMP gave a detailed description of the pilot's clothing, then Finn spoke again. "And the woman?"

"Green slacks and a green sweater. He thinks just regular shoes, but he couldn't remember for sure."

Finn debated about shaking things up and pointing out that there was no loose clothing in the wreckage, no handbag, nor was there any sign of luggage. Then he decided against it. He didn't want to alert Ed Jackson to anything, least of all his suspicions.

Finn took the mug of coffee one of the squad handed him. "What's the latest weather report?"

The game warden spoke up. "Just got off the horn with the base. It's beginning to clear further north, with a possible break coming this way."

Finn downed the lukewarm coffee, tossing the dregs on the fire. "Then get him packaged for transport and break camp." He indicated four members of the team, including the paramedic. "I want you to start moving the patient back along our trail.'' Finn checked his handheld global positioning receiver, then passed it to the game warden. ''You keep this so you can call in the coordinates if you get a break. And keep heading due east. If we can get him moved even a mile further in that direction, we'll pick up the air currents coming through the pass. And if we get some wind, we'll stand a better chance of a break in the cloud cover. The rest of you break camp and wait for us here. If we need you, I'll fire two flares.''

Very deliberately, he selected Chase McCall and the two O'Brien men. ''You three saddle up. I found two sets of tracks leading out of the ravine. One set made by someone weighing about one hundred and eighty pounds and wearing size ten, ten and a half boots. The other set were definitely made by a woman—probably dress shoes with a leather sole.''

He gave Jackson a look deliberately meant to challenge. ''It's going to be hard going. You up to it?''

The other man gave Finn a smooth smile back. ''That's why I'm here.''

It took them a little over twenty minutes to find the dead pilot sprawled under a drift of snow, a pistol beneath his hand. As smooth as silk, Jackson collected the pistol and stuck it in his pocket, making some weak explanation about it being part of the survival gear.

Finn didn't buy that for a minute. A pistol like that was good for one thing, and it had nothing to do with survival. As Finn unloaded the collapsible toboggan from the packhorse, he happened to glance at Chase McCall. The other man was standing with one hand in the pocket of his sheepskin coat, the other hand resting on the swell of his saddle, and he was watching the chief of security with a narrow, thoughtful look, a hard set to his jaw. Finn almost smiled. Chase McCall knew an SOB when he saw one.

The body secured on the toboggan, Finn laid out a new search grid, gradually expanding the area. There was a certain irony about it—here he was freezing his butt off, looking for a missing woman, who was, at that very moment, probably making coffee in his new coffeemaker. It was almost enough to make Finn smile. Almost.

Since there was only one direction they could go, they finally made it to the small meadow where Finn had found her. He located some branches that had been broken in the tangle of shrubs on the western periphery. And he found some green fuzz that had come from her sweater.

Had he had any doubts about Ed Jackson, they would have been answered the moment he showed the security chief the fibers. He got off his horse and approached as Finn held the branch and spoke. "The pilot said she had on a green sweater?"

The look on the other man's face told it all. The whole morning he had been edgy, watching every movement, and in the space of three seconds, Finn could see him relax. "I'll be damned. How did you spot that?"

Letting go of the broken branch, Finn turned back to his horse and gathered up the reins. "I get paid to spot things like that." He swung up into his saddle, gritting his teeth against the urge to drop the guy. He wheeled his mount around, his voice clipped when he spoke. "If she's here, she's got to be close. We're at the eastern end of a narrow valley that's hemmed in by very rough, rocky terrain. The only place she could have gone was along the river, and it's damned treacherous. If she's not here, then there probably isn't a body to find."

The radio clipped to Finn's orange vest crackled, and he remained motionless as he listened. "They think they're going to have a window to bring the chopper in. We need to get the body to the landing site."

Jackson mounted his horse and turned to face Finn, the wisps of fog eddying around his head. "Give it to me straight. What are the chances that she could still be alive?"

Finn stared back at him, trying to keep his dislike from showing. "Has she done a lot of hiking or camping?"

"Not to my knowledge."

"Has she ever had any survival training for this kind of terrain or this kind of weather?"

The other man stared back at Finn, almost as if he were enjoying this game. "Ms. O'Brien? No. Nothing like that."

Finn gave the man a cold tight smile and reined his horse around. "Then her chances are zero to nil."

The weather did clear briefly, giving them just enough time for a rescue helicopter to evacuate the injured copilot and dead pilot. Finn knew damned well that Jackson would have liked to leave with the chopper, but he wanted the man where he could keep an eye on him. They made a second search of the area, and when Finn pointed out that there were signs of more bad weather, it was Arnie Jeffery who suggested they call off the search. Finn's dislike for the security chief intensified when Jackson readily agreed. His response almost made Finn want to balk. But one of the foremost rules in search and rescue was never to put any member of a rescue team in jeopardy. And with the wind picking up the way it was, to stay would put the team at risk.

As Finn mounted up and turned his big bay around, he glanced at the security chief. There was one piece of information he wanted, and he intended on getting it. "I'll be debriefing the team when we get back to the base camp. So I need to know if Mr. O'Brien will be meeting us at some point."

The security chief also mounted up, avoiding Finn's

gaze. His tone was flat when he answered. "Unfortunately, Mr. O'Brien is unavailable."

Finn watched him a moment, then cued his horse forward. Bad answer. He had hoped for something more definite.

The trip back was even worse than the one going in. By midmorning the wind had picked up, driving the snow into dense drifts, and the visibility got so bad that Finn ended up leading his horse. They made camp by late afternoon, and it was after dark the following day that Finn rolled into Bolton. He was so damned beat, he didn't even stop at the fire hall. He knew the base crew would be there, with hot food and hotter coffee, but he just wanted to get the hell home, make sure Mallory was all right, take care of his horses and fall into bed.

By the time he got out of town the cloud cover had started to break up, and ragged pockets of bright stars glimmered through the torn clouds. Because the road to his place ran east and west, the surface had been swept clean by the wind, and deep, wind-sculpted drifts were piled up in the ditches all along the fence lines. It was turning into a beautiful night—the bright starlight making the expanse of smooth unbroken snow shimmer. The cloud cover tore apart even more, revealing the waning full moon, the ribbon of light lying like blue silver against the snow. Another night, Finn would have stopped and appreciated the sight. But tonight, he was so damned tired, he felt as if he didn't have a whole bone in his body.

But he wasn't so tired that his mind switched off. And he spent the last leg of the drive thinking about his departure three days earlier—and how Mallory had made him feel. He couldn't afford to make another slip like that—to get that close to her—to let her get that close to him. She was dangerous to his equilibrium, and he knew it. They didn't even travel in the same universe, let alone the same world. And he had to remember that. He couldn't allow himself to want things he could never have.

But just thinking about how she felt in his arms made his pulse speed up, and he realized that one reason he wanted to come straight home had nothing to do with how exhausted he was. He wanted to get home because she was there, waiting for him. Feeling as if he had a huge hole right in the middle of his chest, he made himself loosen his grip on the wheel, his mood heavy and sober. She was nothing more than an emotional blip in his life—and he had to remember that. In a few hours or days, Mallory O'Brien would be gone from his life, and that was how it would be.

His driveway had been plowed, thanks, no doubt, to Old Joe, the huge pile pushed to one side. Finn pulled slowly through his gateway, his headlights casting a wide swath against the pole barn, the horse trailer rocking as it tracked through the ruts. There was another vehicle parked by the barn, a battered old pickup, headlights turned off, the engine running.

Old Joe got out of the truck and started hobbling toward the long shed where Finn parked the rig. The old man was dressed in heavy coveralls, a hat perched on his head with earflaps sticking out like wings. He was huffing and puffing by the time he reached Finn. "Was in town this afternoon. Heard you was on the way home and that you had one hell of a trip. Figured I'd just wheel in here and give you a hand afore I head back into town. Tonight is my shuffleboard night."

Finn pulled on his gloves, then undid the latch to drop the trailer ramp. "It was pretty bad all right."

His neighbor flapped his hand, shooing him away. "Go.

Get yerself to the house. You look as whupped as Satan's dog. I'll tend these here animals and get the gear stored. You hie your butt in and get some hot vittles into you.''

Finn wearily dragged his hand down his unshaven face. He was cold to the bone and so damned tired, he didn't think he had the energy to get from here to the house.

"Go on. Get," bossed the seventy-eight-year-old. "I can't go out on them rescues, but I can do this. So get. Haul your sorry butt outta here."

Finn dropped his hand on the other man's shoulder. "Thanks, Joe. I appreciate it." He went to the cab of the truck and retrieved his parka, backpack and saddlebags. "I'll likely see you tomorrow."

The old man cackled, coming back with his old standby. "Not if I see you first."

Draping his saddlebags over one shoulder, Finn hitched his pack over the other, clutching his parka in one hand. He was going to do exactly what his neighbor had ordered, haul his sorry butt to the house. And he hoped to hell there was something half-decent to eat—he'd just about had his fill of trail rations.

Rooney bounded around the corner of the house with a stick in his mouth, and Finn stopped and scratched his ears, then threw the stick a couple of times. Then the dog bounded up the road to the barn, off to check the sound of horses being unloaded from the trailer.

Finn entered the porch, latched the door behind him, thinking about what he was going to tell Mallory. He almost hoped she would be asleep. He just didn't want to have to deal with a whole bunch of questions tonight. But she had probably heard both vehicles pull in, and he could just visualize her anxiously pacing back and forth, wondering what he had found. Lord, he just didn't have the energy to deal with that kind of female distress. He was dead tired. All he wanted was some hot food, a hot shower and bed.

Only the track lights were on in the kitchen, and it was very still inside. He unlatched the inner door and toed it open with his boot, letting the backpack slide off his shoulder. He stepped in and set it on the floor, then dumped the saddlebags and parka on top. He turned, finding the living area silent and empty. But Mallory immediately appeared out of the bedroom, her hair tied up on top of her head, loose tendrils corkscrewing around her face and down her neck. She had on one of his blue flannel plaid shirts and a pair of his sweatpants, with the legs rolled up. And she wasn't worried and anxious.

She was bloody well furious. Jamming her hands on her hips, she glared at him. "Where in *hell* have you been? Don't tell me it took three whole days to confirm that I was probably dead! I've been worried sick, for Pete's sake, thinking something had happened to you!"

Finn stared at her as if she'd just launched herself out of a cannon. Tired and weary and sore to the bone, he slammed the door shut, glaring right back at her, his warm fuzzy memories of her all shot to bits. "Just where in hell do you get off, anyway? I've been out there, plowing around in snow up to my thighs for three days, freezing my ass off, looking for you in terrain you can't even imagine. Where in hell do you think I've been, vacationing in Mexico?"

She gave him a scathing look, then tipped her nose in the air and marched over to the fridge, yanked open the door and took out a large pot. She slammed the door of the fridge with her elbow, then banged the pot on the stove, flipping on the gas burner. "Well," she shot back, "it would have been nice if you'd told me you'd be gone for days. Three days—you could have *walked* to Mexico."

Finn stared at her, poleaxed and speechless. A woman he spent what—maybe thirty hours with? And now she was banging around his kitchen like an irate wife, giving him hell for taking so long to find her frozen body? He couldn't believe it!

Hearing the absolute ridiculousness of what was going through his mind, Finn bent his head and gouged at his eyes. Now he really was losing it—ranting on about a rescue mission to find a woman who, at that precise moment, was poking at something in a pot on his stove.

Letting out a heavy sigh, he wearily braced his hand on the wall and pried off his boots, lining them up on the boot rack.

The fragrance of hot, spicy stew penetrated his exhaustion, and he was almost driven to his knees by the smell alone. He hoped like hell he was not imagining the smell, because not only was he half-dead and nearly frozen, he was also so hungry he could eat his own leg.

Certain he wasn't hallucinating, he glanced over at the stove. Her chin still stuck out a mile, Mallory spoke, using that same snippy tone he had already come to recognize. "You'd better go have your shower if you're going to have one. Your supper will be on the table in ten minutes, and if you're not here to eat it, I'll feed it to the dog."

Suddenly feeling as if he were the one who'd just got blasted out of a cannon, Finn dragged his hand down his unshaven face, then shucked his vest. Hell. There was no point trying to make sense of this.

The hot, pounding shower was as close to heaven as Finn figured he would ever get. After he soaped himself from head to foot, he braced his arms on the end of the large enclosure, letting the hot water beat down on his head and sluice down his back, the bathroom filling with steam. He didn't know he could hurt in so many places.

The shower door was suddenly yanked open, and Patrick O'Brien's daughter stood there like an avenging Celtic warrior woman rising out of the steam. Feeling particularly jaded and very old, Finn bowed his head and released a weary sigh. It didn't even really bother him that she'd practically jumped in the shower with him while he was bucknaked. What bothered him was that she was there at all.

The water pounded down as the steam rolled out, and she gave a little cough, then spoke, her voice abject and full of remorse. "I acted like an idiot. I knew I was being an idiot, and I'm sorry. I don't know how come I've turned into such a crazy person."

As if a shower conversation was an everyday occurrence between them, she shut the shower door. "And take your time. Supper is ready whenever you are."

His hands still braced on the wall and the hot water still beating down on him, Finn experienced a small twist of humor. Maybe he had it all wrong. Maybe it was her father who'd had her kidnapped just so he could have a little peace and quiet in his life.

Thinking about her father, Finn opened his eyes, his expression turning sober. Straightening, he shut off the water and opened the door, reaching for a towel. Hell, no wonder she was wound up like a top. Somebody was bent on killing her, and she was probably in knots, wondering what he had found at the crash site. And he hadn't even had the decency to say sweet tweet about it. Drying himself off, Finn made a resolution that he would not let her rile him, no matter what. It might kill him, but he was going to cut her a little slack.

Determined to be nice, Finn walked into the kitchen, doing up the buttons on his shirt. He stopped and stared at the table, not sure if he should be ticked off or amused. She had folded the dish towels into place mats and paper towel into napkins, and there was more cutlery on the table than he would normally use in a week. Obviously she was making an attempt to bring a certain amount of civilized behavior to his uncouth ways.

Dragging up his best manners, he sat down, leaning back in his chair as she set a bowl, arranged on a plate yet, of steaming stew in front of him. And it wasn't a sissy stew. It was a man's stew—big pieces of braised meat, chunks of vegetables, thick, dark gravy. And the smell. Ah, the smell was unbelievable. "Thanks," he said, his voice gruff. "This looks great."

She placed another serving on the other dish towel place mat. He did wait until she sat down, and he did wait until she picked up her fork, then he just couldn't hold off any longer, the smell of that rich-bodied stew kicking his appetite into overdrive. He couldn't ever remember being this hungry. Nor could he remember eating anything that tasted so good.

He was so intent on the food that he had almost worked his way through his second helping before he realized that she was simply pushing her food around, her motions jerky. Recognizing the fact that she had a high personal stake in what he'd been doing the past few days, he rested his forearms on the table and watched her, his gaze intent. Then, without saying anything, he reached into the breast pocket of his shirt, took out the pendant and placed it by her plate.

She went very still; then she grasped it and closed her eyes, clutching the pendant to her heart. It was not a priceless piece of jewelry—just a simple gold pendant, but it didn't take the tears gathering along her lashes to tell Finn it was priceless to her. Experiencing something soft and fluttery in his chest, he looked down as he waited for her to compose herself.

"Thank you," she whispered unevenly.

Propping his elbows on the table, Finn looked at her, lacing his hands together. "You're very welcome."

Avoiding his gaze, she placed the locket on the table, carefully aligning the broken chain. "It was my mother's— she gave it to me just before she died. And my father gave it to her just before they got married." She swallowed hard and traced the worn faded engraving on the back with her fingernail. "I thought I had lost it for good."

His clasped hands resting against his mouth, Finn continued to study her. She was a mess of contradictions.

Her lashes spiked with tears, she lifted her head and met his gaze. "Thank you for bringing it back."

He gave her a small smile. "And thank you for an excellent supper. And just so you know, I would have fought Rooney for it."

She gave him a small grin, still fondling the pendant. "Darn. I should have dumped it in his dish. I would have liked to see that."

Finn's expression altered, and his gaze turned serious. "You aren't going to like what I've got to tell you, Red."

She folded the keepsake in her hand, then sat back in her chair. Drawing up her legs to sit cross-legged, she wrapped her free hand around her ankle, then gave him a small smile. "Okay. I'm ready. Let's have it."

Finn didn't want to tell her. But he knew she had to know the truth. "I'd bet a large sum of money that your father's chief of security is in this up to his neck."

Some of the color drained from her face, and she rubbed her hand across her eyes, and he could see her struggle. It took her a moment to get it together; then she lifted her chin. "I was afraid of something like that." She tucked a loose piece of hair behind her ear; then she looked at him, her face lacking color. "Go on."

Leaning back in his chair, Finn rested one hand on his

thigh, keeping his voice even as he told her. Told her about the O'Brien hotshot security squad, about how Jackson tried to take over the show. Told her about the trip in, and how they eventually found the wreck.

He turned the knife over, then lifted his gaze to look at her. "The copilot was unconscious but alive." He explained the injuries and the extraction from the wreck. Then he told her how he went back the next morning and found the duct tape she'd pulled off her legs, as well as the pendant.

Finn straightened the knife, his face hardening. "I thought about pointing out that there was no coat, no purse, no luggage of yours on board, but I figured it was better to let it go."

"And the pilot?"

Finn didn't want to tell her that—how close the pilot had gotten to where he had found her. He watched her for a moment, then answered. "We found him about a hundred yards from where I found you. He'd been dead several hours, and he had a pistol with him." Finn gave a mirthless smile. "And I don't think he was out hunting bear."

There was a startled flash in her eye; then she surprised him with a low laugh. "No, I guess not."

He liked her laugh. And it was funny how she seemed to fit here, surrounded by such a rustic setting. The amber logs warm and lustrous behind her, her long copper hair piled haphazardly on top of her head, several tendrils hanging loose. She looked like something off the pages of an outdoor catalog, with the sleeves of his blue plaid shirt rolled to her elbows, the garment so big on her that it was sliding off one shoulder. But mostly she looked as if she belonged there, sitting at his table.

Jarred by that thought, Finn abruptly sat back and controlled his expression, a crazy pounding breaking loose in his chest. He'd definitely gone down the wrong trail on that one. And it was a mental slip he couldn't afford to make. Not when she was looking all warm and soft. And especially when she wasn't aggravating him.

Her soft voice broke through his mental jumble. "Did he mention my father?"

Finn glanced at her, his expression going still when he saw how pale her lips had gone and sensed the anxiety in her. He paused a second, then told her what Jackson had said, about her father being unavailable. He could tell the information about her father hit her hard. All the color washed out of her face, and she suddenly had that same trapped look in her eyes that she'd had when he found her. For one awful moment, he thought she might actually get sick.

Hugging herself, she closed her eyes and rocked in the chair, her teeth clenched, the anguish on her face almost intolerable to watch. He wanted to touch her, to just pick her up and hold her, but she was fighting a battle he knew nothing about.

Finally she looked at him, her expression haunted, her face as pale as paste. The green of her eyes magnified because of the glimmer of tears, she spoke, her voice low and uneven. "I think it's time I told you everything."

Chapter 6

Finn stared at her, the realization that she was going to trust him with the whole truth making his belly tighten. That show of trust affected him like little else had, and he had to look away. He pushed his plate and bowl to one side; then he leaned forward and propped his elbows on the table. Once he got his expression contained, he looked at her, his undivided attention prompting her to speak.

Looking down, she realigned the broken chain on the pendant; then she folded her hands in her lap and looked at him. "You know the first part. How they grabbed me out of my car, then injected me with something."

Lacing his hands together, Finn nodded. Mallory eased in an uneven breath, then began pushing the loose ends of the chain around. "They didn't realize it, but I'd regained consciousness just before they loaded me onto the plane. They had blindfolded me, but I was awake. Two people carried me on, and they put me on the floor—on a sleeping bag, I think. Anyway, they were talking." She looked up at him, her eyes so dark and somber, it made his chest hurt to look at her.

She hesitated, then spoke, her voice unsteady. "That's when I found out that they were taking me to my father's hunting lodge in Alaska. And it's only accessible by helicopter, or floatplane in the summer. Or a plane fitted with skis in the winter." She gave him a wan smile. "Anyway, I put up quite a fight when they tried to administer the second dose of drugs, and that's when they taped my feet—once they had me on board." She shrugged and toyed with the pendant. "Just before the drugs kicked in, I heard one of them make the comment that they should have just finished the job right then and there. But the other one—the one who appeared to be calling the shots—told the first one to use his head—that he had to keep 'her' alive until the boss could finish off her old man." She looked at him then, eyes wide with worry, her multitude of freckles standing out against her pale skin. "And the next thing I remember was waking up after the plane crash. When I saw the outside of the plane, I knew someone very close to my father had to be involved. They couldn't have gotten the plane otherwise."

"Is that why you didn't want to phone the police the night I brought you back?"

She nodded, her expression still ashen as she twisted a loose thread on the seam of the sweatpants. "I knew the police would immediately go to my father. And whoever was behind this would know that—and once they knew I was still alive, my father's life would be in jeopardy." She looked up and met his gaze. "It seemed to make sense. As long as they thought I was dead, he would be safe. Other than you, I didn't know who I could trust." She inhaled deeply, then began twisting the thread again. "If we were to call in the police now, Ed Jackson would be the first to find out, and he'd be able to get to my father.''

His elbows still on the table and his clasped hands resting against his mouth, Finn watched her, assessing whether she had given him the whole story. He was certain she had. And what she said made sense. His eyes narrow in thought, he stared at her for a moment; then he spoke. ''Now that you've told me what you know, tell me what you think.''

Her face drawn with worry, she sighed and let her hands fall listlessly into her lap. ''I don't know what to think,'' she said, holding his gaze. ''Nothing adds up. If it were a straightforward kidnapping, they would have taken me somewhere and held me until the ransom was paid. But keeping me alive until...until...'' She waved off the conclusion to that sentence, then tipped her head back to stare at the ceiling. ''I spent the whole time you were gone trying to figure it out.'' She gave him a mirthless smile. ''I even made lists, but I still couldn't come up with a reason why they would do this. Except,'' she paused and frowned, running her finger along the edge of the table, ''except the only thing I do know is that whoever orchestrated this had to be someone in the loop, someone who would have access to the information about the hunting lodge. That isn't common knowledge. And the plane. That makes it someone very, very close to him.''

''Like Ed Jackson.''

Her expression taut, she gave a small nod. ''Yes, like Ed Jackson.'' She stared across the room, tiny worry lines around her eyes. ''What's scary is that Jackson is the first line of defense between anyone and my father. And that's why we still can't go to the police. Even if the police bypassed him, he would be the first one my father would call.'' She shrugged and let out a sigh. ''But that still doesn't explain the comment about having to keep me alive until they finished off my father. If they want us dead, why would the order of killing matter?''

Finn had no answer for that, but he had a damned good idea who did. However, he had no solid evidence to base his opinion on—not a damned thing, other than a gut feeling. And if they went to the authorities with his suspicions, he had no doubt that Jackson had the capabilities to wipe all traces of both him and Mallory off the face of the earth. But one thing he did know, and that was that Jackson could never be the brains behind this kind of operation; Jackson was the muscle.

''Finn?''

He looked at her, keeping his expression passive. ''What?''

Hesitating, she fingered the necklace again, then she looked at him, fear in her eyes. ''Do you think my father is still alive?''

He considered her question and spoke. ''Gut feeling?''

She nodded. ''Gut feeling.''

Finn gave a small shrug. ''I got the feeling that Jackson doesn't know where he is.''

She closed her eyes and let her breath go in a rush, then she pressed her hands over her face, the chain of the pendant dangling between her fingers. She sat like that for several seconds; then she lifted her head and dropped her hands. He could see her turning something over in her mind. When she spoke, her voice was quiet. ''There is something that no one knows, not even Ed Jackson.'' She looked at him, a bit of color back in her face. ''Dad never believed in putting all his eggs in one basket, especially concerning my mother and me—and there had been threats and attempts in the past.'' She gave him a small smile. ''So our chauffeur is really a personal bodyguard, as well as a surveillance, weapons and electronics expert.'' Her smile widened just a little. "I have a sneaking suspicion that Dad hired Malcolm away from Buckingham Palace, but neither one of them will confirm it. However," she said, her expression getting serious again, "the fact is, Malcolm has taken our protection several steps further. And if he had any idea I was snatched, he would have had Dad immediately boxed, and our country estate turned into a fortress."

Finn lined up his utensils, assessing what she had told him; then he responded. "But I don't think that takes the heat off you. Their initial plan went up in smoke the minute you disappeared. But I expect they now have a contingency, and you can be damned sure Jackson is a part of it." He hesitated, then asked the one question that he needed an answer to. "What would your father do if he knew where you were right now?"

She gave him a warped smile. "Seriously?"

"Seriously."

"He would be up here so fast, it would make your head spin."

"With Malcolm's approval?"

The smile was back. "No. Not with Malcolm's approval. My father doesn't believe he needs approval for anything, Donovan. He's a force unto himself."

Finn returned the smile, his mind processing that information. Which scrapped any idea of calling her old man. The last thing they needed was to draw Patrick O'Brien out into the open. Both their lives would be in danger if they did.

Finn didn't want to point out the obvious. She'd already had just about all she could handle, but he couldn't take any chances with her either. She had to see that the danger wasn't over. He gave her a steady look. "We can't take any chances, Red. If they found out you were alive, I think we can assume they'd come looking for you.''

She slanted a look at him, and she tried to make a joke out of it, but he caught a glimmer of annoyance in her eyes. "God, I love the way you sugarcoat things, Donovan. It makes a girl feel so special.''

Finn wanted to grin but he didn't. The stew had kicked in, and he barely had the energy to stay sitting in the chair. He watched her mull things over, sharply aware of the pressure she was under. Then he went back over everything they'd talked about, trying to assemble all the pieces of information into something concrete. He was dead certain that Jackson was involved, but in what capacity was anybody's guess. And right now, he was too damned tired to figure anything out.

He looked at her. ''I need to know what you want to do, Red. We need to come up with some sort of plan.''

She stared back at him, her eyes full of distress; then she looked down and straightened the corner of the makeshift place mat. ''I don't want to do anything right now.'' She let out a sigh and leaned back in her chair, meeting his gaze. ''You're exhausted, and so am I. I hardly slept at all when you were gone. And now with Ed Jackson in the picture, that changes things. I don't want to do anything stupid or rash.'' She tucked some loose hair back, then gave him a dispirited look. ''Can we just sleep on it for tonight?''

He gave her a small smile. ''Sounds good to me.''

Stretching his cramped and aching legs out in front of him, he folded his arms across his chest, considering the woman who sat across from him. She had tried to control her wild mane of hair by tying it up with a piece of string, but silky tendrils curled around her face and neck. And he'd never noticed before how her full mouth was almost pouty—except Mallory O'Brien wasn't a pouter. He almost smiled to himself. Mallory O'Brien was a scrapper and a fighter.

His expression sobered as he noticed that she was chewing on a fingernail, her anxiety getting the best of her. Hell, she had reason to be anxious. It was even getting to him. But he was too tired to think about it anymore. And he didn't want to talk about it anymore. And she probably didn't need to think and talk about it, either. From the way she looked, he suspected she had done nothing but pace and worry the whole time he was gone, and he decided it was time to get her mind off all her considerable problems.

He crossed his ankles, his gaze fixed on her, waiting for her reaction. "That was damned fine stew, Ms. O'Brien. I wouldn't have thought that a woman like you would know one end of the kitchen from the other."

He got exactly what he expected. Her head came up and she turned to look at him with that haughty, regal look, hard-blown annoyance flashing in her eyes. "Just where do you get off making those kinds of assumptions? I'm not a moron, for God's sake."

Finn had no idea why he was deliberately needling her— well, that wasn't exactly true. She did need to get her mind off the mess, but the real truth was that he'd never seen anyone who sizzled the way she did when she was ticked off. Watching her sizzle was kind of like watching fireworks.

He gave her an off-center smile. "I never said you were a moron. I'm just surprised you know how to cook."

Straightening her spine, she placed her hands on the table and narrowed her eyes at him. "Of all the unmitigated, mindless…" Flashing him another irritated glance, she rose and roughly tied the tails of his shirt around her waist; then she snatched away the remainder of his supper, picked up hers and flounced to the sink. "I should have fed it to Rooney. At least he'd appreciate it."

Finn watched her at the sink, her back as stiff as a board. She was tall, with well-defined shoulders and an athletic body. And even as monkish as his life had been over the years, he still had enough red blood in him to appreciate the way his sweatpants molded to her long, long legs and her lush bottom.

But tonight he was so worn down, beat-up and tired, he was certain there wasn't even the smallest chance of arousal left in him. Then she twisted around and bent over as she slammed a dish into the bottom rack of the dishwasher, the neck of the shirt gaping open. And he realized she didn't have a thing on underneath. As if frozen in place, he stared at the soft female flesh, the swell of full breasts, the smooth, freckled skin. Another rush of heat nailed him to the seat, and he broke out in a cold sweat. Gripping the arms of the chair, he clenched his jaw and closed his eyes, his heart slamming against his ribs.

Jarred by his reaction and feeling suddenly trapped, he launched himself out of the chair and headed for the door. Snagging up his mackinaw off the hook, he yanked open the door. "I'd better check the horses," he ground out, then stepped into the porch, pulling the door behind him. The frigid air washed over him, and he rested his forehead against the windowpane in the second door, trying to pull air into his lungs.

But the pulsating heat was not that easy to vent. And it was a long time before he got strength back in his knees. Still half stunned, he raked his hand through his hair. Now he was in big trouble. Very big trouble. For the first time since he'd met her, his rigid self-control had broken down, and he had visions of her naked. Disgusted with that carnal lapse, he ripped open the door and stepped outside, yanking on his jacket as he started striding toward the barn. Damn it, he had to get a grip. He was a grown man, for God's sake—not some hormone-driven adolescent. He swore again. There was something wrong with his head to let that happen.

But there was nothing wrong with his head, prompted a little voice; it held the image of her naked breasts just fine.

As exhausted and as strung-out as he was, Finn found things to do in the tack room until it was a legitimate time to call it a night. With Rooney trotting ahead of him, he headed down the path to the cabin, his collar turned up, his hands in his pockets.

There were only a few clouds left in the sky, and the full waning moon cast a silky sheen on the drifted snow, the stars so bright in the high mountain air that they seemed close enough to touch. It was the kind of night that he would never get enough of, the kind of night that allowed him the space to take a deep, full breath. A shifting band of northern lights shimmered and wavered above the trees and he paused to watch them. If he hadn't felt so battered and tired, he would have stayed outside to appreciate the enormous sense of space in that night sky. Or he might have even strapped on his snowshoes and trekked out to the little meadow where the deer often gathered at night.

But not tonight. Tonight he was just too damned beat to appreciate anything. *Except,* prompted that wicked little voice in his head, *Patrick O'Brien's daughter.*

Giving himself another lecture, he stomped the snow off his boots and entered the porch, the dog preceding him. Okay, he thought to himself, this was no big deal.

The first thing he noticed when he entered the cabin was that the furniture had all been rearranged. He closed the door, perusing the arrangement with a jaundiced eye, then expelled his breath on a heavy sigh. It didn't matter. It really didn't matter. If it made her feel better to shove furniture around, then far be it from him to say anything. Although—hell, he didn't know—it seemed cozier like this.

Shaking his head, he stepped out of his boots, telling himself he was going to go to bed and keep his mouth shut.

She was at the stove, stirring something in a pot, and she glanced at him. He could tell from the redness around her eyes that she'd been crying. Feeling like a heel for baiting her earlier, he made an awkward gesture to the new arrangement. "The living room looks great."

She managed a wan smile, indicated the pot. "I've made some hot chocolate. Would you like some?"

About to take off his coat, Finn hesitated. She had been locked inside for three days, with nothing to do but worry, and then he had to give her a hard time on top of it. He jammed his hands in the pockets of his mackinaw. "Have you ever done any snowshoeing?"

She looked startled for a moment, then gave a low, husky laugh. "No. I've never been snowshoeing, but I'm a wonder on the subway."

Experiencing a weird kind of approval for her not wallowing in self-pity, he awarded her a lopsided grin. Okay. So maybe snowshoes weren't such a great idea. But there was another option. Feeling almost as if he were asking her out on a date, he nodded at the pot. "Why don't you dump that in two of those thermal mugs on the second shelf, and come out and watch the show?"

She stared at him a moment; then acting oddly flustered, she wiped her hands on the thighs of her pants, her smile tentative. "I would love to come out and watch the show."

Ten minutes later, they were back outside, with her wrapped up in his sheepskin coat and an old pair of his mukluks on her feet. Each of them carried a thermal mug as they trudged through the trees. Rooney plunged ahead of them as Finn broke trail through the undisturbed snow, leading them to the little clearing just north of the cabin and situated on the rim of the ravine. His objective was the old tree stump anchored there.

When he finally reached it, he dusted it off as she climbed the last of the trail, her labored breath hanging in the air. "Here," he directed. "Come have a seat. It's the best in the house."

Huffing and puffing with exertion and laughter, she grasped his hand and let him pull her up the last little bit, then she collapsed on the stump. "Ah. Darn it. I am so out of shape." She shivered, then moved over so there was room for him on the stump.

This spot was a particular favorite of Finn's. It was a high spot, clear of the barrier of trees, and the land rolled away from them, giving the impression that they were on top of the world. The vast, unblemished blanket of snow undulated and shimmered in the moonlight. And below, the silver thread of the unfrozen creek snaked its way through the wolf willow that grew in clusters at the bottom of the ravine. If there was a place where he felt almost whole, this was it.

Mallory looked up as she took a sip from the mug, then went perfectly still. "Oh, my God," she breathed, awe-struck by the night sky. Her breathless admiration warmed him, replacing the bone-deep weariness with a surge of pleasure.

"That is so amazing," she murmured. She turned and looked at him, and he could see the sparkle in her eyes in the silvery light. "You weren't kidding. This *is* the best seat in the house." She grinned. "You must know some-body who knows somebody to get these on such short no-tice."

He gave her a half grin back. "I have my sources." He

pointed out the aurora borealis shimmering and wavering in the northern sky, the colors changing from white to pink to a misty shade of green, the bands constantly shifting and changing. Mallory was a fascinated spectator, and that warmed Finn even more.

He'd done this hundreds of times in the past—come out here to watch the night sky and to soak up the unbelievable sense of space. But it was different tonight, with someone there to appreciate it with him, someone to share in the spectacle, someone else's frozen breath hanging in the air beside his. And it was as if the whole universe was putting on a display for them. And the countryside was so still, it was like sitting in a perfect crystal dome.

They sat there watching the northern lights and sipping their hot chocolate, silently viewing nature at her most spectacular. It was so huge and impressive, neither of them spoke, the need to communicate taking second place to the awesome display. And Finn discovered something significant about Ms. Mallory O'Brien. She might have an unpredictable temper, and she might be as opinionated as hell, but she was also very comfortable with silence. That was a rare gift. And one that suited him.

They had been sitting out there close to half an hour when the northern lights finally began to fade. Finn drained the last of his hot chocolate, preparing to call it a night when Mallory spoke, her voice quiet. "Finn?"

He turned and looked at her, waiting for her question. She held his gaze, her face unsmiling in the moonlight. "Would you mind telling me about your wife?"

Finn stared at her, then roughly stuck his hands in the pockets of his mackinaw, his throat suddenly cramped shut, an age-old pain rolling through him. His sweet, sweet Sally. How could he ever explain Sally to another woman?

His face feeling almost paralyzed, he took a deep, uneven

breath, trying to ease the constriction in his chest. Not aware of making any conscious decision to answer her, Finn found himself responding. "What do you want to know?"

Her response was very soft. "What was she like? What happened?"

Finn plowed snow into a heap with his foot; then he took another uneven lungful of cold air and started at the beginning, his voice gruff with remembering.

Mallory never said a word. She just sat there looking out across the snow-laden ravine, quietly listening.

Finn had never told anyone the whole story before—not from beginning to end. For one reason or another, he had always given an abridged version of the tragic circumstances leading up to her death. The version all depended on who he'd been telling it to. But tonight was different. Tonight he told it start to finish, unburdening the whole ugly, devastating end to that part of his life.

He was pretty torn up when he was through, and she didn't say anything. Instead she took off one mitt and slipped her hand into his pocket, lacing her fingers through his, silently offering him the kind of comfort he hadn't had in years. She just held his hand for a long time, then softly, so softly, she spoke. "I completely understand why you did what you did," she said, giving his hand a firm squeeze. She paused for a moment, then eased in an unsteady breath. "And I am so sorry about your wife."

Her words went straight to his heart, and Finn clenched his jaw, the surge of emotion nearly blinding him. Rubbed raw by her absolution, he closed his eyes and swallowed hard, tightening his hand around hers. Those words and the warmth of her hand were the kindest, most thoughtful gestures anyone had ever extended to him since Sally's death so many years ago. And her kindness and compassion made his chest hurt. It was almost as if that single touch had broken the chains around his heart.

Ice crystals had begun to glimmer in the cold night air, coating the trees and shrubs with a fine layer of hoarfrost when Mallory finally broke the silence. As if needing to confide, she started talking. "My father and I have been in a battle of wills ever since I can remember. He wanted to take control of my life, and I wanted to take control of it myself. It was a constant fight between us." She let go an uneven sigh, a definite wobble in her voice when she continued. "Now I don't even know where he is or if he's all right. And I wish I could take back all the arguments we've had."

He gave her hand a reassuring little shake. "We're eventually going to get this all sorted out, Red. And with your chauffeur looking out for him, I'm sure he's being well taken care of. The really important thing is that we keep our heads on straight until we figure out what to do."

As if bolstered by his reassurance, she turned and looked at him, a hint of a smile around her mouth. "What exactly does that mean—keeping one's head on straight? It's never made any sense to me. What has a straight-on head got to do with anything?"

He gave her a wry smile. "You're a pain in the butt, you know that?"

She grinned at him, withdrawing her hand. "Speaking of butts, you look very comfortable, perched there on yours."

It wasn't really a question, but she seemed to be waiting for a positive response. Actually, in spite of how tired he was, he'd gotten pretty darned comfortable. At least with her. He gave her another half smile. "I have no complaints."

He didn't know how it happened. One minute he was

sitting on the stump beside her, and the next he was flat on his back in the snow. Looking totally pleased with herself, she dusted her hands together and had the audacity to laugh at him. "Well, now you do." Whistling for Rooney, she headed down the trail toward the house. "Don't forget to bring the mugs," she called back to him.

Still flat on his back, Finn stared up at the blanket of stars, feeling just a little ticked. He'd spent the last three days wading through snow up to his armpits trying to find her downed plane, then instead of hauling his sorry butt off to bed, he'd dragged himself out here tonight—for her benefit—to give her a break from being locked up in the house for three days. And then she showed her appreciation by dumping him in the snow?

"What did you do that for?" he yelled, feeling aggravated.

"Because you looked too darned complacent," she yelled back.

He lay there for a moment longer, irritation building in him. She was a crazy woman. Wearily getting to his feet, Finn dusted himself off, digging snow out from the neck of his jacket, catching himself almost wanting to smile. And he wasn't pleased about that either.

She was already inside and had her winter gear stripped off and hung up when he entered, and he was so intent on nursing his annoyance, he nearly tripped over the dog.

Slamming the mugs down on the shelf over the boot rack, he opened the door wider, giving a stern hand signal that indicated the porch. "Rooney. Out!"

Mallory looked at him as if he'd taken leave of his senses. Giving him one of her determined, narrow-eyed looks, she snapped her fingers and indicated the floor beside her. His tail wagging and looking totally pleased with himself, Rooney waddled over to her, looking up with puppy-love worship. Finn could not believe his eyes. She had his dog taking sides, for Pete's sake.

Fixing her with a baleful look, Finn said nothing. Okay. He was too tired to even fight with her over it. And after spending another hour outside with her, he was too damned tired to care. He'd let her win this one.

The effects of the past three days hit him like a locomotive, and he felt his knees wobble. No wonder he was cranky. He hadn't had more that nine hours of sleep since he'd left. Dragging off his coat, he felt the room wavering. It was time to call it quits. He was bloody well retiring from the battlefield.

Once in his room, he flipped the switch that turned on his bedside light, then grabbed his shirt by the back of the neck and pulled it off over his head, his insides going very still when he saw his bed. Pillows stacked up. A novel spread open on the covers. The lamp moved. He let out an exasperated sigh. Someone had been sleeping in his bed, and it sure in hell wasn't Goldilocks.

But right then, he was too tired to care. He dragged back the covers, revealing the dark blue sheets and flipping the book to the floor. Shucking the rest of his clothes, he sprawled facedown on the bed, sure every vertebrae in his spine had been disconnected. He was getting too old for this crap. Way too old.

Dragging up enough energy to move, he braced himself up on one elbow to pull up the covers and shut off the light. And he saw dog hair—on the sheets and on the pillowcases—all kinds of dog hair. Another flicker of irritation almost gave him enough energy to pile out of bed and go give her hell. She was going to ruin the best dog he'd ever had if she kept that up.

But it just wasn't worth the effort—having to put on some clothes and walk all the way back out there. He'd deal with the dog issue tomorrow. Too tired to even think straight, he closed his eyes and let the first stages of unconsciousness take him under.

Finn dreamed about the plane crash that night, and Jackson, and he woke up abruptly, the dream still clear in his head. He stared into the darkness, his pulse racing, his mind turning over. What would anyone gain from keeping her alive only until they could do away with her father? Suddenly wide-awake, he considered all the pieces. She had no siblings, and her mother was dead. So who would benefit if Mallory O'Brien, heir to millions, were to survive her father, then turn up dead?

Certain he had stumbled onto a critical piece of the puzzle, he threw back the covers, intending to go across the hall to wake her up. But a grunt came from the end of the bed, and a weight shifted beside him. Rising up on one arm, Finn turned, his night vision focusing. He had to shake his head to make sure he wasn't still dreaming.

Rooney was asleep on the foot of the bed and the daughter of Patrick O'Brien was asleep beside him. Now how in hell had she managed that? How had she gotten into bed without waking him up? Feeling totally discombobulated, Finn scrubbed his hand down his face, not at all happy about the circumstances he found himself in. Especially when he had already envisioned the daughter of Patrick O'Brien naked. Even more annoyed for remembering that slip, and determined not to let it go any further, he caught her shoulder and shook her. "Damn it, Mallory." She rolled on her back and smacked her lips, then opened her eyes and looked at him.

"What," she muttered groggily.

He had intended on telling her she couldn't crawl into his bed whenever she felt like it, that he was a red-blooded male. But that was just begging for trouble, so he changed his mind. "You can't let Rooney sleep in the house," he growled. "He's an outside dog, and it's not good for him. It's too hot inside—and he gets sores."

Bracing herself up on both her arms, she opened her eyes really wide, then glared at him. "Did you wake me up from a sound sleep just to tell me I shouldn't let the dog sleep in the house?"

"Yes." He snapped, then his honesty kicked in. "Well, no."

She continued to glare at him. "Which is it, Donovan? Yes or no?"

Lord, she looked so right in his bed, with moonlight streaming over her, one shoulder temptingly revealed, her hair begging to be touched. Jerking his thoughts away from that track, he said the first thing that came into his head. "It's no." Feeling a little as if he'd just been launched out of a cannon again, he turned to look at her squarely. "Who would benefit if you were to survive your father, then turn up dead?"

She glared at him, her tone huffy when she retorted, "You could have worded that a little more tactfully. Turning up dead sounds pretty darned callous."

She was right. It was callous. But how come he was always the one in the wrong here? Letting out an exasperated sigh, he stuffed two pillows behind his shoulders and folded his arms across his chest. "I didn't mean for it to sound callous, Red," he said with exaggerated patience. "I was just trying to make some sense out of what's going on. And I need a place to start."

Without responding, Mallory rose from the bed, snapping her fingers at Rooney to follow; then she left the room. *Now what,* he thought, staring after her. Talk about the vagrancies of a woman's mind. This one could wear him right out.

He heard the outside door close, and a flicker of humor surfaced. Maybe she'd gone out to cool off in the snow.

He was amusing himself with that image when Mallory reentered the room—without the dog—turned on the light and crawled up beside him. She had a bottle of rye in one hand and two glasses in the other. Finn hitched himself up higher so he was sitting up, the sheet firmly tucked around his hips.

Her face furrowed with thought, she opened the bottle, splashed a slug into one glass, then handed it to him. The thoughtful look still on her face, she repeated the process for herself before screwing the cap back on and wedging the bottle beside his pillows. Turning to face him, she drew her legs up to sit cross-legged. She took a sip from her glass, then looked at him. "What made you ask that?"

He frowned and rolled the amber liquid around in his glass. "You said something earlier, about why the order of killing was so important." He shrugged. "And I started wondering. Who would benefit if your father were to predecease you?"

She thoughtfully watched him, then tossed back the rye, shuddering as it went down. Finally she gave him a small, tight smile. "Have you any idea how much I don't want to start wondering about stuff like that?"

Understanding her reticence more than she would ever know, he stared into space. Hell, he didn't want to make it worse for her, but she had to realize it wasn't over yet. He swirled the amber liquid around his glass again, then downed it all. He waited for the heat to hit his belly before he looked at her, his expression somber. "You have to know that your life could depend on just that, Red. These aren't kids playing cops and robbers in the park. These guys are playing for real."

She ran her finger around the lip of her glass, sighed and looked at him. "I don't even know where to begin."

Drawing up one knee under the sheet, Finn rested his forearm across it, his expression thoughtful. "Okay. Let's start at the beginning." He looked at her. "Are you sole beneficiary to his estate?"

Mallory shrugged. "Well, there are other sizeable bequeaths, but yes, I'd inherit the bulk of his estate."

"Okay. Next step. If your father was to predecease you, where would the bulk of your estate go?"

Mallory studied the glass, then she began pulling at the frayed cuff of his sweat top, and he could swear she was deliberately avoiding the question. He prompted her. "Where, Red?"

Finally she shrugged, looking very sheepish. "Well, umm," she stalled, "actually, I don't have a will." She finally looked at him, making a little grimace. "Well, I *had* a will. I just don't have one anymore."

No will? Someone with that kind of fortune, and she didn't have a will? Finn didn't know whether to be appalled or amused by her admission, but one thing was for sure: he definitely wanted to hear this story.

She got all fidgety and evasive, and it was obvious she was trying to avoid something. Humor lifting his mouth, he prompted her again. "And?"

She heaved a sigh and looked at him. "Well, I sort of lost my temper."

Watching her, Finn allowed his amusement to show. "That's hard to believe."

She gave him a sharp look, and he grinned and prompted her again. "Go on."

She heaved another sigh and told him. "I was at my father's office for other reasons—or what I thought were other reasons. But then he insisted it was time I reviewed my personal affairs with his battery of lawyers. I didn't think it was necessary, so we got into this huge fight. Then this stuffy personal lawyer of his—the very stiff and proper Mr. Delleware of Delleware, Johnson, McGinnis and Fogalty,'' she rhymed off, her tone disparaging, "brought out another set of documents, insisting it was time I made some amendments to my last will and testament.'' She gave another shrug, avoiding his gaze as she picked at the hem. "My father is always trying to run my life—he always thinks he knows what is best for me. Anyhow, this really ticked me off, so I grabbed the stack of legal documents out of the very proper Mr. Delleware's hands, and I stuffed them through the paper shredder.'' She grinned suddenly and looked at him, a gleam of delight in her eyes. "It was one of the industrial-strength paper shredders, and it just ate that stack of paper up like nothing.'' Then she heaved a sigh. "I was so furious. I said that's what I thought of his amendments, and I stormed out of the office.''

Finn couldn't help it. He laughed out loud. Looking at her, he shook his head. "Maybe I had it right all along. It crossed my mind that maybe it was your father who had you kidnapped, so he could get a little peace and quiet.''

Mallory looked totally pleased with herself for making him laugh, and she sloshed another shot into his glass and hers. Clinking her glass against his, she grinned. "To my father.''

Slouching down lower on the pillows, Finn stared into space and took a swallow from the glass, his mood altering. He wished he didn't have to make her dig through this. But if he was going to keep her safe, he had to know. He took another swallow, then looked at her. He didn't say anything, but the question was there.

She heaved another sigh. "Okay. The people who would benefit by my death.'' She started listing them.

Another idea occurred to Finn almost immediately, one that made far more sense. He held up his hand to stop her. "Whoa. Just a minute. I think we're on the wrong track." He frowned, looking for a hole in his theory, but could see none. It would make sense—a whole lot of sense. He looked at her again, his expression intent. "Let's back up. Who would stand to inherit if you died intestate—and who could have found out that you had no will?"

Mallory stared at him, comprehension finally dawning in her eyes. She looked absolutely stunned for a moment; then she pulled herself together. She let her breath go in a rush. "God, that is so scary. But there are quite a few." Placing her glass in the cradle of her legs, she tucked loose hair behind her ears. "My father was an only child, and both his parents were only children, so there are only very distant relatives on his side. But my mother's side is a different story. She came from very old, old money." She smiled, a tone of amused cynicism in her voice when she explained. "And some very pedigreed blue blood. Frankly, I can't stand any of them. Snobs, every one."

Resting her forearms on her crossed legs, she frowned as she began to absently pleat the top sheet. "There are three remaining brothers—my uncles—on the Tyson-Reed side, along with several cousins." She looked up at him. "My grandfather disowned my mother when she married Dad. It was all very ugly, and they treated my mother like a leper while my grandfather was alive." Her chin came up and her tone turned hard. "I wouldn't give any of them the time of day, let alone leave them anything in my will." She looked up at him, wry amusement in her eyes. "But to be fair, after Grandfather died, my uncles went out of their way to effect a reconciliation with my mother. But I was always suspicious of that—I figured there were ulterior motives."

"So," Finn muttered, narrowing his eyes, thinking that maybe they had zeroed in on a motive, "is it safe to assume that they were also excluded from your father's will?"

Mallory actually laughed. "God, yes. He can't stand them, either. He thinks they're nothing but a nest of maggots."

He asked another question that had popped into his head. "If you were to predecease your father, where would the bulk of his fortune go?"

She shrugged. "The same bequeaths would remain in place, but the bulk would go to various international charities and scholarships. No one could touch his will if I predeceased him. It's ironclad."

She finished her drink and handed him her empty glass. He set it, and his own, on the night table. Then he laced his hands behind his head and stared at the ceiling, thinking how her information lined up. But with that kind of money up for grabs, it could be anybody.

Swiveling his head on his stacked hands, he turned to look at her, a funny feeling surfacing when he saw how abjectly she was folding and refolding the corner of the sheet.

As if sensing his gaze upon her, she looked up, her expression bleak. "Could we not talk about this anymore tonight?" she whispered unevenly.

He wanted to reach out and touch her, but he kept his hands safely anchored under his head. "No," he said, his own voice husky, "we don't have to talk about it anymore."

Before he had time to react, she curled up beside him, resting her head on his shoulder, her hand flat against his chest. She might as well have stuck him with a live wire. And just like that, he found himself holding her, his one hand cupping the back of her head, his other arm around her back. Finn closed his eyes and clenched his jaw, an enormous feeling unfolding in him. He was exhausted and his defenses were down, and right then, he didn't have what it took to pull away, to suggest she go back to her own bed. He wanted her there. And he wanted a whole lot more.

The muscles across her back contracted as she rose up on one elbow, her breasts pressing against his chest as she leaned over and turned off the light, the softness of her setting off a chain reaction in him. Letting go a long sigh, she snuggled closer, tucking her arm tightly around his chest. Just as if she had done it a hundred times before.

Her settling in like that set off another reaction in Finn, and feelings he didn't even know he was capable of rushed in on him. But of all the things that got to him, it was the comfortable familiarity that got to him most. It was as if this was the most natural thing in the world, for her to snuggle down and go to sleep in his arms.

Easing in a deep, unsteady breath, he carefully cradled her head just a little tighter against him, his chest so full it was hard for him to breathe. God, he had been alone so long. So long. And it was almost enough to simply hold her. Almost. Turning his head as if changing positions, he brushed his mouth against her forehead, the feel of her assaulting his senses. If he wasn't careful, he could end up in big trouble here. Very big trouble. He had never met anyone like her. Never. And she made him feel things he thought he'd never feel again.

Mallory sighed and settled deeper into his embrace, pressing her head more firmly against his mouth. And if Finn didn't know better, he would have sworn he felt her smile. He closed his eyes tighter and tried to swallow. He must be out of his mind, allowing her to get this close. But could he make himself pull away?

Not a chance. He adjusted his head and tightened his hold. Not a damned chance.

Chapter 7

When Finn woke up the next morning, daylight was already seeping in around the closed blinds, the sharp brightness piercing his closed eyelids. He was lying spreadeagled facedown on the bed, his whole body aching, his head thick and throbbing. He felt as if he'd been run over by a compactor.

Groaning slightly, he slowly rolled over on his back, his stiff, aching muscles protesting. Served him right for sitting out on a damned log, getting another bloody chill, just so she could see the northern lights. Wetting his mouth, he forced his eyes open, squinting at the clock on his bedside table. He squinted harder. Not possible. He massaged his eyes with his thumb and forefinger, then looked again. 9:23. He'd seen right the first time. He hadn't slept in that late in his entire life.

Bracing himself, he glanced over at the other side of the bed. Neat. Tidy. Blankets straight, as if she'd carefully covered him up. Nobody had ever covered him up. Nailed with a sudden ballooning sensation in his chest, he picked up a long red hair off the smoothed pillow, his heart giving an odd little falter when he wound it around his finger. It felt just like silk.

Swearing under his breath, he tossed the hair on the floor and levered himself out of bed, every muscle and bone protesting. All right. He had to get a grip. He should have never let her stay in his bed last night. It was a dumb thing to do, and he had to be more careful in the future. Mallory O'Brien could be damned hard on a man's mental health. Among other things.

He pulled on his jeans, his head so thick it felt as if it was stuffed with wet cement. He'd had two drinks last night; his head felt like he'd had a dozen.

Focusing on a spot straight in front of him, Finn made his way out to the hallway, feeling decidedly hungover. Diffused sunlight blazed through the windows in the great room, and he squinted against it, the smell of coffee reeling him in toward the kitchen. Coffee. He needed coffee.

Mallory was seated at the big round kitchen table, her long, long legs wound around the chair legs, her elbows hooked on the edge of the table, a book open in front of her. There was an empty plate off to one side and a steaming cup of coffee by her elbow. Her hair had been shampooed and was drying in thick curls around her shoulders, the sunlight streaming in through the windows making it shine like polished copper. She had obviously raided his closet again and had on another pair of his sweatpants and his favorite green plaid shirt.

Feeling unaccountably cranky, he spoke, his tone surly. "If you stick around much longer, we're going to have to get you some clothes of your own."

Propping her head on her hand, she turned to look at him, not at all intimidated by his sour attitude. Instead, there was a glimmer of amusement in her eyes. "And a good, good morning to you, merry sunshine," she said, watching him as he sat down, the sparkle of amusement intensifying. Unable to cope with either sunshine or morning, Finn tipped his head back and closed his eyes, hoping that the blood pounding around in there would run someplace else. He made a mental note not to do or say anything that might get her Irish up—he was sure his head would explode if she slammed so much as a dishcloth on the table.

He heard her push her chair back, then a few seconds later he felt her brush against his arm. Now what was she up to? Taking care not to set off the throbbing, he lowered his head and opened his eyes. Not only had she brought him a cup of freshly made black coffee, but she had also set a basket of steaming biscuits on the table in front of him. Fresh biscuits? She made fresh biscuits? He wanted to kiss her. No. No. He didn't want to do that. Just the thought made his blood heat up.

The fog finally cleared out of his mind, and he almost smiled as he watched her do the dish towel, paper towel, cutlery thing again. He was also going to have to clean up his act if she stuck around much longer—he couldn't remember the last time he'd bought napkins, and he didn't even own place mats. He glanced at her face as she brought the butter and a container of warmed honey to the table. She placed the butter and honey by the basket of biscuits.

Her tone was businesslike. "We're going to have to get groceries. There's hardly anything to cook with."

Right then, Finn couldn't have cared less about the state of their larder. All he cared about was that basket of steaming biscuits. "This looks really great," he said, his voice still rusty from sleeping so long.

She sat back down and started reading again, and Finn literally tore into the biscuits. He felt as if he hadn't eaten in a week, and he had nearly eaten his way through the entire lot when he decided it wouldn't kill him to be half-way sociable. He turned his head to look at her. She was engrossed in the book, and as she continued to read, she wound a long strand of hair around her finger. There wasn't anything remotely sensual about that preoccupied habit—but there was, and Finn got a rush of heat in his middle, which immediately spread lower. The sensation nailed him so hard, he just about choked on the last bite of biscuit. Fixing his gaze on the table, he blew out his breath, his heart going like a locomotive in his chest. He closed his eyes, and willed in some common sense. She was Patrick O'Brien's only daughter, for Pete's sake. And the whole thing was insane. And he was not going to let this happen. He was not. Come hell or high water, he *was* going to keep his mind from slipping below his belt buckle. If he'd been wearing a belt buckle.

More annoyed by the minute by his response to that one little gesture, Finn silently berated himself. Not only was she the daughter of one of the richest men in North America, she was too young, and most of the time she drove him crazy. And she was pushy. And she fit perfectly beside him in bed.

Whoa! Where in hell had that thought come from? Feeling as if he'd been poleaxed, Finn opened his eyes, his teeth clenched so hard his jaw ached, a hot-and-cold feeling breaking out all over his body. He was supposed to be getting a grip, not letting his mind wander. Somehow or another, he was going to have to get a damned grip. Feeling a whole lot like a cornered animal, he shoved his chair back, trying to scrape up the grit to thank her for breakfast. But she was so intent on what she was reading that she didn't even lift her head.

Getting away while the getting was good, he all but

bolted for the bathroom. A shower, a shave and a dose of common sense, and maybe he'd be able to get back in his own skin.

Except in the bathroom he encountered a very lacy bra and equally lacy French-cut panties hanging over the shower door. His insides immediately clutched up into a hard little ball, and he had another panic attack. He should have never gone to bed last night. He'd been able to keep a lid on it when he'd been dead tired. She hadn't tempted him that much. He shook his head. God, now he was lying to himself.

Swallowing hard, he reached out to snatch the garments off the door, but the silky sensation reminded him of her hair, and he jerked his hand back. Watching two pieces of very slinky, sensual underwear as if they were a pair of rattlesnakes, he let out a roar. "Can't you dry your damned dainties somewhere else? I want to have a shower!"

He heard her slam something on the table—probably the book—then he heard her stomp across the great room and down the narrow hall. She pushed past him, snatching the garments off the glass door. "For heaven's sake—they aren't contaminated. And they wouldn't have lowered your testosterone level if you'd taken them down yourself." Finn wasn't worried at all about his testosterone level. At least not at the moment. All systems were fired and ready to go.

But in spite of the state he was in, he was smart. He held the bathroom door so she couldn't slam it behind her.

The long shower helped, and by the time he'd showered and shaved, he felt almost restored. And almost in control.

Rolling back the sleeves of his clean shirt, he entered the great room, his insides going still when he spotted Mallory. She was standing in front of the windows, her arms tightly folded, and there was a pinched look on her face. It hit him that she'd pretty much been forced to remain inactive because of him. And he suspected that along with the worry, that inactivity must be driving her nuts. His expression turning sober, he finished rolling his sleeve. He realized that she hadn't complained once.

Moving to the stove to pour himself another cup of coffee, he spoke, his voice quiet. "We're going to have to come up with a plan, Red," he said, his tone serious. "I think the longer you stay hidden, the more the odds go up."

He saw her shoulders move as she heaved a big sigh. "I know."

He could hear the dejection in her voice, and he decided that more than anything, she needed to get out. "But before we do anything, we've got to get you some clothes. If we want to maintain your anonymity, that means a trip to Calgary."

She turned to look at him, her eyes not quite so bleak, a tiny smile playing with the corner of her mouth. "Are you humoring me?"

He grinned, indicating the shirt she had on. "No. That's my favorite shirt, and I want it back."

Before they left, they made a half-decent effort to disguise her. She stuffed her hair under a cap and put on a pair of Finn's sunglasses. Mallory pointed out that it really wasn't necessary—no one would recognize her without, as she put it, her glamour face on. Finn had to agree with her.

He was careful to get her out of the district without anyone seeing her. Granted the windows of his big SUV were tinted, but anyone who met them would have known he had a passenger with him. And it wasn't that often that Finn had someone in his vehicle. It wasn't until they were on the main highway leading into Calgary that he was able to really relax.

It struck him again that she was very comfortable with silence, more interested in the passing scenery than talking.

He didn't want to intrude on that space, but he had been doing a whole lot of thinking, and he needed to discuss his thoughts before they got to the city.

Bracing one elbow on the ledge by the window, he shifted in his seat. "I assume that Ed Jackson has the capability to listen in on all your father's phone calls."

She heaved a long sigh and looked at him, her face nearly obscured by the aviator glasses. "Pretty much."

"Then would there be any way that you could get in touch with your father's personal bodyguard—"

"You mean Malcolm?"

"Yeah, Malcolm. Could you get in touch with him without going through the monitored phone lines?"

Her expression brightened and she sat up straighter. "Yes, I could," she said, her tone full of hope. "He has a sister just outside of Chicago." Her expression brightened even more. "God, that's brilliant." Excitement bubbling from her, she looked at Finn and explained. "Malcolm always calls me Marigold when nobody is around. I could phone Joyce, his sister, and have her pass on a message to call Marigold. Malcolm would figure it out." She reached over and touched his arm, her smile energized. "Oh, Finn. If I could just find out my father was okay, that would make such a difference."

He cast her a smile, then refocused on the road, his arm tingling from where she'd touched it. "Fine then. That's what we'll do. Do you want to do it now or later?"

She looked at her watch. "Later. I know she works, and she won't be home yet. And I don't want to talk to anyone else." She looked at him again. "We'll go shopping first."

It was almost as if a terrible weight had been lifted off her shoulders. She perked right up, and her mood turned almost festive. She teased him, telling him she was a monster shopper, and that all of New York would quiver and quake whenever she went shopping there. Finn didn't ask for a definition. He figured he was better off not knowing.

She insisted that they take advantage of the accessibility and economy of shopping at one of the big, discount stores situated in the huge strip mall located on the southern outskirts. She wouldn't even consider going to one of the upscale malls.

Although he felt obliged to argue with her, Finn had to agree that it was a smart choice. Even if Jackson and his crew were actively looking for her, they would never conceive of the idea that Patrick O'Brien's daughter would go shopping there. And with the getup she had on, he doubted if even her own father would recognize her.

Finn thought he'd just hang out in the hardware section while she was getting what she needed. Wrong. Mallory had a different plan altogether. Suspecting that she was not all that keen on being on her own, he grudgingly gave in. He expected shopping with her would be the equivalent of getting his eyeballs scraped, but she charmed him right up front, worrying about how much money he was going to have to spend on her. Looking very earnest, she promised she would pay him back every penny.

He stuck with her program, but he took an abrupt hike when she started down the personal hygiene aisle, and he kept his eyes forward as the purchases were being scanned. There were some things he just didn't want to know.

An hour after they arrived, and several hundred dollars lighter, Finn stacked the bags of purchases in the back of his SUV, slightly bemused by how delighted she was over her good deals. It hit him again that she was not at all what he expected.

And it was the same when they went for groceries. It took about ten minutes for him to realize that she knew her way around the produce department. And he said as much.

She gave him a scathing look. "Honestly, Donovan. You have a very narrow opinion of me. My mother died when I was thirteen. Mildred—she's our head housekeeper—insisted that I learn to look after myself." She checked the price on the butternut squash, then reached for one. "And besides, I've been living on my own since I was eighteen. And I'm a damned fine cook." She followed him over to the grapefruit bin and took the piece of fruit he'd picked up out of his hands. "This is a lousy grapefruit, Donovan. Hasn't anyone ever taught you how to shop?" Suitably chastised, Finn stuck his hands in the pockets of his mackinaw, a flicker of humor surfacing. He wondered if she was so impossible to live with that her father had kicked her out when she was eighteen.

The grocery shopping done, they loaded the bags in the back of the vehicle, and Finn looked at her. "Would you like to grab something to eat?"

She shook her head, looking suddenly anxious again. "I think I'd like to call Malcolm's sister. But I need to leave a number where he can reach me, and I don't want to leave him yours."

Finn reached into the inside breast pocket of his mackinaw, and handed her his cell phone. "I don't think anyone is going to connect the dots on that one, Red. They won't be watching his sister. And if he's as smart as you say, you can be darned sure he's going to go to an outside phone to call you."

Suddenly nervous, she took a deep stabilizing breath and took the phone. "All right. Let's do it."

She climbed in her side of the vehicle as he turned on the ignition. Mallory took off her new mittens, then dialed for Chicago information and asked for the sister's number. She wrote it on the back of one of the bills she'd stuck in her pocket. Taking another deep breath, she dialed the number, pressed Send and put the phone to her ear.

Leaning back against the door, Finn draped his arm over the wheel and watched her. And he could tell by the way her expression altered that there was no answer.

Her face was impassive when she lifted the phone away, pressing End. "No answer," she said softly. "And no answering machine or voice mail."

Hating to see her like that, with the hope knocked out of her, he resisted the sharp urge to pull her onto his lap and hold her. Shedding that idea, he spoke, his voice gruff. "What if I were to try to call your father. It would be legitimate, seeing as I was team leader for the search."

Picking at the cuff on one of the mittens, she shook her head. "They'd never put you through to him. Someone would field the call, and if we used one of his private lines, they'd make a darned good guess that I was alive. It would be the only logical explanation for your having those numbers." She lifted her head and looked at him. "And I think they're going to want to find out what happened to me before they make another move."

Finn stared out the window, silently agreeing with her. Providing they had it figured out right.

Clouds had moved in, turning the sky dull and overcast and filling the interior of the cab with gray light. Her profile to him, Mallory continued to pick at the mitten; then she lifted her head and looked at him, her face showing the effects of the strain she'd been under. "Let's go home," she said softly. "I don't want to stay here, waiting around."

He nodded and shifted in his seat. He suspected that the reality of her situation was beginning to really get to her, igniting a whole new level of anxiety. And he could understand that. He also knew they could not remain in limbo much longer. They were going to have to make a move soon. That thought made his gut knot.

Checking his rearview mirrors, he pulled out of the parking spot. "Then let's go home."

Dusk was just beginning to settle in when they pulled into the yard, and Rooney trotted out to meet them, wagging his tail. Finn gave a small smile when the dog went to Mallory's side of the car before he came around to Finn. Smart dog. He knew what side his bread was buttered on.

Finn got some of the bags out of the back, and handed a couple to Mallory when she came around, then got another bunch and followed her to the house.

Mallory kicked off her shoes and immediately took her purchases to her room. Gazing after her with a thoughtful expression, Finn watched her disappear into the shadows. She hadn't said one word since they'd left Calgary. Feeling uneasy about her, he went back outside to get the groceries. When he reentered, Mallory was by the kitchen sink, and she was just replacing the cell phone on the counter, her expression strained. She turned to stare out the kitchen window. He didn't even ask. He knew from her expression that she had tried to reach Malcolm's sister again, and there was still no answer.

His arms full, he kicked the door shut behind him, his insides going cold when she turned and he saw her face. Setting his load down on the kitchen table, he continued to watch her as he peeled off his gloves.

She stared at him across the dimly lit room, her eyes wide, her expression transfixed by anxiety. She drew a deep uneven breath, then made a nervous gesture with her hands, not a speck of color in her full lips. "I did nothing but think about this all the way home," she said, her voice breaking. "I'm going to have to go back. I have to find out about my father."

His gut clenched at the thought of her leaving, and Finn broke eye contact as he stuffed his gloves in his pocket. Needing time to get his expression under control, he stripped off his mackinaw and hung it on a hook. Finally he turned to look at her, his own expression schooled. "Have you thought about trying to reach Malcolm directly?"

She made another gesture with her hands, only this one was almost beseeching. "I can't do that," she whispered.

"Why not?"

Looking more distraught than he'd ever seen her, she abruptly stuffed her hands up the sleeves of her sweat top, then swallowed with great difficulty. "I can't call anyone directly," she said, the deepening twilight making her face indistinct. "They would be on your phone number so fast, it would make your head spin. And I don't want to drag you into the middle of this."

Resting one hand on his hip, Finn stared at her, annoyance making his face hard. "For God's sake, I'm already in the middle of it. So a phone call isn't going to make much difference."

She leaned back against the counter and looked at the ceiling; then she looked back at him. "I need you to listen to me, Finn," she said, her tone just a little stronger. "I need you to hear me out and see if this makes any sense."

Resisting the need to slam something, Finn locked his jaw and stared at her. Finally he let his breath go on a long sigh. "Fine. I'm listening."

"The public knows that I'm missing, right?"

He nodded.

"Which means they must have filed a flight plan, and they probably made sure that whoever they filed it with knew I was on board. That would substantiate my having gone to my father's hunting lodge. Right?"

Resting his hip against the end of the cupboard, Finn folded his arms, continuing to watch her. "Right."

She chewed her bottom lip, her expression intent. "Okay, but the crash screwed up that plan. And now the whole world knows I'm missing. And I think as long as they don't know for sure what happened to me, everything is on hold. They aren't going to make a move on my father until they know for certain. But the minute they suspect I'm alive—and they would certainly suspect something if strangers started calling highly classified phone numbers— they would try to go with the original plan. It would be even worse if I called Malcolm directly, and they were monitoring that call. So as long as they believe I'm dead, my father is probably safe. But if they find out I'm alive, I think he's in real danger."

Considering what she'd said, Finn looked down at the floor, turning everything over in his mind, looking for holes in her theory. He couldn't see any. His arms still folded, he looked back at her. "Do you think your father would change his will if you were declared dead?"

"Not a chance." She tried to smile, but she couldn't hold it, and Finn saw the first glimmer of tears in her eyes. "I am going to have to go," she whispered, then she abruptly turned away and pressed her hand to her mouth, and Finn saw her shoulders heave. He could stand a lot of things— but he could not stand to see her break down. A huge ache rose up in him. It was as if some invisible hand reached into his chest and squeezed his heart.

His own expression tight with strain, he went over to her and grasped her shoulder. More than anything, he wanted to sweep her up and hold her, to use his size and strength to protect and shelter her. But he couldn't do that—not after the way he'd dropped his guard last night. He didn't dare hold her—he couldn't trust himself to get that close to her right now. She made him want things he couldn't have, to feel things he shouldn't feel. And he couldn't cross that line—it would be too damned hard when she was gone out of his life. But he could deal with the loneliness just as long as he could keep her safe.

Bracing himself, he hooked his knuckles under her chin and made her look at him, his heart giving another painful lurch when he saw the misery in her eyes. He forced a smile. "Just so you know. There is no damned way I'm going to let you leave here on your own, Red. Not a chance in hell."

Her fingers were trembling when she tried to quickly wipe away her tears, her eyes bleak. "I would feel so awful if something happened to you because of me. I couldn't live with myself."

It was as if the huskiness in her voice cut something loose in him, and he had to touch her face. His chest jammed with emotion, he gazed down at her, gently stroking one cheek with his thumb to dry away her tears. He could feel the heat of her, and he could feel her trembling, and God, but he wanted to hold her. The need was so intense it was almost more than he could control, and he knew he was going to be damned sorry later for getting even this close to her. But she looked so pathetic he just could not walk away. Unable to stop himself, he smoothed his thumb across her full bottom lip. "Hey," he said, his own voice very gruff. "We're in this together, Red. And if we're careful, nothing is going to happen."

More tears spilled over and she tried to swallow. "I hate this—hate feeling scared," she whispered.

Deciding that it was time to talk about the nuts and bolts of getting her back to Chicago, he took her by the hand, led her over to the sofa and made her sit down. Still clasping her hand, he sat on the coffee table so he could face her; then he reached for her other hand. Trapping both of her cold hands between his, he looked directly into her eyes. "We need to talk, Red. And these are the givens. First of all, I'm not letting you go anywhere without me. That's a hard cold fact. The second given is that you're going back." He looked down and rubbed his thumb along the topside of hers; then he looked back at her again. "That's going to present a bit of a problem. You don't have any identification, no Canadian birth certificate, no passport, so they aren't going to let you on a plane without it. So that means we're going to have to drive across the border."

She stared at him, her lips dry, her eyes wide with apprehension. "But won't that be risky for you?"

He gave her a wry smile. "Only if they ask. I'm not going to tell them I have a criminal record." Seeing the alarm in her eyes, he gave her hands a little shake. "If they catch me, all they can do is deny me entry into the U.S., Mallory. They can't toss me in jail for trying."

"But what if they catch you *after* you're across the border?"

He looked at her with dark humor. "The trick is not to get caught, Red." He gave her hands a reassuring squeeze. "Once we're across the border, we can try to call Malcolm directly. There'll still be a bit of risk, but since we're going to be on the move, it will afford us a certain amount of safety. We'll just have to be really careful."

She closed her eyes, trying to compose herself, then she let her breath go and looked at him. "I don't like the idea of phoning Malcolm," she said, her voice stronger. "I think that's just asking for trouble. You have no idea what my father's security force is capable of."

"Okay. Then the other alternative is for me to call your

father and tell him I found the necklace—that I'm going to be in Chicago on business, and I'd like to return it to him."

She gave him a sharp look. "No. Definitely not. Jackson would be on you within an hour." Absently she toyed with his fingers, tracing an old scar along the side of his index finger. It was as if she'd touched every nerve ending in his body, and it was all he could do not to jerk his hand away. He concentrated on keeping his breathing even and controlled as she continued. "I still think the best bet is to get to Joyce, Malcolm's sister. That would set off the fewest number of alarms at the security center of O'Brien Industries."

She abruptly let his hands go and got to her feet, jamming both hands through her hair, her anxiety back in full force. "I can't afford to make any mistakes. I can't." She paced to the window and back several times. Finally she looked at him, nervous energy radiating from her. "I need to get out of the house," she stated forcefully. Then as if reining in the tension inside her, she took a deep breath. "I need to go for a walk or something. Do you think it would be okay if I climbed up to the stump and back?"

Understanding that she needed to burn off tension by doing something physical, Finn nodded. "It should be all right. Just take Rooney with you, and be sure to stay out of sight of the road. If someone turns up here, I'll whistle for the dog."

Her face suddenly drawn, she got dressed and went out, calling for Rooney to come. After he closed the door behind her, Finn went to the window overlooking the ravine. His hands in the back pockets of his jeans, he watched her wade through the snow, Rooney romping along beside her. Somehow he had to stay in one piece through all this, and he had to be damned careful that he never lost sight of who she was or where she was going. It all came back to that.

And even if she weren't Patrick O'Brien's daughter, she was still years younger than he was. And she was in a situation where she might see him as something he wasn't. But Lord, she did make him feel things he thought he'd never feel again. And he knew, as sure as he was standing there, that Mallory O'Brien could very easily be a whole lot more than he wanted her to be. The realization made him feel very old and dull inside. A surge of aloneness piled in on him, and he turned away from the window, his throat tight. He wasn't sure he could go through this again.

Chapter 8

Mallory was gone for well over an hour, and it was dark by the time she finally came in, covered in snow and smelling of cold air. Her cheeks were rosy, and there was a bright sparkle in her eyes. "Rooney and I walked all the way down to that little clearing at the far end of the ravine. Did you know there was a herd of deer down there?" she asked, her voice lifting in amazement.

Leaning back against the stove, Finn watched her, amusement altering his expression. "Yeah. I knew."

"Wow! That is so fantastic—your own private herd of deer." She stripped off her coat and hat, her hair sticking out all over from static electricity. She set her boots beside his. "God, I'm starved. What smells so good?"

He considered giving her a hard time, telling her it was venison, but decided against it. She'd tear him apart.

"T-bone steak, baked potatoes and beans."

She made a sound of approval as she pulled her hair

behind her head, rewrapping the elastic band. "That sounds absolutely fabulous. What can I do?"

The amusement got away from him, and the corner of his mouth lifted. "You could set the table."

Her eyes brightened, and she whipped into her room and came back, carrying four brightly patterned place mats and four coordinating cloth napkins. "I got you these," she stated, placing them on the table. She grinned at him. "You need to get civilized. You've been living on your own too long."

The sight of her so pleased with herself as she set his table nailed Finn right in the chest. The sense of loss was so immense, it was almost too much to handle and he abruptly turned back to the stove, his throat tight, the muscles in his jaw jumping. He didn't know how she had managed to worm her way into his life in such a short time. But she had, and he knew that once this was over, he would never be able to look at those place mats again.

He wasn't sure how he did it, but he pulled himself together. And in spite of that small falter in his mental discipline, the meal itself went fine. She asked him dozens of questions about his business, and she even managed to amuse him again, when she started making suggestions on how he should expand. It was obvious that her father's entrepreneurial spirit was genetic.

He went out to feed the stock while she cleaned up the kitchen, and when he came back in, he heard her moving around in the spare bedroom. She came out, dressed in her new blue jeans, but she had put on one of his plain white T-shirts and had knotted it at the waist. She had her hair all gathered together, and she was holding it in one hand. "Where are your scissors?" she demanded.

He set his hat on the hook, then slipped out of his boots.

He didn't like the sound of that bossy tone, and he became immediately suspicious. "What do you want scissors for?"

"I'm going to cut my hair," she announced, her mind clearly made up. "It's too recognizable."

Finn looked at her as if she'd just taken leave of her senses. "There is no damned way I'm letting you cut off your hair, so forget it."

She gave him an outraged look. "Excuse me. It's my hair, and I'll do what I damn well please."

Finn could feel the veins on his neck starting to bulge as he glared back at her. "So does that mean you're going to cut off your face as well?"

She let go of her hair and jammed her hands on her hips. "Who crowned you king?"

Realizing they were doing it again, Finn bent his head, took a deep breath and held it as he mentally counted to ten. Back in control, he lifted his head and looked at her, taking a different tack. "I like your hair the way it is," he said, his voice gruff. "Don't cut it."

It was as if his simple request threw a switch and she suddenly acted all flustered. As if not quite sure what to do with her hands, she stuck them in her pockets. "All right," she said, the belligerence gone, a faint flush creeping up her cheeks. "I won't cut it."

Watching her like a hawk, Finn assessed her response. Convinced she meant it, he turned and took off his coat. So, he thought, letting go a small smile of victory, there was a way around Miss Spitfire. Ask. Don't demand.

Combing his fingers through his hair, he went over to the coffee table and picked up the channel changer and turned on the TV, muting the sound. Then he went over to the cupboard he used as a liquor cabinet, taking down a bottle.

"You get CNN?" she asked, her voice oddly compressed.

He took out two glasses and set them on the counter. "I'm not some weird hermit, Red. I've got a satellite dish, and I get over a hundred channels. And yes, I get CNN." He poured one glass. "Do you want a drink?"

"I think I'll go out for another walk," she answered, her voice sounding strangled. He turned around, alarm shooting through him when he saw how pale she'd gone. Then he glanced at the TV, his insides dropping when he saw an image of her on the screen, the mouth of the announcer moving. She was so glamored up, he barely recognized her. Swearing, he crossed the room, grabbed the remote control and switched the set off. Hell, he never even thought before he turned the damned thing on.

Finn glanced at her, his insides doing another nosedive when he saw her standing there, her head bent, one hand clasped over her face. He had some idea of how helpless and misplaced she must be feeling, and that was bad enough, but what made him feel really lousy was how she kept trying to swallow.

He knew the worst thing he could do right now was make any comment, so he pretended not to notice as he snagged her wrist. "Nah. You don't want to go out again. I'll bet you twenty bucks I can find a John Wayne movie."

Wiping her face, she managed an uneven chuckle as she allowed him to tow her along. "You're on." He couldn't find a John Wayne movie, but he did find a really bad western that was so awful it made her laugh. They sat there side by side, drinks in their hands, their feet propped up on the coffee table, making rude comments about the plot and the acting. Finn couldn't remember ever enjoying a bad movie so much.

It was just after ten when the movie ended, and as much as he didn't feel like it, Finn went and checked the horses.

There was no sign of Mallory when he got back, and he experienced a sharp rush of disappointment. Shutting off the lights, he went to his room, the sound of her brushing her teeth coming from the bathroom. Trying to ignore that hollow feeling in his belly, Finn pulled his shirt from his jeans, and without undoing the buttons, grabbed the back of the neck and dragged it over his head.

Just as he tossed it on the chair, he heard her shut off the light in the bathroom; then she entered his bedroom, wearing another one of his blue flannel shirts, her long naked legs nearly putting him into cardiac arrest. It was the first time he'd seen them naked, and it was almost more than he could handle. They made him think about things he had no business thinking about. With great effort, he dragged his gaze higher. She had her wealth of hair secured on top of her head with an orange scrunchie thing, and she was rubbing something fragrant into her hands.

And as if she had every right to be there, she walked around to the other side of the bed, pulled back the covers and climbed in.

Nailed with such a rush of relief, Finn closed his eyes and locked his jaw, feeling almost light-headed. Easing in an uneven breath, he unsnapped his jeans, his hands suddenly unsteady. He wanted her there—God, but he wanted her there. And he didn't want her there. Somehow he was going to have to go back to the way it was before she turned up in his life, and every moment he spent with her was going to make it all the harder when she was gone. But he was also pretty damned sure his heart was going to give out on him altogether if he didn't get to hold her pretty soon. And he just might lose it altogether if he did.

Using at least a shred of common sense, he left on his

briefs as he slid his jeans down his hips, then sat on the edge of the bed. Feeling as if he couldn't get enough air into his lungs, he kept his back to her as he stripped off his jeans and socks. This had gone too far to turn back. But he didn't have a clue how to play it out. She had him tied up in so many knots he felt like a teenager on his first date.

His heart hammering in his chest, he switched off the light and slid into bed. And before he had a chance to wrestle with his conscience, Mallory came into his arms. Tightening his jaw against the surge of sensations, he turned toward her. On a ragged intake of breath, she wrapped her arms around him and welded herself against him, and suddenly Finn couldn't breathe, let alone think. Clenching his eyes shut, he tightened his arms around her, his pulse going berserk when he realized she had nothing on under his flannel shirt.

Struggling not to let the heavy, pulsating rush get away on him, he tried to control his pumping heart and labored breathing, her softness and strength pulling him under. Lord, but he wanted this. Wanted her. Wanted to lose all his loneliness in her.

Flattening her hand against his naked back, Mallory choked out his name, clutching him with a desperate strength, almost as if she was trying to climb right inside him. "Don't let go," she whispered urgently, her voice breaking. "Please, don't let go."

Beneath the sexual fever in her, Finn detected a thread of terror, and suddenly he was overwhelmed with such a burst of feelings for her, it was almost as if his heart had exploded in his chest. Easing in a ragged breath, he roughly turned his head against hers and crushed her against him, his heart pounding, his pulse labored. Above all else he wanted to protect her, to give her comfort, to intercept her fear and replace it with himself. More than anything, he needed to do this, to simply care for her.

Cupping her head, he pressed his mouth against her forehead, his voice rough. "I'm not going to let anything happen to you," he whispered, clutching her head tighter. "And I'll hold you for as long as you want."

It was as if his words stripped away any pretense, and she gripped him tighter, her chest heaving. "I'm so terrified that something has already happened to my father," she choked out. "And I hate feeling so damned helpless, knowing someone wants to kill me. And why would they? I'm not a bad person—it's not fair that they want to kill me for the money—especially when I never wanted the damned stuff in the first place."

A tiny sob escaped, and she pressed her face into the curve of his neck, holding him even tighter. "And I didn't mean to cry. I just wanted to go to bed with you really bad, now I've ruined everything."

Her honesty about wanting to go to bed expanded the sensation in his chest, and it certainly didn't help the pulsating heaviness in the lower half of his body either. But that hot, heavy need took second place to a far more compelling need—the need to just hold her and comfort her. A need to care for and protect. Sex was nothing compared to that.

Overcome with a thousand tender feelings for her, Finn swallowed hard, holding her with careful strength. Feeling as if his heart was climbing right out of his chest, he somehow drew a deep, unsteady breath, then managed a gruff chuckle. "From the way I'm feeling, I'm pretty sure that's not ruined." He tightened his hold on her head, trying to reassure her. "And just so you know. I'm pretty damned happy to be right where I am."

Her face wet against his neck, she tried to twist in his

arms, but Finn held fast, whispering against her hair. "Just let me hold you," he said, his voice very gruff. "I like holding you, Red."

She clutched him, abruptly pressing her face tighter into the curve of his neck, a shudder coursing through her.

So saturated with feelings for her that he felt as if he was drowning in them, Finn began to stroke her. "You've been hanging on a long time, and I think maybe a good cry is in order," he said, massaging the small of her back. "It's not every day you find out someone wants you dead."

As if his gruffly spoken assurance gave her permission to let it all go, she began to sob in his arms, holding on to him with a kind of desperate strength.

His chest clogging up and his throat cramping, Finn closed his eyes and thrust his hand deep into her magnificent hair, trying to provide the kind of comfort she needed. He made himself swallow, trying to ease the ache in his chest. He had wanted to be careful—to maintain some distance. But it was far too late. This little wildcat had somehow managed to climb right into his heart, and there wasn't a damned thing he could do about it. And it felt so good to hold her. So good. Holding her was almost enough.

Mallory eventually cried herself to sleep, still snuggled deep in his arms. Staring into the darkness, Finn continued to rub her back, savoring the simple pleasure of having her there. He hadn't felt this whole for a very long time. Closing his eyes, he listened to her breathing, her face warm on his neck. He wished he could stretch this moment out forever.

Finn wasn't sure how it happened. One minute, he was holding her, thinking how damned good it felt. And the next moment the ringing of the phone was dragging him out from under a deep sleep.

Mallory stirred in his arms, and he eased away from her,

pulling the covers up over her shoulder. "It's okay," he mumbled gruffly. "Go back to sleep." Rolling over, he glanced at the clock. Then he propped himself up on one elbow and reached for the phone. Who in hell would be calling him at twenty minutes to midnight?

It was Arnie Jeffery's voice on the other end of the phone. "I'm sorry for calling so late, Finn, but I just got word that Ed Jackson has decided to mount another search. He claims that Mr. O'Brien wants his daughter found. According to Jackson, her old man isn't convinced she's dead. And apparently he's prepared to pay big bucks to make it happen."

Finn spoke, his voice clipped. "Are you sure these orders are coming from O'Brien?"

"Don't have a clue. All I know is what Jackson said, and that he, meaning Jackson, is going in to recover Mallory O'Brien, dead or alive, come hell or high water." Finn heard the RCMP officer heave a weary sigh before he continued. "I just wanted to forewarn you that you can expect a visit from Jackson first thing in the morning. He wanted directions to your place, and my cross-shift was stupid enough to give them to him."

Braced on one elbow, Finn stared into the darkness, a cold feeling churning up in his gut. Now Ed Jackson wanted Mallory's body—come hell or high water. And right now, he needed something to get Jackson off his trail. But most of all, he knew he had to get Mallory out of there, and he had to get her out of there fast.

His whole body on alert, Finn managed to keep his tone light. "Well, Jackson can run his own damned search. I have to attend to some urgent personal business—I'm leaving tomorrow morning. And I'm not changing my plans to suit him."

The constable sounded sour. "Well good luck with whatever it is. I almost wish I could be called away, too. This guy is driving us nuts.''

After thanking Arnie for the warning, Finn hung up the phone, his pulse running heavy as he stared into the darkness. The last thing he needed was Ed Jackson on his doorstep. The security chief was no fool, and having him get that close to Mallory was a risk he wasn't willing to take. Especially when Ed Jackson was bent on recovering a body. Her body.

That was bad enough, but the feeling in his gut made it even worse. Something did not feel right. And he didn't like those kinds of feelings. They made him uneasy. Very uneasy. Which meant there was only one solution, and that was to move her someplace safe.

Turning on the light, he rolled over and shook her awake. ''Come on, Red,'' he growled. ''We've got to haul our butts out of here.''

Turning over, she squinted at him, clearly muddled by sleep. ''What?''

''We've got to clear out of here.''

Fighting back blankets, she sat up, still looking very groggy. ''Why?'' she demanded.

Yanking on his jeans, Finn told her about the call. Then he shoved his arms into a clean T-shirt. ''I don't like it,'' he stated flatly. ''It just doesn't feel right. And I don't trust him. I've seen Ed Jackson at work, and he's damned good at what he does, and he doesn't miss a trick. And to make matters worse, he's a ruthless bastard. So I'm getting you out of here.''

She stared at him, alarm in her eyes. ''But where are we going to go, Finn? We just can't go haring off without some sort of plan.''

Finn yanked on his socks. ''Somehow or another, we have to get in touch with your father to warn him. I think this could all blow up in our faces if he gets drawn out over a phony search.''

Mallory got out of bed, her face ashen, her eyes wide with fear. Unable to handle that look in her eyes, Finn reached out and caught her wrist, pulling her to him. Tucking his head against hers, he wrapped his arms around her, trying to envelop her in some sense of security. ''I'm not going to let anything happen to you, Red,'' he said, his voice very husky. ''Not while there's breath in me. And we're going to do all we can to make sure nothing happens to your father, okay?''

She took a deep breath and nodded. ''I know I'm safe. I'm just worried about my dad.''

Her softly spoken words did unbearable things to Finn's heart and he closed his eyes and pressed his face against the wild tumble of her hair. Knowing that she believed she was safe with him was the greatest gift she could have given him.

Allowing himself a moment to absorb the wonder of her, Finn stroked her back, sharply reminded that she was naked except for his shirt. Taking a deep breath, he reluctantly let her go. Brushing her hair back with both hands, he smiled into her eyes. ''I'd like to spend a whole lot of time doing this,'' he said, his voice gruff, ''but we've gotta get out of here.''

He felt her pull herself together, and she also took a big breath and squared her shoulders. ''What do you want me to do?''

He held her gaze, his mouth lifting. ''First of all, I want you to smile.''

She stared at him, then rewarded him with an off-kilter grin. ''You're nuts to get involved in this, you know.''

He rubbed his knuckles along her jaw. ''Hell, I don't know anything. I'm in it to the end, Red.''

She gave him a wry, skeptical look, but he could see the flash of relief in her eyes. And for some reason the tension in his gut let go.

Aware that they were wasting valuable time, Finn told her his plan. And the plan was to get her to Chicago—and her father.

As soon as he mentioned Chicago, she started shaking her head. "No, Finn. We can't do that. You said it yourself that they'd never let me on a flight. And I'm worried about you getting caught if we drive across the border."

He held her gaze, his expression intent. "That can't be helped. We're going to drive. It's much easier to cross in a car. And I have some of Sally's old papers and documents here—including her birth certificate and her social insurance card. And I've got our marriage certificate."

The expression in Mallory's eyes changed and she stared at him with the strangest look.

Needing to touch her, he smoothed her hair back again. "If we get stopped by U.S. customs, we'll pass you off as Sally Logan Donovan."

The light in her eyes changed and she looked down as she did up a button on the shirt she was wearing. "All right," she said, her voice very soft.

He grasped her hand and gave it a firm squeeze, then moved away from her. "But we've got to clear out of here, and we'll have to make damned sure there's not a single trace of you left. I don't trust Jackson. And if he got even the least bit suspicious, I wouldn't put it past him to search the house. And if for no other reason than he's got the hard, cold nerve to do it." He started tucking in his T-shirt as he headed for the door. "Get dressed. I've gotta make a phone call."

Turning on lights as he went, Finn headed for the phone in the kitchen. Before he did anything, he had to call Old

Joe. Tonight was the old bachelor's bingo night—the stock-man's night to howl—and he knew that his neighbor rarely got home before midnight on bingo nights.

Damned glad that he had done this before—just taken off on the spur of the moment, Finn picked up the phone and punched in a number.

The bachelor answered the phone on the second ring. "Jest walked in the door. Won me the jackpot tonight, boyo," he announced, pleased with himself.

Finn congratulated him on his good luck, then got to the point. "I have to head out of town for a few days. I won-dered if you'd keep an eye out for Rooney and take care of the stock while I'm gone."

"I surely will."

Hooking his thumb in the front pocket of his jeans, Finn stared across the room. "I'm going to be heading out early, so I'll leave Rooney here and you can collect him later. And I'll also leave your paycheck on that old table in the porch."

"That sounds fine, too." There was a slight pause, and Finn heard the other man scold his cat; then Old Joe cack-led and spoke into the phone. "Say, you wouldn't have a lady friend visiting, would you? Thought I saw someone of the female persuasion out walking down in the ravine."

A cold sensation slithered through Finn's gut and he abruptly turned his head and stared across the room. Damn it. Now they were in big trouble. Finn hauled in a deep breath, then spoke, forcing a joking tone into his voice. "Your eyesight must be giving out on you, old man. It must have been me you saw—I went down to check on the deer."

The old man chuckled. "Well, you need a new cook. You were looking a might slender."

Deliberately changing the topic, Finn gave Old Joe in-

structions, then hung up the phone, the edgy feeling intensifying. Old Joe liked to talk and he was an inveterate storyteller, and Finn knew there was a damned good chance that
his stockman might have already said something to his
bingo-playing cronies. Which left Finn with one very large,
dangerous loose end. His gut twisted into a cold, hard knot.
He didn't like those kinds of loose ends. Not with Jackson
breathing down their necks.

Making a decision not to tell her that Old Joe had seen
her, Finn headed toward the storage room. She had enough
on her plate without worrying that her carelessness had
jeopardized their safety.

His expression tight, Finn collected a couple of small
duffel bags from one of the shelves, then opened the gun
safe and the strongbox that was sitting inside. He took out
a handful of cash and Sally's old documents.

Trying not to second-guess his strategies, he returned to
the bedroom and started packing, watchful of any subtle
traces that she'd been in the house. Now that he knew Old
Joe had seen her, it was even more critical that he leave
nothing to chance. He remembered finding the long red hair
in his bed—and that was just the kind of evidence that Ed
Jackson would spot if he decided to check Finn out. And
if Jackson ever got wind of Old Joe's sighting, he definitely
would check Finn out.

Yanking back the bedding, Finn began a search for trace
evidence just as Mallory reentered the room. She gave him
a bemused look. "What are you doing? I thought you
wanted to get out of here?"

"Your hair is pretty distinctive, Red," he said, sweeping
his hand down the bottom sheet. "And I don't trust Ed
Jackson."

Using language that startled him, Mallory snatched the
comforter off his bed, then began gathering up all the bed-

ding. "See?" she snapped, wadding it all up together and heading toward the door. "If you'd let me cut it, we wouldn't have had this problem."

Finn stared at her, irritation suddenly blooming in him. "Hey," he interjected, his tone annoyed. "This has nothing to do with the length of your hair. It's the damned color that's the problem."

She gave him one of her looks. "Oh. So now the color of my hair is a problem. Anything else?"

Realizing he was damned if he did, and damned if he didn't, Finn jammed both hands on his hips and stared at the ceiling. He was getting really good at counting to ten. Letting his breath go in a controlled exhalation, he looked at her. "Have you ever considered taking up wrestling as a profession?"

She stared at him as if he'd lost his mind, then she suddenly smiled. "Ah, Finn," she cooed, her tone syrupy. "Did I take you down for the count again?" Looking smug, she marched out of the room, the bedding in her arms. "You might want to get the vacuum out."

Finn never knew anyone could be that thorough. And bossy. He'd wanted to clear out of there as fast as possible. But not Mallory. No. Mallory was on an eradication mission. By the time they had everything packed in his SUV and set to move out, Finn was ready to strangle her. But Mallory had done such an impeccable job of housecleaning, Finn doubted if Ed Jackson could find a piece of lint, let alone even the most minute trace of her.

Then they had a fight about the dog. Mallory said they were not leaving him behind. Finn insisted that they were. And the only reason that Finn won that argument was because he pointed out that he didn't have the required veterinary documents on hand to get the dog into the U.S.— did she want Rooney held at the border? That stopped her cold, but she made a big production of saying goodbye to the dog.

Finn didn't realize what the big production was all about until she climbed into the passenger seat and he caught the glimmer of tears in her eyes. And it hit him that she was indeed saying goodbye to the dog. That hit him even harder, realizing she was saying goodbye forever, and it left him feeling very hollowed out inside. Placing his cell phone in the charger mounted in his console, he tried not to think about what that meant. He could not allow himself to think about what it was going to be like without her here. Not when he had to concentrate on keeping her safe.

It was the thought of her safety that made him think of the wallet-sized documents he had stuffed in his vest pocket—the ones that would identify her as Sally Logan Donovan, should they get asked at the border. He turned on the overhead light, fished them out, checked through the three cards, and without saying anything, handed them to her.

As if she didn't want him to know about the tears, she quickly wiped them away and shuffled through the cards. Then she folded them in her hand as if they were something precious. "Thank you," she whispered.

Shifting in his seat, Finn reached across the cab, caught her by the chin, forcing her to look at him. "We're going to pull this off, Red," he said, his tone quiet with reassurance. "I don't want you to worry, okay?"

Her eyes filled up again and he saw her try valiantly to swallow, such distress in her expression. And it made his heart hurt just to look at her. He wiped away a stray tear with his thumb, holding her gaze. "What's the matter?" he asked, his voice gruff.

She stared at him, worry in her eyes. "It's not just my hair that could give us away," she whispered, her voice uneven. "It's me—Patrick O'Brien's daughter." She eased in a shaky breath, the despair in her eyes intensifying. "My face will have become public knowledge, and it scares me to death what could happen to you and my father if someone recognizes me."

Resting his hand on the steering wheel, he held her gaze. "We'll just have to be careful to keep that kind of exposure to a minimum." He forced a smile. "So are you ready to get this show on the road? Or do you want to vacuum the barn before we go?"

That got a husky chuckle out of her, and she reached back for the clasp of her seat belt. "I don't do barns."

It was two minutes to five when they finally rolled out of the yard. Wanting to avoid driving through Bolton, Finn backtracked on a secondary highway, which would add a good forty-five minutes to the journey.

Her hair stuffed into a fuzzy hat she'd bought on their shopping trip, Mallory reclined the seat and snuggled down under Finn's coat, her face turned toward the window, watching the illumination from the headlights glance across the snow-covered landscape. By the time they reached the turnoff for the road that would take them to the main highway, it was obvious by her breathing that she had fallen asleep.

Finn drove through the early morning darkness, his gaze fixed on the road, considering the trip ahead of them. There were several border crossings, but some had restricted hours. He decided they would be less noticeable at one of the major ports of entry, and he preferred to travel in sparsely populated states like Montana and Wyoming. Which meant crossing at Coutts.

The crossing went without a hitch—the standard questions about destination, how long and country of birth. And that was it. Finn made one quick stop to change his money, but as he was heading back to the vehicle, his cash turned into U.S. funds, a feeling of unease settled in his belly. It was almost as if he felt someone watching him, and it was all Finn could do not to check over his shoulder.

The first time he ever had the feeling—that distinctive prickling up the back of his neck—he had been eight years old. He'd been out in the bush, and had had that same sensation—that he was being watched. When he turned, he'd spotted a cougar on a high ledge, watching him. From that point on, he had developed a sizeable respect for instinct. And he never ignored it. And he didn't ignore it now.

Once back on the road, he never said anything to Mallory, who spent more time asleep than awake, but he kept an eye on his rearview mirrors. He hoped the feeling would go away, but it didn't. It remained like a persistent knot in his gut.

They stopped only for gas, bathroom breaks and to grab drive-through food, heading right through to North Dakota. And they only stopped then because he knew that if he didn't get some sleep, they'd end up in a wreck. And he was not prepared to let Mallory drive and risk her getting stopped without a license. After another heated argument, which he won simply because he was driving, they stopped at a decent-looking motel off the interstate. There was a convenience store right across the street, and after he got Mallory safely settled in the room, he went across and bought a bagful of fruit, some nuts and some fresh-looking cellophane-wrapped sandwiches. He didn't know about her, but he had just about hit his limit of fast food.

She was just coming out of the bathroom when he entered, her hair wrapped in a towel, wearing a dark green T-shirt thing that skimmed her knees. She looked freshly scrubbed and bright as a new penny—which figured, seeing as she'd slept more than she'd been awake.

He handed her the bag, then dragged off his mackinaw. "Go crazy," he said.

She responded with a grin, the grin fading when she looked up at him. Her expression softening, she reached up and touched his face. He'd had two hours of sleep the night before, he needed a shave, needed a shower and, most of all, he needed about ten hours of sleep. He was nearly dead on his feet, but that one touch sent loneliness streaking through him, and he sorely wished she were somebody else's daughter.

His heart slamming against the wall of his chest, he stared down at her, wishing she wasn't Mallory O'Brien—that she was just the girl from down the road—someone who could be a part of his life. But she *was* Mallory O'Brien, and she was not from his world, and after he got her back safely to her father, he would never see her again. He wished he didn't like her so damned much—or want her the way he did. Because no matter the circumstances, she was going to leave one hell of a hole in his life when she was gone. And he knew he was going to do a whole lot of hurting for a very long time.

Trying to smile at her, he grasped her hand and gave it a light squeeze, then brushed by her as he headed to the bathroom. "I need a shower," he said gruffly.

He expected her to be in bed when he came out, but she wasn't. The bedside lamp was on, and she had the bedding stripped back. But she was standing by the bed, her still-damp hair curling around her face, rubbing hand lotion liberally on her hands. "Facedown," she commanded in that bossy tone.

Tightening the towel around his waist, Finn felt obliged to argue, but he just didn't have the energy. The hot shower had depleted what little strength he had left, and more than anything, he just wanted to lie down. It was just easier to do as he was told. He stretched out and closed his eyes, giving up a groan as his body settled into the bed. Lord, he'd been sitting so long, he felt as if he'd been turned into a pretzel.

The mattress shifted, and he abruptly opened his eyes, his pulse lurching when he felt her straddle his hips. "I'm going to give you a massage," she stated, and he felt something warm spill on his back, and a familiar scent assailed his senses. How in hell had she warmed up the hand lotion?

"Put your arms under your head," she directed.

He was too damned tired to argue with her—hell, all he seemed to do was argue with her. So he complied. Just being able to lie down, stretch out and close his eyes was enough. And he was so damned beat, he figured he was safe from anything happening. Besides, it wouldn't kill him to humor her.

What he expected was a few token strokes. What he did not expect was a full-blown massage, the kind that made him groan, the kind that found muscles and sore spots he didn't even know he had, the kind that made his whole body turn to putty. He didn't know anything could feel like that.

Letting the muscles in his back go slack, he forced himself to comment. "You've got pretty good technique going there, Red."

She chuckled and moved to the small of his back, eliciting another groan from him. "I should. I took a two-year course."

Finn opened his eyes, frowning slightly. That didn't compute. "You took a course?" he verified, not believing what he'd heard.

She dug the heels of her hands into muscles along his spine. "I've taken all kinds of courses. Mostly out of personal interest. And some," she said, working on another group of muscles, "just to annoy my father."

His eyes open, Finn turned his head, his curiosity piqued. "Like what?"

She gave a soft laugh. "Like a mechanics course for women—I practiced on his prized cars. He had a fit when he found out."

Too relaxed to answer her, he focused on the sensations, her hands working magic on his tired body. And it was an experience like he'd never had before. He had never expected it to feel so good—or to have the effect it did. Finn closed his eyes, the sensation spreading through him like liquid honey.

But then she massaged the small of his back, the pressure of her hands doing unbelievable things to his body, and his heart stumbled. And in the space of that heartbeat, his exhaustion was no longer a defense. And his whole body responded. Concentrating on his breathing to keep it even, Finn clenched his jaw, the feel of her hands on his body making his blood run thick, a male need unfolding in him.

He tried to focus, to keep his mind blank, but she shifted on top of him, her long legs tensing and shifting against his hips. And with that one small movement, his self-imposed discipline—the discipline he had used to shut himself off—crumbled, and all he could think about was the intimacy of her legs clutching him, and the feel of her hands all over his body. A long denied need pumped through him, and he tightened his hands into fists and abruptly turned his face into his folded arms, forcing air into his lungs.

He thought he had gotten a grip; then she leaned forward and grasped one of his clenched hands, releasing his grip. "You've gone all tense," she said, her voice soft as she began to massage the palm of his hand. Fighting the fevered sensations throbbing through him, Finn locked his jaw, every cell in his body responding to her touch. Just when he had reached the point of no return, she let go of his hand. His heart pounding, Finn struggled to bring himself under control, and he thought he'd made it when she took hold of his other hand.

That palm was even more sensitive than the first, her touch more caressing, and just like that, all his good intentions got blown to bits. And Finn could not remain passive any longer.

Needing to stop her marauding hands—needing to tell her how much her touch restored him, he twisted underneath her.

Her hair wild around her shoulders, the hem of her nightshirt shoved up, she stared down at him, the pulse in her neck running wild. Finn held her gaze, then ran his hand up her naked thigh. She shifted her hips, aligning herself to his throbbing hardness. The only thing that separated them was the thin motel towel, and she reacted as if she'd been scalded. Making a low, ragged sound, she closed her eyes and moved against him.

Feeling as if he was about to explode, Finn grasped her face and pulled her down, taking her mouth in a restrained kiss, the blood pounding in his ears. And even then, maybe he could have pulled back, but her breath caught and she opened her mouth. It was too much. Too much. Clutching the back of her head, he ground his mouth against hers, pouring his heart and soul, all his aloneness into that kiss.

And even with need clawing through him, Finn still thought he would be able to pull back, but then she slid into his arms, her body molding against his, skin against skin. The feel of her on top of him, of her heat pressed tightly to his hardness, made his whole body go hard, and a red haze filled his mind.

His lungs expanding on a surge of need, Finn altered the angle of his mouth on hers, desperate for the taste of her, desperate for her. Drawing her knees up, Mallory twisted against him, and Finn groaned, the pleasure so intense it was almost like pain. Tangling his hand in her damp hair, he tightened his hold on her head, then locked his other arm around her hips as he worked his mouth against hers, starved for the heat of her.

He wanted this. More than his next breath he wanted this, wanted her. His mind consumed with the red haze, Finn roughly rubbed his hand across her buttocks, aware that only the towel prevented him from thrusting into her. That awareness escalated the fever in him, and desperate to taste even more of her, Finn opened his mouth wider. Driven by the kind of hunger that consumed, he feasted on her, the raw hunger coursing through him. But even though he plundered her mouth again and again, he couldn't get enough of her, and he crushed her hips against his, trying to pull her under him.

But nothing was ever easy with Mallory O'Brien, and she struggled free, keeping her mouth welded against his. Knowing where this was going and unable to stop himself, Finn shoved her T-shirt up, a shudder coursing through him as his thumbs skimmed the peaks of her perfect breasts.

On a ragged sound, Mallory broke off the kiss and sat up, her weight on his groin nearly sending him over the edge. Her mouth swollen and her eyes glazed, she grasped the bottom of her nightshirt but Finn beat her to it. His whole body engorged with blood, he whipped the shirt off over her head, her hair spilling around her shoulders, his pulse stumbling when he saw the dark, urgent look in her eyes. Whispering her name, he clasped her head and pulled her down and claimed her mouth again. Fighting for air, he dragged his mouth away and dragged her beneath him, the towel no longer separating them as she wrapped her long legs around him. He couldn't contain the ragged sound ripped from him as he settled his weight on top of her, his hard flesh pressing against hers. The rush of pleasure was so intense it nearly took him under. So good. It felt so damned good.

His breathing raw and labored, Finn twisted his head against hers, fighting to put on the brakes. More than his next breath he wanted to thrust into her moist heat, to lose himself inside of her, but he clenched his teeth and forced himself to remain still, his whole body trembling. He couldn't use her this way. Especially when he had nothing to protect her.

Clutching at him, she moved under him, thrusting her hips upward. "No," she sobbed out. "You can't stop."

Nailed with another rush of need, Finn shuddered, his hardness pressed against her. He clutched her hips even tighter against him. Feeling as if both his heart and lungs were about to explode, he pressed his mouth against the curve of her shoulder. "I can't take that kind of a chance with you," he whispered raggedly.

Grasping his head with both hands, she made him look at her. Her eyes were almost black and glistening with tears, a kind of panic in her face. "It's okay," she pleaded. "Don't stop."

Forcing in another unsteady breath, he took her face between his hands and tipped her head back, then covered her mouth, her desperate plea giving him back some control. This might be his only night with her, but he did not want it to be just a one-night stand. Not with her. Never with her. He wanted to taste every inch of her, find every pulse point. He wanted to acquaint himself with every inch of her body, to lose himself in her. He wanted to make this night last forever.

Letting his breath go, he brushed his mouth back and forth across hers. "I won't stop," he whispered. "But I'm not going to be in a big rush, either." He took his time with another soft, searching kiss—a kiss so soft, so slow, so deep, he felt the effects all the way down to his feet.

Mallory tried to fight him, tried to take him inside her, but he dragged her arms from around his neck, then held them on the bed above her head. Stroking her palm with his thumb, he gazed down at her, telling her exactly what he was going to do to her. She stared up at him, her eyes dilated and unwavering. Then he stroked a pulse point in her wrist, and she made a ragged sound and closed her eyes, arching her head back.

It was as if her incoherence gave him another element of control, and Finn dropped his head and dragged his open mouth down the pulsing vein in her neck. Still gripping her wrists, he moved lower, and Mallory moaned and arched beneath him, thrusting her breast toward his mouth. Closing his eyes, Finn suckled on her, giving her what she wanted—what she needed. And what he wanted and needed.

He tasted her, made love to every inch of her, wanting to take her higher than she had ever been. Her physical responses and ragged moans, her involuntary shudders gave him rush upon rush of such agonizing satisfaction that he nearly lost it several times. He didn't want it to ever stop, this chance at loving her.

But the touch of his mouth at the very heat of her took her too close to the edge, and Mallory wrenched free of his hold, then grasped his hair and pulled him up. "No more," she whispered brokenly. "I need you now."

She struggled beneath him, trying to align herself with him, first ordering him, then begging him. Unable to deny the release she was offering one second longer, Finn shoved his arm under her, lifting her hips to meet him. It was as if all the years of his self-imposed solitary confinement piled in on him, and she was his only hope of salvation. His face contorting with the agony of being so close, he found her mouth and thrust into her, desperate for the heat of her.

Feeling as if he was going to explode into a million pieces, he cupped her buttocks and rocked against her to trigger her response. Mallory arched and cried out, her nails scoring his back. Squeezing her legs around him, she tilted her hips, taking all of him inside her, her spasms of release contracting around him and drawing him deeper into her soft, moist heat.

It was too much. Too much. And Finn could not hold back one second longer. Crushing her against him, he thrust into her, gloving himself in her heat, driven to give her all he could. Stiffening beneath him, Mallory tried to find the rhythm. Finn ground his teeth together, using every ounce of skill he had to take her over the top one more time. Then she shuddered and clutched at him as she convulsed around him again, her heavy contractions milking him. The red haze turned brilliant white, and he jammed his face against her neck as his own release came, his reality splintering into a million bright lights.

Chapter 9

Blinded by the aftermath of sensation, Finn held Mallory in the tight cradle of his arms, his breathing still ragged, his muscles trembling. Being with her, being buried deep inside her was like nothing he'd ever experienced before, and he hauled in a ragged breath and roughly turned his face against her neck. He felt as if his spine had just been stripped from his body.

Totally emptied and his whole body quivering, he roughly pressed her head against him, hundreds of emotions jammed up in his chest. He'd never felt this way before—so purged, so emptied—so restored. And he wasn't sure how he was ever going to pull away.

She was hanging on to him for dear life, and Finn finally got it together enough to realize that tears were slipping down her temples. He gathered what little strength he had and braced himself on his elbows, his throat cramping up again as he gazed down at her. Her eyes were tightly closed, the tears spilling out, her hair spread like wildfire

on the white sheets. Another surge of heavy emotion nailed
him, and he had to swallow hard. God, but she mattered to
him. His heart wedged painfully in his chest, he bracketed
her face between his hands, carefully wiping away the tears
with his thumbs. Then he closed his eyes and lowered his
head, covering her swollen mouth with a soft, gentle kiss,
trying to tell her by touch alone what a miracle she'd given
him.

Letting her breath go in a sob, Mallory locked her arms
around his neck, holding on to him like a lifeline. His own
throat so constricted he couldn't swallow, Finn gathered her
up and held her tight, his own eyes damp. He wanted to
say something to her. But he didn't want his first words to
be the old standby, to ask her if she was okay. He needed
to tell her that she had just brought him back to life. But
he couldn't say that either.

Unable to find the right words, he smoothed down her
hair, then trailed a string of soft kisses across her face. He'd
never thought he'd ever feel like this again—whole, complete. Alive.

Sensing she was just as raw as he was, and that she
needed him to break the emotion that bound them, he
kissed the curve of her neck, then gave her a little squeeze.
"I gotta tell you, Red," he said, his voice very gruff, kissing the hollow under her ear. "That was the best body
massage I ever had."

She hugged him back, rewarding him with a husky
laugh. "I hope you don't tip all your masseuses this way."

Finn chuckled and gave her another squeeze, his chest
packed tight with feelings for her. Knowing that he was in
so deep there was no way out, Finn shut out the stark reality
he would eventually have to deal with. He had this night
with her, and that was more than he'd ever hoped for.

Shifting his position, he gazed down at her, smoothing

tendrils of her bright hair away from her face; then he dropped his head and kissed the tracks of freckles across her nose and down her face. It was the first time he'd ever been to bed with a natural redhead, and the expanse of freckles fascinated the hell out of him, especially when she had them everywhere. "I think I've just become a freckle man," he murmured, kissing the freckles across the swell of her breasts.

"There is no such thing as a freckle man," she sniped, sounding genuinely miffed as she tried to push his head away. Finn wasn't about to be budged from his exploration.

He smiled against her soft flesh, following the freckles lower. "There is now." He did dot-to-dot with his tongue, moving still lower. "I've always liked Appaloosas," he said, deliberately baiting her.

He didn't think she could ever do it twice. But one moment he was on the bed; then the next, he was flat on his back on the floor, half the bedclothes down there with him.

Not quite sure how it had happened, he stared up at her, his expression stunned. She hung her head over the edge of the bed, resting her head on her folded arms, her thick hair spilling onto his chest. She gave him a deceptively sweet smile. "You might want to rethink that, slugger."

Amused by her smugness, Finn reached up and snagged her arm; then using his considerable strength, he dragged her off the bed.

She was laughing and struggling, but the instant her weight settled on top of his, her expression changed, and Finn's pulse accelerated, the feel of her flush against him setting his heart into overdrive. Her eyes dark and full of promise, she cupped her hand along his jaw, then bent her head and brushed her mouth against his, her touch soft, teasing, inciting. His lungs jammed up, and Finn ran his hand up her back, pressing her closer, his hunger no longer sated.

Struggling with the sensations she was arousing in him, he managed to hold himself in check. "I shouldn't take any more chances with you," he whispered gruffly against her mouth.

She shifted against him, her naked body molding with his. "Take chances with me, Donovan," she whispered back, her mouth moving against the sensitive hollow under his ear, her lips moist and tormenting. "I *want* you to take chances with me." Then tightening her hold on his head, she slid her body down his, her mouth blazing a trail of sensations. Finn tightened his fist in her hair, a ragged sound wrenched loose as she began to move against him. And in the space of a heartbeat, he was lost in her. Surrendering his strength to her, he let her take him under. And the urgency started all over again.

The thin light of dawn was seeping around the venetian blinds on the window when reality finally checked in. Struggling with the groggy feeling of disorientation, Finn opened his eyes; the only thing he was conscious of was that Mallory was snuggled up in his arms with her head on his shoulder, her breath warm against his flesh.

Tightening his arm around her, he smoothed down her hair and brushed a soft kiss against her forehead. Then lifting his head slightly, he looked at the cheap clock radio on the nightstand. Hell, he'd wanted to be long gone by now.

Dropping his head back on the pillow, he stared into the fading darkness, trying not to think how damned good it felt to wake up with her. He hugged her against him, saturated by her warmth and softness, her hair like silk against his skin. Being careful not to wake her, he gently repositioned her head, releasing pins and needles in his arm; then he tightened his hold again and began stroking her soft, soft skin.

He was sure he had never been this exhausted in his whole life. He'd had maybe two hours of sleep the night they bolted, and he had even less the past night. His eyes throbbed and his head felt as if it was full of gravel, but he really didn't give a damn. He had lost count of how many times they made love, and waking up with her asleep in his arms was worth any amount of discomfort.

He smiled to himself, remembering. Thank God they ended up back in bed. He didn't even want to think what he would have felt like if they'd spent the night on the floor.

The scent of their lovemaking assailed his senses, making his pulse speed up, and he closed his eyes and grasped the back of her head. If he could, he'd stay here all day. But with Ed Jackson on the loose, they just couldn't risk it.

Sobered by that thought, Finn opened his eyes, the backlog of exhaustion gone. For one entire night he had lost himself in her, putting every one of his instincts on hold. And that was a damned dangerous thing to do—especially with her. This one he had to keep safe, no matter what.

Wanting to give her a few more moments of sleep, Finn eased out from under her, smiling a little when she mumbled something and rolled onto her stomach, her face toward him, her back bare to the waist. He gave in to one powerful need and carefully swept her hair back from her face as he pressed a kiss against her temple. Letting go a sigh, he covered her up. Hardening his jaw, he slipped from the bed and headed toward the bathroom. He didn't allow himself even one look back.

Once showered and shaved, he went back into the room,

a twist of humor surfacing when he saw how she was sprawled out, all the pillows clutched under one arm. He plugged in the electric kettle provided in the room, dumped a packet of instant coffee into one of the mugs, then opened one of the packaged sandwiches and spread the road map out on the tiny table. They had covered a lot of ground the day before. And if they could hold that pace again today, they should be in Chicago the following day. Sticking to the speed limit, that would mean nonstop driving for at least eighteen hours, and he wasn't too optimistic he could manage that. Not with as little sleep as he'd had over the past forty-eight hours.

"You're a dead man if you ate them both."

He turned his head, his heart faltering when he saw her. She was sitting up in bed, the sheet twisted around her waist, her perfect breasts exposed, her hair a tousled riot around her face. With the dusky light, the white of the bedding, the creamy color of her skin and the vibrant color of her hair, she was like something off an old master's canvas. It hit Finn so hard, his heart constricted, seizing up his entire chest. She was all woman, every inch of her. Then Mallory yawned, a huge, waking-up yawn, totally ruining the image.

Finn gave her a wry grin. "How old were you when you started getting so territorial over food?"

She yawned again and dragged her hair back with both hands. "The moment I starting eating."

Amused by her sass, Finn continued to watch her as he took a sip from his cup of coffee. She did, indeed, have freckles everywhere.

Catching where his eyes were drifting, she narrowed her eyes at him, then snatched up the sheet and flounced off the bed, displaying a tantalizing field of freckles on her bottom. As if reading his mind, she yanked the sheet around her. "You should learn to raise your sights—and your mind—a little higher, Donovan," she snapped. "You might be surprised what you discover."

She marched into the bathroom and slammed the door, and Finn grinned to himself. He was beginning to enjoy her flashes of temper.

It was just going on seven when they hauled their stuff out to Finn's vehicle. There the ground was bare, but frost covered the windshields of the cars in the parking lot. An early morning breeze rustled dead leaves across the pavement, and somewhere a dog barked, the sharp sound perforating the stillness.

They rounded Finn's big SUV—and stopped dead in their tracks. Chase McCall was sitting on the back bumper, his legs stretched out in front of him, his arms folded. His black Stetson was pulled low over his eyes, and he was so still, Finn thought he was asleep.

But before Finn could step in front of Mallory, Chase tipped his hat back with one finger, giving her a lopsided smile. "Howdy, ma'am."

The muscles in his jaw locked, Finn stared at the other man, anger making his pulse accelerate. He had a feeling someone had been following them, but he never would have figured it was Chase McCall on their tail.

Refolding his arms, Chase studied his boots for a moment; then he spoke, his tone almost conversational. "I never did have any use for Roddy Bracken."

Angered because he'd got caught with his guard down, and even more angry because they'd been so easy to track, Finn stared at Chase. "What in hell are you doing here, McCall?"

Chase McCall looked up at Finn, his expression somber. "I thought you should know that Ed Jackson has his tail in a twist. Apparently he got wind of the story Old Joe told at bingo, that he figured you had a woman staying with you.''

He studied his feet again, his arms still folded. ''I saw you pick up the locket, and I got a feeling from the way you put it in your pocket that the lady was still very much alive.'' Chase looked up and stared across the street, watching a battered pickup pass, the faulty muffler echoing loudly in the early morning quiet. ''Then I heard from Arnie that you'd been out to your line shacks the day before, and I put two and two together.'' He grinned up at Finn. ''I may be a bit slow at times, but I can add.''

Her face pale, Mallory moved toward Finn and slipped her hand into his, her eyes wide with alarm. Certain that Chase McCall meant them no harm, Finn gave her hand a firm squeeze and tucked both their hands in the pocket of his mackinaw.

He fixed his gaze on the rancher and challenged him, his voice clipped. ''But that still doesn't explain what you're doing here.''

Chase studied his boots for a second, then met Finn's gaze, his own very serious. ''I went to your place this morning. I wanted to let you know that Jackson was looking for you—and that I'm damned sure he's put it together, too. When I got there, you were already gone. I figured you headed south.'' He grinned. ''Nearly shot past you when you stopped after you crossed the border.'' His expression hardened, and a cold look appeared in his eyes. ''I don't like Jackson, and figured I'd better keep an eye and make damned sure he wasn't on your tail.''

Finn didn't know what to say. He'd gone it on his own for so long, he'd forgotten what it was like to have someone stand shoulder to shoulder with him.

Mallory looked up at Finn, an odd expression softening her gaze; then she withdrew her hand from Finn's pocket and extended it to Chase. "I'm Mallory O'Brien," she said, her voice husky. "Thank you for looking out for us."

Chase got to his feet and grinned at her. "Chase McCall. And you're most welcome, ma'am."

Letting go of Mallory's hand, the rancher shoved his hands in the back pockets of his jeans and turned toward the motel. "Think I'm going to grab me another couple of hours in the sack before I head back."

Finn had to clear his throat before he could speak. "McCall."

Chase McCall turned, his unshaven face looking dangerous under the black Stetson.

Finn gave a single nod of recognition. "Thanks. I appreciate you watching our backs."

Chase stared at him a moment, then spoke. "If it was my lady in trouble, I figure you'd do the same for me." Then without another word, Chase McCall sauntered toward the motel, juggling the room key in one hand.

It wasn't until they had pulled out of the parking lot that Mallory turned to him. "Who is this Chase McCall?"

Finn checked for oncoming traffic, then made a right turn that would take them onto the highway. "He's a local rancher and horse trainer. Don't know much about him, except his family has been in the district for years. Married a native girl a few years back and has three kids. Bought some horses from him a few years ago, and I've been on a couple of searches with him." His voice got gruff. "I'd never considered him much more than an acquaintance."

She looked at him, her expression unsmiling, her gaze steady. "Well, you can now."

Finn felt as if the rising sun was too bright, the first rays scalding his eyes. Maybe he'd misjudged a whole lot of people over the past few years. "Yeah," he responded, his voice gruff. "I guess I can."

After that brief conversation, they both fell silent, neither one of them wanting to talk. Finn knew they probably should, but the news about Jackson was a grim reminder that their situation was very real. And no matter how many times Finn turned it over in his mind, there was only one explanation for the threat against her—that someone from her mother's side of the family was trying to get their hands on her money. It was the only thing that made sense. And right now they were very much on their own. And he figured that talking about it would only make it seem worse.

He glanced across the cab, his gut reacting when he saw her stark profile. "Why don't you try to get some more sleep," he said, his voice quiet.

She gave her head a small jerk, then folded up his coat and placed it on the console. Without looking at him, she curled up, getting as close to him as she could possibly get, her hand warm against his thigh, her head nestled against his rib cage. She closed her eyes, and Finn could see her try to swallow. He covered her hand with his own, giving her a reassuring squeeze. There was nothing he could really say. He knew she was afraid for her father, and he also knew that she was dealing with that worry the only way she knew how. And all he could do was be there as a kind of bulwark between her and the terror. She shifted her head and turned her hand palm against palm, then tightened her fingers around his. As if comforted by that connection, she released a soft sigh, and Finn felt the tension leave her.

That one small act did painful things to his heart, and Finn found himself struggling with emotions so big, so intense, they nearly suffocated him. God, but he wanted so many things with her—a life, a future—he wanted forever, but he knew that was impossible. He was a realist, and he knew his time with her was probably marked in hours.

It was crazy. So damned crazy. She had knocked him

for a loop from the moment he'd laid eyes on her, and he could count the days he'd spent with her on one hand. But none of that mattered. Time didn't matter. Because he knew that Mallory O'Brien was going to be lodged in his heart until the day he died.

And God, it was going to damned near kill him to walk away—and he was going to have to walk away. He would only hurt her more if he dragged it out. And that was the black and white of it—in a very short time, he was going to be left with one hell of a hole in his life.

Realizing where he was headed with those kinds of bleak thoughts, Finn tried to block it all out of his mind. He reached over and turned on the radio, the distraction working until a particular song came on—a haunting sad ballad with beautiful lyrics. The song itself was bad enough but one phrase—"I could fall in love with you"—nailed him right in the chest and he reached out and abruptly shut the radio off. His throat so tight he could barely see, he lifted her hand and pressed it against his mouth, the scent of her hand lotion making his throat cramp up even more. She was there with him now, and he had to make the most of it. Maybe if he could imprint it deep enough—the warmth of her hand and the weight of her head against him—maybe he could make it last him a lifetime.

By noon, Finn knew he could not drive safely any longer. Not wanting to pull over on the shoulder, he took an off-ramp into a small town and pulled into gas station. Just about drunk with exhaustion, he filled up the truck, then took a bathroom break.

He almost smiled—almost—when he came back out and found Mallory now wide-awake in the driver's seat, the window down, both hands on the wheel, her seat belt done up and a determined look on her face. He opened the driver's door. "Not a chance," he stated.

She yanked the door out of his hand and slammed it. "Not a chance," she parroted, giving his words right back at him. "Get in. I'm driving, whether you like it or not."

Too tired to argue with her, Finn rested his hand on the open driver's window, giving her a weary look. "Do you have any idea of the consequences if you get caught driving without a license?"

She gave him an annoyed look and tightened her hands on the wheel. "No. But I do know the consequences if you get caught here with a criminal record. So you can be damned sure I'm not going to do anything stupid. So just get in the damned truck."

Her response floored him. He had been so intent on keeping her safe it had never occurred to him that she might be concerned about him. No one was ever concerned about him.

As if reading his thought, she looked at him and shook her head, an odd look in her eyes. "You are," she said, a husky quality in her voice, "the thickest man I've ever met. Now get in the truck."

Knowing he was going to be dead on his feet if he didn't get some sleep soon, Finn finally relented with a sigh. He turned, then stopped and looked back at her. "Do you want to try and call your chauffeur from here?"

She stared at him, her lips paling; then she looked away and shook her head. "No. Not yet," she responded, her voice suddenly uneven. "I don't want to spend the whole day in a panic if I can't get him."

Reminded of the enormous strain she was under, Finn rounded the truck. Maybe letting her drive was the best thing for her—maybe it would give her something to do and help keep her mind off the grimness of her situation.

Knowing that he would not get any kind of decent sleep in the front seat, Finn rearranged the cargo area, then flattened half of the back seat, fixing an adequately sized bed with the sleeping bag and pillows they had brought. And the moment he crawled in and lay down, his head started to swim, and he had to close his eyes. "You better wake me in four hours, Red, or your driving days are over."

She reached between the bucket seats and patted his head, real amusement in her voice. "Do you think you can quit giving orders for that long?"

"Four hours," he insisted.

She started the ignition and put the vehicle in gear. "Four hours," she agreed.

The rest of the day turned into an exhausting road marathon. They stopped only for gas and bathroom breaks, and eventually for one restaurant meal. Finn was not a good traveler. Being locked up in a vehicle hour after hour was just a little too much like being in prison, and they both got irritable and cranky.

Their plan was to drive through the night. He was in the back taking his four hours of sack time when the change in road sounds brought him awake. He lifted his head, the headlights cutting through the darkness, the clock on the dash showing 1:00 a.m. He realized it was the sound of the vehicle slowing that had wakened him up, and it took him a second to figure out that Mallory was pulled off the highway onto an unused approach. Before he could clear the sludge from his mind, she turned off the lights and ignition, then crawled through the space between the bucket seats and into the narrow space beside him.

Realizing she was shivering in the dark, Finn rolled on his back and gathered her snuggly against him, then pulled his coat over her. "I'll get you warmed up," he murmured softly, smoothing her hair down, "then I'll drive."

She abruptly turned her face into the curve of his neck.

"I don't want you to drive," she whispered unevenly. "I want you to hold me."

That kind of emotional honesty shook him—really shook him—and he closed his eyes and swallowed hard, drawing her more securely into his embrace. He could tell by the tension in her that it wasn't cold that was making her shiver—it was fear, and he tightened his hold, tucking her hair back. He wanted to tell her that he'd gladly hold her forever, but he had already exceeded boundaries he never should have crossed with her. Her thick hair curling around his fingers, he nestled her head snugly against his neck. Wanting to lighten her fear, he spoke. "You sure know how to park," he muttered, tucking the coat against her back.

He felt her smile. "I do, don't I?"

Her response made him smile, and Finn turned his head against hers, taking a deep, releasing breath. Having her in his arms neutralized his edginess, and he breathed in the scent of her, the confinement no longer pressing down on him. She was his salvation, and she didn't even know it.

Five hours of solid sleep with her in his arms altered his mood, and they managed a thin veneer of normalcy until they were within range of Chicago, then Mallory got very quiet again. Her expression taut with tension, she picked up the cell phone, then closed her eyes and leaned her head back against the headrest. It was as if she were collecting herself before she spoke. "Pull into that rest stop up there," she commanded quietly. "I'm going to try to reach my father."

Finn cast her a quick glance, the rising sun glinting off her sunglasses. His own expression altered. He didn't know what changed her mind about trying to reach Patrick O'Brien, and he wasn't entirely sure it was a good idea.

He checked the rearview mirrors and pulled into the rest stop. Putting the vehicle in park, he switched off the engine. His arm resting on the wheel, he looked at her. "I'm not sure that's a good idea, Red."

She gave him a tight smile. "I know that. But I have to try." She looked away, then took a deep, stabilizing breath and met his gaze again. "I don't dare use any of the classified numbers—that would be a dead giveaway. But what if I tried to get through to his private secretary? There are some business associates who have that number."

Finn watched her, not liking the idea a whole lot, but understanding why she felt compelled to call. Finally he tipped his head in agreement.

Without looking at him, she dialed a number, the pulse in her neck erratic as she stared out, her whole body rigid. Taking a deep breath, she finally spoke, using a damned fine imitation of a proper English accent, her voice so strained it didn't even sound like her. "This is the law firm of Delleware, Johnson, McGinnis and Fogalty calling. Mr. Delleware would like to speak to Mr. O'Brien."

Mallory looked at Finn, her eyes wide with alarm, a stricken expression on her face. Then she swallowed hard and spoke, still using that very clipped English accent. "Thank you. Mr. Delleware will try to reach him later."

She dropped the phone and covered her face with both hands, and Finn picked it up and hit the End button with his thumb, the knot of unease back in his belly. "What happened?" he demanded gruffly.

Hauling in a deep breath, she raked her hands through her hair, then turned to look at him, her face very pale. "It was Ed Jackson who fielded the call." That was something Finn did not want to hear, and his insides knotted. The fact that Jackson had called off the second crash-site search and was now back in Chicago did not bode well for Mallory.

He wanted to touch her but he didn't. Setting the phone down on the console, he thought it through, then spoke. "For what it's worth, I think he's here to do some serious damage control. And I also suspect your father still thinks he's one of the good guys, so you aren't going to have a hope in hell of contacting him."

She stared out the window, her face very stiff. "Then you think my father is still alive?"

Finn rested his arm on the steering wheel and continued to watch her. "With Jackson standing guard? Yeah, I do. I also think that Jackson is damned worried that you're going to turn up and blow his plans to smithereens—and I also think he's going to do whatever he can to stop you."

She took a drink from a bottle of water, then meticulously screwed the cap back on. "I have to get in touch with Malcolm."

Finn nodded and reached for the ignition. "Yes." Checking for oncoming traffic, he accelerated along the shoulder, then pulled into the right lane. "But now we're going to need another phone to do it—and one that can't be traced."

She finally looked at him. "Why?"

"For two reasons. I expect the good Mr. Jackson is already intimately familiar with my cell phone number. And I think it would kick off fewer suspicions if you could leave a local number. For anyone to call my cell phone, they'd have to dial long distance."

Mallory stared at him, then nodded and looked away. She never said another word. Instead, she sat silently beside him, watching out the window, and he couldn't even see her profile. He could tell by the way she had her hands clenched together that she was struggling to keep her panic contained.

It wasn't until they could see the city rising out of the

horizon that she spoke again, her tone quiet. "I'll drive from here."

Finn wasn't sure that was such a good idea either, but he didn't say anything. She was so tense it was as if she was held together by a thread, and he understood that she needed to do something. And that made his own mood turn grim. They were, without question, heading down to the wire.

The solution to a second cell phone presented itself at a red light in a seedy part of the city. Finn happened to glance across at Mallory, and he noticed the passenger in the car next to her was talking on a cell phone. Finn had learned to read more than body language in prison, and the tattoos covering the passenger's arms said it all. This dude had spent a lot of time on the wrong side of the law, and most of it in prison. And ten chances to one, the phone was illegal. Finn grabbed his own cell phone and launched himself out of the truck.

Mallory gave him an alarmed look as he slammed the door, commanding her through the open window. "Drive around the block and find somewhere to park. I'll find you."

It took him one green light, with horns blaring because of blocked traffic, to negotiate a deal. Before he handed over the cash, he used his own phone to dial the number they'd given him. When the phone rang, he handed the dude three hundred dollars, then dodged oncoming traffic. He would have paid twice that amount.

Finn found Mallory parked in a garbage-filled loading bay of a grimy brick warehouse, and he could see the relief in her eyes when he climbed back into the cab.

He held up the second cell phone. "We're in business, Red."

She gave him a weak smile. "I don't even want to know

how much I owe you." Looking behind her, she backed into the street, then pulled into traffic. There was an odd silence; then she spoke. "I'm taking us to my place."

Finn stared at her, a hard knot settling in his belly. "I think that could be a big mistake."

She checked over her shoulder and moved over a lane, a hint of her old stubbornness in her tone. "Why?"

"For one thing, how are you going to get in? You don't have any keys. And secondly, if I were Ed Jackson, that's the first place I would have staked out, just in case."

She gave him a tight smile. "Not if he doesn't know about it. This is the apartment that no one, not even my father, knows about. And I can get in."

Still, he did not like the idea one little bit. With Ed Jackson's connections, no place was safe. As far as he was concerned, they were walking straight into the lion's den.

It wasn't until they were about to pull into a gated underground garage that she spoke again. "I'm not going to do anything stupid," she commented, as if adding to an existing conversation. "My neighbor is away on a Mediterranean cruise, and I know her security code." Stopping at a keypad mounted just in front of the gate, she punched in seven numbers, then the gate slowly rolled up, allowing them to pass under.

Finn's survival instinct kicked in, and the knot in his gut got worse. They were going into the lion's den—in more ways than one. And it made him uneasy. Damned uneasy.

Mallory parked in the wide empty space between a silver BMW coupe and an older Rolls-Royce. She put the vehicle in park, switched off the ignition, then got out—and immediately disappeared from view. Not liking the fact that she'd dropped out of sight, Finn got out and went behind the vehicle. He found Mallory on her back under the tail end of the BMW. "What in hell are you doing?" he demanded, the last couple of hours of tension getting to him.

Muttering something under her breath, she reached up under the vehicle, then a few seconds later she scrambled up, a magnetic key holder in her hand. She waggled it at him. "I have a bad habit with keys." She opened the case, took a key out and put it in the passenger side door lock. "I either lock myself out, or I leave 'em somewhere, or I lose them."

Mallory opened the door, leaned in and began rummaging in the glove compartment. Presented with a perfect view of her jean-clad bottom, Finn discovered he wasn't as tired as he thought. "That's not a bad habit," he felt obliged to point out. "That's pathological."

He heard her chuckle; then she backed out, dangling a key chain with a single key on it under his nose. "Voilà! The key to my apartment."

Finn gave her a wry half smile. "How come you don't have a set in the heels of your shoes?"

Mallory grinned and reached into the back seat of the SUV. "Wrong shoes."

Swinging out his duffel bag, she handed it to him, then picked up hers. "I don't mean to be inhospitable, Donovan, but I can't say I'm sorry to see the last of your truck."

He frowned and turned, looking at the BMW. "I thought you said you were in your car when they grabbed you."

She gave him a speaking glance. "I do have more than one car, you know." Her duffel in her hand, she started walking toward a security door, an off-center grin appearing. "You're in my territory now, slugger. You're going to have to follow me."

To avoid security cameras, she took him up a poorly lit and little-used stairwell, using one of the keys on the chain to unlock the security door on the top floor. "You can get out by these doors, but they automatically lock behind you when you leave.'' She shot him another small grin over her shoulder. ''Just in case you should need to know.''

Finn did not want to step into that hallway for a whole lot of reasons, not the least being another security camera. Every instinct in him warned him to stay where he was, but his gut feelings had nothing to do with any threat. It had to do with the fact that he was going to be forced to come face-to-face with the reality of Patrick O'Brien's daughter. And all that it entailed.

He tried to stall. ''I expect you have staff. What are you going to tell them?''

She gave him an annoyed look. ''I don't have staff *here,* Donovan,'' she said, her tone pointed. ''I had too many years with people hovering. And I hated it. I have a live-out housekeeper who comes a couple of times a week, and that's it.'' She gave him another half smile that did not reach her eyes; then she glanced through the narrow window, waited a second and opened the door. ''Don't wander off,' she warned. ''We gotta do this fast.''

Mallory waited as the camera made the rotation to scan the hallway that ran at right angles to the one the security door opened onto. She then took the key out of the lock, opened her door and shoved him inside. Abruptly shutting the door, she looked up at him, mischief in her eyes. ''How's that for artful dodging?''

He gave her an amused look. ''Don't you ordinarily unlock your door like a normal person?''

She dumped her duffel and jacket on the floor and smiled. Then she tucked the key chain in the breast pocket of his jacket and patted it. ''Just in case you need it later.'' Looping her hair behind her ear, she reached for the switch.

Light flooded the windowless foyer, and Finn's response

died on his lips, a sick feeling rising up in him. It was even worse than he expected.

The evidence of her immense wealth was everywhere. He wasn't sure what he expected, but it definitely wasn't this. Exquisite Persian rugs, priceless Chinese porcelains, rare period antiques, crystal chandeliers and the kind of art that international museums would kill for. He remembered her comment that he needed some bright rugs on his plain wooden floors, and the sick feeling intensified. He didn't realize until that instant—when that second rush hit him— that he had been hoarding some vague hope that this was not the end. But one look at her elegant, priceless surroundings, and he knew it was. This was who she really was.

Aware that Mallory was watching him, as if assessing his reaction, he arranged his face into an unreadable expression, then forced himself to look at her. He experienced another surge when he saw how she was watching him. "I needed you to see this," she said, her voice soft and uneven.

Feeling dangerously off balance, he didn't know what to make of her reaction. And she threw him for another loop when she slid her arms around his waist and hugged him hard, her whole body quivering. "It's only me," she whispered brokenly. "It's just me."

A hollow feeling settling around his heart, Finn closed his eyes and gathered her up in a fiercely protective embrace, his throat getting very tight. He'd never expected to get a second chance at the kind of suffocating feelings that were welling up inside him—he thought he was damned lucky to have it happen once in a lifetime. But twice? No, he'd never expected it to happen twice, and not like this— not as if she were his next breath—not as if the constant ache was eating him up alive. He wasn't sure how he was ever going to be able to walk away, but he'd known all along that he'd have to. She didn't fit in his world, and he sure in hell wouldn't fit in hers. But it was going to nearly kill him when he finally left her. It was going to rip him in two.

Swallowing hard, he thrust his hand into her hair and roughly pressed her head against the curve of his neck. He didn't want to think about tomorrow, or the day after that. It was now that counted.

Whispering his name, Mallory pressed a soft, intimate kiss against the tight cords in his neck, the effects of the caress making his knees want to buckle. Doing unbearable things to him, she slid her hands down the back of his jeans, pressing him against her. And Finn hauled in a ragged breath and clutched her tighter, an age-old desire roaring through him. It was as if those soft wet caresses ripped open something inside him, and the only way he could survive was to climb right inside her brightness.

Mallory abruptly shifted her hold and clasped the back of his head, her breathing just as ragged as his as she pressed her face against his neck. Locked in a common need, they remained motionless, clinging to each other. Finn felt so exposed, so raw with wanting, he didn't think he could let her go. He really didn't.

As if fighting to collect herself, Mallory remained motionless for a moment; then she pulled away and grasped his hand. Without looking at him, she led him up the curved suspended staircase to her loft bedroom.

The space was nearly as large as his entire cabin, with a huge tester bed centered in the deep burgundy room. White gauzy fabric hung draped over the crossbars of the bed, the enclosure as airy as a dream.

Finn allowed her to lead him to the bed. Then, bracing himself for an agonizing surge, he grasped her head and tipped her face up, covering her mouth with a soft, featherlight kiss. But softness backfired on him, and the moistness of her open mouth pulled him in, nailing him with such a surge of need it compressed the air right out of his lungs. Kissing her was like drowning in moist heat, and he fought for air as she fumbled with the buttons of his shirt, her mouth offering him everything.

Unable to tear himself away from her, he fought with her clothing, stripping it off piece by piece, her urgent, questing hands setting off one throbbing response after another. The kiss turned more frantic, more urgent, more desperate. It was like being trapped in a fever, but finally they were rid of the confining barriers of their clothing.

His blood racing thick and heavy, Finn carried her down onto the huge bed, the feel of her hot naked body beneath him making him shudder. It was too fast, too frantic, too out of control, and he tried to stop, to slow down, but then Mallory wrapped her legs around him, rubbing the tip of his hardness against her moist heat. And right then, he lost what little control he had left. His face contorting, he thrust into her, the hot, slick sensation wrenching a ragged sound from him. He was drowning. Drowning in the heat of her, the tightness of her, the frenzy of her. But he was not alone. She locked him to her, thrusting up against him, calling to him, taking him deeper and deeper. Then the blackness exploded, and he was lost in the bright white light.

When Finn finally surfaced, he was damp with sweat, his arms were trembling and he was so emptied and weak he couldn't move. But he was still holding her, his arms locked around her, their bodies tightly fused together. Collecting what little strength he had left, he braced his weight on his arms and tightened the hand tangled in her hair, then kissed her with every ounce of gentleness he could muster, his throat jammed up tight. In the space of days, she had become the air he breathed, and he wasn't sure how he was going to survive when he had to leave her.

A tight ache formed in his throat and he cradled the back of her head, pouring everything he felt into that one gentle kiss. He could never say the words—but he could feel them. By God, he could feel them.

His hand cradling her head, he looked down at her, his expression softening. Managing a smile, he used his thumb to dry her mouth. "This is some bed, Red. We could play tag football in here."

She ran her hand up his back, pulling his head down, then whispered against his mouth. "I like the way you tackle me. Are you ready to play?"

He didn't think so, but she proved him wrong. The next half hour nearly destroyed him. And when he surfaced that time, he was flat on his back with her astride him, her hands braced on either side of his head, her hair a wild tumble around them. Behind her the gauzy fabric seemed to float. And he knew he'd carry that image of her to his grave.

Catching her by the back of her head, he drew her down into his arms and gave her a long kiss, then nestled her head beside his on the pillow. Closing his eyes, he smoothed his hand up her back, trying to tell her by touch alone what she meant to him.

They lay like that for a long time—not speaking, not moving—just absorbed in the feel of each other. Then finally Mallory took a deep uneven breath and hugged him hard, her grip almost desperate. Feeling the change in her, Finn tucked her head under his jaw and tightened his hold, his own expression turning sober. Ever since she had tried to call her father and got Ed Jackson instead, Finn had sensed a barely controlled dread in her, and he sensed it again now. And he knew, in spite of how much he'd like to keep reality at bay, they could not drift any longer.

He held her for another few seconds, then let his breath go as he gave her a reassuring squeeze. As if reading his mind, she pulled out of his arms and sat up, then reached for his shirt. Her back to him, she buttoned it, then rose. Still avoiding his gaze, she disappeared down the stairs. His expression sober, Finn stuffed one hand under his head and stared at the ceiling. He wished to hell they had a Plan B.

He heard her footstep on the stairs, then Mallory appeared with the illegal cell phone. Her face stiff with tension, she climbed up beside him, flipped open the mouth-piece, then looked at him, fear shimmering in her moss-green eyes. Running his hand up her thigh to reassure her, he held her gaze and nodded. Drawing in a deep, fortifying breath, she punched in the numbers. Then tossing her head to flip back her hair, she lifted the phone to her ear, her hands visibly trembling.

Her face like wax, she drew lines on her bare leg with her thumbnail, her whole body tensed. Finn could tell by the reaction in her eyes when the call was answered, and he saw her eyes brighten with relief. She put a smile into her voice. "Hi, Joyce. I'm an old friend of Malcolm Bainbridge, and he gave me this number sometime ago. I'm going to be in Chicago for a few days, and I was wondering if you could pass a message on for me?"

There was a small pause; then Mallory spoke again. "That would be great. Would you please tell him that Marigold called, and he can reach me at this number." She repeated the number twice. As soon as she disconnected, she dropped the phone on the bed, then looped her arms around her upraised knees and pressed her face against them. She sat like that for just a moment; then she abruptly got up and went to stand before the windows overlooking

Lake Michigan. Her arms folded, she stared out, her profile stark in the heavily shadowed room.

His expression unsmiling, Finn pulled on his jeans and went over to her. Without speaking, he slid his arms around her, pulling her back against his naked chest. As if emotionally exhausted, Mallory rested her head on his shoulder, then shifted so her forehead was pressed against his jaw. Tightening his arms around her, Finn tucked his head against hers. Now all they had to do was wait.

Chapter 10

And they waited. Afternoon dragged into early evening, early evening dragged into night, and the illegal phone did not ring. Unable to stand the growing panic in her eyes, Finn took her to bed and made love to her until neither one of them could think straight. And then he held her, quietly telling her stories of his wilderness until she drifted off, curled up in his arms.

After she fell asleep, Finn stared into the darkness, dread rolling around in his gut. Either her father was already dead, or his bodyguard had taken him so far underground no one could reach either of them. Which meant that he and Mallory were very much on their own. Thinking of the rifles locked up in his gun safe at home, Finn clenched his jaw. The cell phone was useless. He should have bought a damned gun instead.

It was still dark and very early when Finn got up the next morning. Leaving Mallory asleep in bed, he left the loft without making a sound and went downstairs, the knot in his gut getting worse. He retrieved his shaving gear and clean clothes out of his duffel bag, then used the bathroom adjacent to what appeared to be a guest room. Trying to block out the signs of immense wealth around him, he had a long, hot shower, the hollowness in him continuing to expand. He had trained himself a long time ago not to think about the future. And he was going to have to learn to do it again. Except without her in his life, there wasn't going to be much of a future.

Nailed with a sense of loss so strong that it was physical, Finn braced his hands on the shower wall and bent his head, grief slicing through him. Without her, nothing much mattered a damn.

It took Finn a long time to get it together, and early morning traffic had already started to move when he went into the living room. The sound rose up from the street, invading the silence of the apartment. Finn stared out, his arms folded, his shoulder braced on the casement. Like a moving chain, the headlights of an assortment of vehicles moved along the drive, and Finn watched it, wondering how people could live with the constant noise, the constant hustle and bustle.

Feeling deadened inside, he went into the kitchen and found a small jar of instant coffee, the brand unfamiliar, the crystals dark. He heated a mug of water in the microwave, then dumped some of the crystals in. Noticing the clock on the built-in oven, he picked up the mug and left the kitchen, on the prowl for a TV. It was nearly the top of the hour, and he wanted to find out if there were any new releases concerning Patrick O'Brien's daughter.

There was a small TV in what he supposed was the library—if the wall-to-ceiling, overflowing bookshelves meant anything. He found the remote and switched on the

TV, then stood drinking his coffee, waiting for the headline news.

If he'd thought Mallory O'Brien might get only a passing mention, he was dead wrong. The story of the missing heiress was the lead story, and it was more than Finn ever bargained for. In fact it was stunning, breaking news.

George Tyson-Reed and his wife, Marion, had been shot to death as they returned to their country estate the previous night. That alone was bad enough, but what made Finn's blood run cold was a news release read by Edward Jackson, the chief of security for O'Brien Industries, stating that they had reason to believe that Mallory O'Brien was still alive and being held by a convicted felon from Canada. And police on both sides of the border were on the lookout for Finn Patrick Donovan. They believed him to be armed and dangerous, and the authorities were asking for any information on his whereabouts.

It was like history repeating itself, and when a police photo of him flashed on the screen, a feeling of cold dread sliced through him.

"Oh, my God," came the whisper of horror from behind him, and he turned, his gut clenching even tighter when he saw the look on her face. But before he had time to even wonder what was going through her head, she launched herself into his arms, clinging to him with terrified strength. And for the first time since he'd found her, Mallory O'Brien's fear had the upper hand.

Her voice quivering with terror, she locked her arms around him. "Oh, God," she whispered. "What have I done to you? What have I done to you?"

Her frantic concern for him made his heart stumble, and he shut his eyes and crushed her against him. Against all odds, her belief in him had never wavered, and Finn buried his face in her hair, his chest so tight he couldn't get his lungs to function. He felt as if she had just turned him inside out. "Hey," he whispered gruffly against her hair. "It's okay, Red. This is Jackson's doing. We both know that."

She locked her arms even tighter, as if she wanted to climb right into his body. "But the police don't know that."

He gave her a hug, trying to lighten the tone of his voice. "You know, and that's what counts."

A warning of impending danger gnawed along his nerves, and he gave her another hug; then he eased her away from him. Taking her face in his hands, he made her look at him. Trying to lighten his own expression, he stroked her cheekbones with his thumbs as he managed a small half smile. "I'd like nothing better than to stand here all day with you, but the dogs have been turned loose." He carefully tucked a handful of hair behind her ear, keeping his touch light and gentle. "And if I were tracking us, the first place I'd check out would be your home base. Especially when Jackson knows damned well that if I have you, you aren't a hostage." He bent his head and gave her a quick kiss of reassurance, then met her gaze again, his own serious. "So I think we'd better get out of here— before Jackson and his crew show up. They might have found out about this place."

They threw their stuff together and tried to eradicate as much evidence as possible that they'd been there. Mallory even had the presence of mind to grab a city map. Making sure she had the illegal cell phone in her small handbag, Finn threw his stuff into his duffel.

They were out of the apartment in less than twenty minutes. Skirting the security cameras once again, they headed for the stairwell and the underground parkade. Knowing they couldn't leave Finn's vehicle for Jackson to find, they borrowed the front plate off the sedate Jag two stalls down and threw Finn's single plate in the cargo hold. Then with Finn behind the wheel, they roared up the ramp to the street.

And directly into the path of a blue sedan with the O'Brien Industries logo on the side.

Swearing, Finn cranked the wheel and stepped on the gas, shooting across oncoming traffic, barely missing the blue sedan and a city bus as he veered in front of it. Cutting off the vehicle on his right, he made a sharp right turn. Her hand on the dash, Mallory turned to look out the back window, her face ashen.

"I can't see them," she said, her voice shaking.

Caught in the middle of morning rush-hour traffic, Finn had nowhere to go. He thought maybe, just maybe, he had outmaneuvered them, then he saw the blue car swing out from behind a truck that was following him, and he swore again. It was bad enough that they'd been spotted. But Jackson's crew had them in their sights, and that made his gut ball up. The blue sedan bullied its way through traffic, until it was only two cars behind them.

It took Finn one long look in his wide side mirror to realize two things. The man in the passenger seat had a weapon, and the driver was talking on a cell phone. Finn had done enough tracking himself to know what was happening. If they were talking on a cell phone, his guess was that reinforcements were being mustered in—and it wasn't going to be the Chicago police department. And that upped the odds. The only way that Ed Jackson could save his own ass was for Mallory to turn up dead. And it was evident from the news release that Jackson planned to hang her death on Finn.

Mallory spoke, her voice barely controlled. "If I remember correctly, there's some construction about four blocks ahead.''

Knowing they could not risk getting boxed in, Finn made another right-hand turn, and horns blared behind him as he cut through traffic. Spotting an alley and a God-sent break in the traffic, he made an immediate left turn, following the alley down to a less congested side street. Watching every intersection for the blue sedan, he gripped the wheel. Damn it, they couldn't just keep driving around, hoping they'd lost them. Finn glanced at her. ''Where's the nearest police precinct?''

Twisted in her seat, she watched the traffic behind them, fear imprinted on her face. ''We can't go to the police,'' she said, her voice shaking. ''If they spot you, they're going to shoot first and ask questions later.''

He managed a small grin. ''Now who's sugarcoating things?''

She looked at him, a dark stricken look in her eyes. ''Don't joke,'' she said, her voice breaking. ''Didn't you hear what they said on the news—that you're believed to be armed and dangerous?''

Trying to keep his tone calm and rational, he answered her. ''We can't just keep driving around, Red.'' Not with Ed Jackson's armed men on their tails. Finn glanced at her, his expression fixed. ''Now, where is the nearest precinct?''

''Oh, God.''

He swiveled his attention to the traffic ahead, his insides dropping when he saw the blue sedan pull out directly in front of them. That was bad enough. But now there were two blue sedans. The second one was waiting at the next intersection, and Finn knew the net was about to close.

Spotting a loading bay tucked in the back of a big brick warehouse, Finn wheeled into it, slammed the truck into park, snatched the keys out of the ignition and threw open his door. "Get out and run, damn it!" he commanded, grabbing his own cell phone and hitting the automatic door lock.

She never hesitated. She hit the ground running, her handbag slung across her chest, and headed down a narrow alleyway. His whole body braced for the impact of a bullet, he stayed right behind her, trying to shield her.

The alley spilled out onto the adjoining street, and as they turned on the sidewalk, Finn saw two men pounding up the alley behind them. Knowing he had to get her some place safe damned fast, he grabbed her hand. "Come on!"

Breathing hard, she sprinted beside him, gripping his hand. "Is this supposed to be fun?" she managed, her breathing harsh and labored.

He might have smiled but he was too busy scanning ahead for a possible escape route. The light at the crosswalk changed just as one of the blue sedans shot across the intersection, the driver slamming on the brakes when he spotted them.

Men behind them. Men in front of them. They darted across the street, running for their lives. "The office building," Finn directed. They dashed in through the big glass doors and through the marble lobby, the security guard shouting at them. Just as they burst out the other side, Finn spotted the taxi, the wheels cranked, the driver watching for a break in traffic.

Finn banged on the roof, then yanked open the door and shoved Mallory in. The driver pulled into traffic just as Finn slammed the back door. "Where to, folks?"

Fighting for breath, Finn grabbed Mallory by the back of the neck and forced her down on the seat. "Just drive. We got some thugs chasing us." This was not his type of wilderness, but it was wilderness just the same, and he considered their options. The more he thought about it, the more he realized that the police were not viable options. After the smoke screen Ed Jackson had laid down, the good men in blue *were* apt to shoot first and ask questions later. And if they happened to take him down, Finn knew that Mallory didn't stand a chance.

The muffled ring of an unfamiliar cell phone shattered the tense silence, and Mallory abruptly sat up, fumbling for her handbag. "Oh, God," she breathed unevenly. "Let it be Malcolm."

Her hands shaking, she flipped open the mouthpiece and pressed the connect button. Her face white, she stared at Finn as she put it to her ear. "Yes?"

Abruptly she pressed her hand to her face, a tremor coursing through her whole body. "Oh, God, Malcolm. Ed Jackson is trying to kill us."

She lifted her head and stared at Finn, listening. Finn knew they were sitting ducks. It was only a matter of time until Jackson's crew located them, which meant they had to get out of this damned cab and somewhere safe. The cab pulled up beside a city bus, and the huge ad painted on the side jumped out at Finn. And he got a shot of pure adrenaline. Why in hell hadn't he thought of that earlier—like the day after he found her? It was a solution to end all solutions.

His voice was sharp when he spoke. "Tell him we're heading to that TV station," he ordered, indicating the huge ad. Checking behind him, he gave the cabby their destination, his gut knotting as he spotted one of the blue sedans coming through traffic. "And tell him to be quick with help. We've got trouble on our tail."

It took them fifteen minutes to get to the station—and it was the longest fifteen minutes Finn had spent in his life. Finn stuffed some cash into the cabby's hand, and once again they hit the sidewalk running. He managed to shoot

Mallory a tight smile. "How do you feel about appearing on TV, Red?"

They managed to bluff their way past the receptionist at the TV station, but they weren't so lucky with the security guard. But Mallory, pale and shaking, made things happen by announcing who she was. And lucky for them, the security guard recognized her.

Within minutes, they were seated in the office of the station manager, with the security guard posted at the door, and several other personnel standing by. Her legs finally gave out on her and Mallory sank into a chair, still clinging to Finn's hand. Taking a deep breath she squared her shoulders, and looking very much the wealthy industrialist's daughter, she told her story.

The station manager was an old news director, and his reaction was immediate. Not only did he have the scoop of the decade sitting in his office, he also recognized that Ms. O'Brien's safety depended on how he handled the situation. He immediately moved Finn and Mallory to an inner corridor, barred by heavy security doors. Leaving two more security guards posted outside, he ushered them both into a control room. And before Finn really had time to assess what was going on, he found himself standing in a darkened corner of a brightly lit studio, a dozen people milling around him, instructions being shouted from every direction. He never took his eyes off Mallory, who was huddled with the station manager, discussing the content of a hastily written script.

With cameramen positioned behind their cameras, a woman with a headset handed the script to the announcer, then raised her arm and began the countdown. The instant she pointed at the announcer, the red light came on, and the man behind the news desk looked directly into the camera.

"Good morning. This is Chicago AM and I'm Brian Black with breaking news." Then, reading from the script he'd just been handed, he announced that there were new developments concerning Mallory O'Brien, the missing daughter of Patrick O'Brien. Looking straight into the camera, he said that in an exclusive interview with the station, she had told about her abduction, about the plane crash and how Mr. Donovan had stumbled across her in the wilderness. And how, at great personal risk, Mr. Donovan had gotten her safely back to Chicago. The announcer concluded the newsflash, and the woman with the headset turned and pointed to the control room for a hastily assembled profile on the case. The red light immediately switched off and everyone started milling around.

The whole thing lasted maybe three minutes, and Finn got a sick feeling in his gut when he realized his mission was completed. He knew that with the airing of that report, the authorities would be looking for Ed Jackson. His face set in stern lines, Finn shifted his position, his gaze never leaving Mallory's pale face, the heavy, empty feeling unfolding in him. Clenching his jaw against the rush of emptiness, he looked away, his throat knotted. He had accomplished what he had set out to do—to keep her safe. Now she would be enfolded in her father's millions, and he would go back to his high country. And that would be that.

Swallowing hard, he gouged at his eyes, the hollow feeling climbing higher. He had known her only a matter of days, and she had taken over his entire life. And he wasn't sure how he was going to survive without her.

Mallory had just started toward him, a smile on her face, when the studio door burst open and a heavily armed tactical team rushed in and fanned out. Someone shouted, "Everybody freeze! Hands on your heads!"

One of the team grabbed Mallory and shoved her in the

corner; two other members hemmed her in. Finn saw her stumble and fall, and she yelled his name, and he exploded. He was across the room before anyone had a chance to contain him, managing to tackle two of them before the others shut him down. It all happened so fast Finn could barely assimilate it. One moment he was standing there feeling like hell, then in the next instant, he was restrained by three men, his face shoved against the wall and his arms twisted up behind his back. Fury slicing through him, he collected his strength, prepared to take his assailants down; then he saw the police flash on the shoulder of one of the men and he forced himself to go slack. For one terrifying moment, he'd thought it was a team of Jackson's men. And he'd thought he'd lost the game after all.

His heart slamming against the walls of his chest, adrenaline still pumping through him, Finn closed his eyes, his face twisted against the wall. Above the racket, he could hear Mallory putting up a hell of a fight.

"Let me go!" she demanded, her voice rising in fury. "And you take your damned hands off him!"

There was the sound of a tussle, and somebody swore, and the cop holding Finn jammed him harder against the wall. Finn felt the bite of tie-wrap handcuffs around his wrists. He heard another scuffle and saw the flash of red hair very close to him, then a wall of black uniforms. Hauling in air, he turned his head, his face scraping against the rough texture of the wall. "It's all right," he said, trying to keep his voice calm. "Don't fight 'em, Red. These are the good guys."

The man holding him grabbed him by the hair and yanked him upright, jamming a baton under his chin, his tone threatening. "You got that right, buddy. Now, march. We're going for a little ride."

And the last glimpse Finn had before he was taken away

was of Mallory trying to fight her way free of the security around her, her face white with alarm. "No! No! I'd be dead if it wasn't for him!" Each arm restrained by the two police escorts, Finn got shoved into the hallway, Mallory's voice rising in a mixture of fury and panic. "Damn it! Why won't you listen?"

Finn knew damned well why they wouldn't listen. He had walked this walk before. His expression completely shut down, he looked straight ahead, his jaw locked, the hole in his chest spreading. It was a hell of a way to say goodbye.

Sitting with his back against the cinder block wall, Finn stared across the jail cell, the smell and the layers of graffiti on the dirty green paint dragging him back to a time he'd never wanted to recall. And although the plastic cuffs had been removed, he could still feel where they had cut into his flesh.

He hadn't been photographed or fingerprinted, but his personal effects had been confiscated. And he had been interrogated by two detectives from the Chicago police department and by four FBI agents. At this point, he really didn't give a damn who came through the door anymore. Once he had been assured that Ms. O'Brien was safe, he answered their questions, offering up nothing and trying not to think. But there was nothing like being held for four hours in a dingy, stinking cell to remind him of who he really was.

Tipping his head back, he closed his eyes and clamped his jaw together, trying to will away the feeling of claustrophobia—the feeling of being trapped. He knew why he was there. No one got away with slugging two cops, especially an ex-con, and especially someone who'd been accused by Ed Jackson of being armed and dangerous. He understood their caution—he didn't like it, but he understood it. He also knew they couldn't hold him for long. Which meant he was going to have to just damned well grit his teeth and tough it out. Things would happen when they happened.

Using a technique he had learned from his years in prison, he tried to block everything out by holding one clean bright memory of Mallory in his mind. But in some ways, that only made it worse. It reminded him of just how damned alone he really was.

He heard the door open, then a male voice spoke. "You're free to go, Mr. Donovan."

Finn opened his eyes and stared at the detective who'd interviewed him, then picked up his jacket and wearily got up, his face stiff. "Who do I see about my truck?" he said, his voice flat.

The other man stood back to allow Finn to pass in front of him. "That's all been taken care of."

Finn stepped out into the main room, noticing a small nondescript man in a chauffeur's uniform standing off to one side. His expression flat, Finn signed for the brown envelope holding his personal effects, then dumped out the contents. He experienced a sudden tightness in his chest when the key chain with Mallory's apartment key slid onto the countertop. His jaw locked against the sensation, he put his wallet and the two sets of keys in one pocket. And he was just shoving his cell phone into the inside breast pocket of his jacket when the uniformed man came over to him and smiled, then spoke in a very proper English accent. "Mr. Donovan? I'm Malcolm, Mr. O'Brien's driver. I'm here to take you to your lodgings."

Finn considered the other man, a thin sliver of humor surfacing. This was Malcolm—the bodyguard? He would never have guessed it. Aware that the detective was leaning

against a desk watching, Finn only nodded. Malcolm tipped
his head at the detective, then went to the door exiting the
squad room and opened it, giving Finn a pleasant smile.
"This way, sir."

Once outside, Finn snapped up his jacket, then stared at
the O'Brien's driver. "Where is she?" he demanded.

The small man opened the back door of a Mercedes.
"She's safe, Mr. Donovan."

Finn was in no mood for games. "I'm not going anywhere until I know what in hell is going on. And I want
to know where she is."

His gloved hand on the door, the other man looked up
at Finn, a twinkle appearing in his eyes. "She is at her
apartment with her father, under heavy guard." The twinkle
intensified. "And not very happy about it, I might add. Ms.
Mallory doesn't like anyone making her decisions for her."

Finn made his muscles relax. "What about Jackson and
his crew?"

The chauffeur gave Finn the coldest smile he'd ever
seen. "Two of Mr. Jackson's cohorts are currently resting
comfortably at the morgue. Mr. Jackson is resting not so
comfortably with several FBI agents. They don't know if
they have everyone, so Mr. O'Brien has given orders to
have Ms. Mallory held until the FBI can verify her safety."
The twinkle reappeared. "Now if you would get in the car,
sir."

After they started driving, Finn considered trying to
pump Malcolm for more information, but he was just too
used up to push it. It was as if four hours in jail had sucked
him dry. Recalling his last look at Mallory, he closed his
eyes, the familiar hollow feeling eating a hole in his chest.
He was going to miss her. God, but he was going to miss
her.

Twilight was encroaching when they finally turned onto

a narrow drive, stopping at an electronically controlled wrought-iron gate. The gate swung open, and they drove through. Finn stared out the window, reminded again of Patrick O'Brien's immense wealth, the heavy feeling in his chest getting worse.

It was like something out of a novel. The cobbled roadway was lined with trees and the acres of landscaping stretched out, dotted with huge sculptures. If Mallory's apartment had had a sobering effect on Finn, the estate was a hundred times worse. It was like coming face-to-face with the full force of Patrick O'Brien's influence and money.

Aware that Malcolm was watching him in the rearview mirror, Finn tipped his head back and closed his eyes, a kind of soul-deep weariness washing over him. All he wanted to do was go home.

They rounded the last curve, and Finn spotted his SUV parked on the wide cobbled terrace in front of the sprawling mansion. He wondered how they had managed that, when he had the keys stowed in his jacket pocket. The vehicle had been freshly washed and waxed, the license plate restored, and even the chrome had been polished. After the craziness of the past few days, the sight of his polished vehicle was almost surreal. It might have amused him if he hadn't felt so damned beat up inside.

It was a bad scene all around. At every turn, he was reminded of Mallory's absence and how damned alone he was. Malcolm personally ushered him to his room, then showed him where everything was, telling Finn he'd find his things in the armoire. Finn did give up a small smile when he opened the mirrored door and found his clothes, all freshly laundered and perfectly pressed. Even his jeans had sharp creases in them.

But that little flicker of amusement lasted a split second; then a surge of aloneness nailed him, making his eyes burn.

His face set in rigid lines, he picked up some clean clothes and headed for the bathroom. The foul smell of jail clung to him, and suddenly he could not tolerate it any longer. He turned on the shower and shed his jeans, but as he pulled his shirt off over his head, he caught a whiff of Mallory's hand lotion, and that nearly took him down. The loss of her hit with such impact, it was as if he'd just been shot, and another surge of aloneness rolled in on him. Bracing his hands on the wall, he clenched his jaw and closed his eyes, the pain in his chest incapacitating him. He wasn't sure how he was going to make it through the next hour, let alone the rest of his life.

It was a long time before Finn could pull it together, then he wearily straightened, shed the rest of his clothes and stepped into the steaming shower. He hoped to hell he could learn to switch off again. It was the only way he might be able to make it through this. Not that making it mattered a damn.

The shower helped a little, and plain old exhaustion helped to numb him. Trying to keep his mind blank, Finn went to stand before the floor-to-ceiling casement windows staring out into the deepening night, looking down at an arched, vine-covered pavilion and the softly lit elongated reflecting pool. He had never seen anything like it in his life.

A soft knock sounded on the door, and he exhaled heavily and straightened. "Come in."

An older woman in a plain black dress with a white collar opened the door, a gold watch pinned to her breast pocket. She was pushing a linen-draped trolley. She gave Finn a warm smile. "I thought you might prefer dinner in your room, Mr. Donovan."

His throat suddenly tight, Finn nodded. "Thank you." Other than the cup of coffee he'd had at Mallory's, he hadn't had anything to eat all day. But just the thought of food made his stomach churn.

She laid out a table by the fireplace, even including an arrangement of fresh flowers. She completed her task, then straightened and met Finn's gaze. "I want to thank you on behalf of everyone here for bringing Ms. Mallory home safely, Mr. Donovan. She means a great deal to all of us."

Finn studied the older woman, recalling Mallory telling him about the head housekeeper who had taught her how to cook. He managed a small smile. "You must be Mildred."

The woman's eyes immediately filled with tears, and she looked down and fumbled in her pocket for a tissue. "She told you about me, then."

Finn had to swallow hard before he could speak. "Yes, she did."

Mildred dabbed at her eyes, then looked up at him. "She's a very special young lady."

Hit with a rush of grief, Finn clenched and unclenched his jaw, knowing he had to make some response. His voice was very gruff when he finally answered. "Yes, she is."

Mildred stopped what she was doing and stared at him, and Finn suddenly felt so exposed that he had to turn back to the window. An hour. He had nearly made it through a whole hour.

Her voice was very gentle when she spoke behind him. "If you need anything, just dial twelve on the phone to have me paged."

Unable to see for the pain welling up inside him, Finn grasped the window frame. "Thank you."

He heard the door close behind her, but he didn't move. Everything was suddenly closing in on him, and more than anything, he wanted to bolt. But he had to be absolutely sure she was safe before he left.

He never touched his meal, and he considered heading outside, but the thought of running into anyone, even a member of the staff, made him freeze up inside. Finally needing something other than his own thoughts, he checked his watch and realized it was nearly ten o'clock. Trying to curb the restlessness pressing down on him, he located a TV hidden in the matching armoire. The remote in his hand, he switched channels, hoping to find something that might grab his attention.

Finn changed again, and he was suddenly confronted with a clip of him and Mallory walking down the corridor of the TV station. He vaguely remembered a cameraman preceding them, but the fact never struck until now. Mallory had on the pair of blue jeans they'd bought, one of his white T-shirts and a rust suede jacket almost the exact same color as her hair. She was hanging on to his hand, at one point she looked up at him, and Finn could feel the effects of that look right through him.

He didn't even hear what the voice-over was saying— all he could see was her, and far too quickly, the image was gone. He experienced a stab of panic, and started scrolling through the channels, trying to find the same clip on another station. Finally realizing what he was doing, he switched off the TV and threw the remote on the bed, another sudden rush of claustrophobia pressing down on him. He needed to get the hell out of that room. Snatching up his jacket, he headed for the door and yanked it open, only to be confronted by a young man with his hand up ready to knock. The staff member took a step back, looking very flustered. ''Umm. Mr. Donovan. Mr. O'Brien wonders if you could join him in the library.''

Finn didn't want to join anybody anywhere, but he locked his jaw together and drew a steadying breath into his lungs. Forcing himself to ease off, he tossed his jacket on the chair just inside his room, then faced the messenger. "Fine."

The library was indeed a library. Vast high ceilings with groined arches, high narrow windows draped with dark green velvet, ornate bookshelves from floor to ceiling filled with leather-bound books, a huge fireplace with a heavy black walnut mantel, andirons that had to be centuries old. Even the floor was a work of art, inlaid with rare and priceless woods.

The only light came from a matching pair of Tiffany lamps on either end of the enormous antique desk, the heavy shadows somehow appropriate. It was an impressive room, and it suited the man standing by the huge antique desk, staring out the window.

Finn heard the door close behind him, and he stood in the shadows, assessing the man by the window. From various reports, Finn knew that Patrick O'Brien was in his late sixties, but he appeared younger. He was wearing casual khaki-colored pants and a dark brown shooting sweater, leather patches on one shoulder and the elbows. His thick, curly hair was the same color as Mallory's, only his was heavily streaked with white, and his neck resembled that of a bull. Wry humor tugged at Finn's mouth. He could recognize a street fighter when he saw one.

Patrick O'Brien turned. "Ah. Mr. Donovan. Thank you for joining me."

Finn stared at the other man, sizing him up. Finally he spoke, his tone clipped. "How is she?"

Patrick O'Brien tossed the gold pen he'd been holding onto the desk. "She's fine." He looked back at Finn. "A man who cuts right to the chase, I see."

As far as Finn was concerned, that statement didn't warrant an answer. Patrick O'Brien gave him an amused look and came around the desk. "My daughter tells me if it hadn't been for you, she would have never survived."

Finn stared at the man, feeling unaccountably bad-tempered. "I think Mallory sells herself short."

Patrick O'Brien chuckled. "My daughter rarely sells herself short, Mr. Donovan. I've got the battle scars to prove it." He picked up a carved alabaster paperweight off the desk and weighed it in his hand, his expression very thoughtful. "I appreciate what you did, Donovan. She means a great deal to me."

Finn got an abrupt tightness in his chest, and he looked away, trying to keep his expression passive. That was another statement he wasn't about to answer.

"I understand Malcolm brought you up to speed on what's been going on."

Finn lifted his head and looked at Mallory's father. "He told me a bit."

Patrick O'Brien set the paperweight down, then sat back on the edge of the desk and folded his arms. There wasn't a trace of expression on his face. "Jackson is in custody, and two of his henchmen are dead. There was a shootout late this afternoon. We now know that there were also two other men who were involved, all of them hired by Jackson, and employed by my company." He stared at his shoes for a moment, then looked back at Finn, bitter anger glinting in his eyes. "Needless to say, I'm not very happy about that. So I've already brought in a reputable security firm to do an entire personnel audit." His eyes turned cold and hard, contained fury making the muscles in his jaw flex. "I will make damned sure nothing like this ever happens again."

Finn watched the other man, assessing his face, assessing his body language. "Did they find out anything from Jackson?"

Mallory's father nodded. "Yes. And you had it figured correctly. My brother-in-law and his wife instigated the whole scheme and approached Jackson. Apparently they were in serious financial difficulty and saw this as a solution. Jackson claims it was one of the dead men who murdered them—panicked and acted on his own, or at least that's the story he's sticking to. I suspect that's not entirely the truth."

He refolded his arms and stared at the floor, lines of strain showing on his face. "Just to be on the safe side, I've ordered this new security company to keep Mallory under lock and key until the other two are captured. They felt her apartment offered the best immediate security, since she kept it such a secret." He lifted his head and looked at Finn, a glimmer of amusement in his eyes. "And I'm afraid my very willful daughter is not too happy about that. I expect you already know just how willful she is."

Finn met the other man's gaze, his expression softening, a small smile hovering around his mouth. "Yeah, you could say that."

Mallory's father chuckled, but he didn't say anything for a space. Finally he let go a tired sigh. "The real irony is if they had made it all the way to Alaska with her, their whole plan would have fallen apart." Finn looked up and met Patrick O'Brien's gaze, and Mallory's father gave a wry smile. "They weren't aware of it, but Malcolm and I were already at the lodge. I'd wanted to get away from everything for a bit, so I never told anyone where we were going. We didn't get back until three days ago." His expression sobered and he looked down, shaking his head. "I didn't even know she was missing until then." There was another brief pause; then he lifted his head and looked at Finn. "Mallory told me how well you looked after her, Mr. Donovan. I owe you a huge debt of gratitude."

Unable to hold the other man's gaze, Finn stuffed his hands in the back pockets of his jeans. "You don't owe me anything."

There was an odd silence, then Patrick O'Brien spoke, his tone slightly amused. "Ah. So that's how it is."

Finn shot him a sharp, hostile look, but Patrick O'Brien turned and picked up the paperweight again. His tone was casual as he handled the carving. "I'm sure Mallory told you that her mother was considerably younger than I— sixteen years, as a matter of fact—and I expect that made me somewhat protective."

He looked up and met Finn's gaze, his expression casual. "Which was probably not a bad thing, seeing as my daughter is as willful as she is." He gave Finn a lopsided smile. "And I imagine she's making the security team's life a living hell as we speak." He stared into space for a moment, then let his breath go in a heavy sigh. "I think I should forewarn you that the FBI wants to talk to you again, and there could be an issue over your entering the country with a criminal record." He met Finn's gaze again, his own solemn. "The media is having a field day with all this. I will, of course, try to do what I can—and I do have considerable influence. But that's where it stands at the moment."

It was almost as if Finn was suddenly trapped on a high, narrow ledge, with no way off, and he was faced with a hard, cold choice. There was no way in hell he was going to stick around, just so the FBI could toss him out of the country. And he had no intention of letting his past become part of the media feeding frenzy. He couldn't drag her into the middle of that. He *wouldn't* drag her into the middle of that.

The second certainty came hard on the heels of the first, making his throat close up and his insides twist. It was over.

And he would never wake up again with her beside him. He would never again experience her warmth and humor, her comfortable silences. And he would never again lose all his aloneness in her.

He abruptly turned, blinded by the gripping sense of loss. It was time to cut his losses and get the hell out. Needing a minute to pull it together, he reached out and touched the fine old weather vane mounted in a stand by the door. Finally he spoke. "I don't want her subjected to that kind of media circus," he said, his voice very gruff. "She's been through enough as it is." Stuffing his hands in his pockets, he turned and met Patrick O'Brien's gaze, his expression fixed. "I think it would be better for everyone if I cleared out now."

Patrick O'Brien stared at him, his expression steady and intent. It was a moment before he responded. "I understand your position. But my daughter won't be very happy about that, Mr. Donovan."

Finn forced a small half smile. "She'll get over it."

Finn knew he couldn't say the same for himself.

Chapter 11

Finn went back to his room, a heaviness in his gut that he had never experienced before. Not bothering to turn on the lights, he went to stand before the window. It had started to rain when he was in the study, and he watched the slicing drizzle, a mixture of dread and reluctance eating away at him. It was time. He knew it was time. There was nothing more he could do, and staying would only complicate matters for her.

In another lifetime, he'd had personal experience with the media. They were like vultures, hovering around a carcass, just waiting for any damned scrap to feed on. And if he were deported because of his criminal record, there would be a media frenzy to end all media frenzies. He could just see the headlines—and he knew what that would do to her. And he'd do whatever was necessary to prevent that from happening.

Feeling dead inside, he turned from the window and crossed to the armoire. His jaw locked, he opened the doors and took his neatly folded duffel and began stuffing his belongings into it. If he cleared out now, he'd be hundreds of miles away by morning. And out of everybody's reach.

There was a light knock on the door, but Finn ignored it. He didn't want to see anybody, and he sure in hell didn't want to have to talk to anyone, either.

His nonresponse didn't get him the results he wanted. The door opened anyway, and Malcolm entered. Only it wasn't the chauffeur that stepped into the room—it was, without question, the highly trained bodyguard. He was dressed all in black—black pants, black shoes, a black turtleneck. And Finn spotted a telltale bulge under his black leather jacket. He cast the Brit an impassive look, then tossed his bag down on the end of the bed.

Malcolm spoke. "Mr. O'Brien told me you have decided to leave."

Finn cast him another look, then went into the bathroom to collect his shaving kit and the clothes he'd had on earlier. When Finn reentered the room, Malcolm was standing in front of the muted TV, watching something on the screen. It gave Finn a bit of a start when he realized the bodyguard had switched to closed-circuit TV.

Malcolm turned, indicating the view of the front gate, where a snarl of media vans was clustered, along with technicians and reporters huddled under umbrellas. There was annoyance in the bodyguard's tone. "Quite a nasty bunch, actually. I assumed they would have given up by now." A twinkle appeared in his eyes, and he gave Finn a small smile. "I suspect you'd rather avoid that scene, so I will show you another way out—one that is quite private."

Finn held his gaze for a second, then stuffed his shaving kit in the side pocket of his duffel. Without looking at him, Finn responded, his tone abrupt. "Thanks. I'd appreciate that."

"I just returned from Ms. Mallory's."

Experiencing a sudden bottomless ache in his chest, Finn rolled up the jeans and roughly stuffed them in the bag. "How's she doing?"

Finn heard the click of the remote control; then the bodyguard shut both doors on the second armoire. There was an undercurrent of humor in Malcolm's voice. "Ms. Mallory, to use the local vernacular, is a bit ticked. The security people have shut down the telephone system and confiscated her cell phones—they don't want anyone having access to her. She was not at all pleased about that. She wanted very badly to talk to you."

It was almost as if he taken a severe blow to the heart, and Finn couldn't have responded even if he'd wanted to. Feeling exposed and vulnerable and absolutely raw, he jammed the remainder of his clothing into the duffel, pain radiating through his chest. It hurt just thinking about her.

Malcolm came over to the bed, then withdrew a small gift-wrapped package from his pocket and placed it with great care beside Finn's duffel. The bodyguard's voice was oddly muted when he spoke. "Ms. Mallory knew you would be leaving before she got a chance to see you," he said quietly. He pushed the small package in Finn's direction. "She wanted to give you something to remember her by."

Finn stared at the package, the sense of loss so huge he was paralyzed by it. He had no idea how long he stood there, staring at that gift, feeling as if his heart and soul had just been pulverized. She had wrapped it in gold paper and tied it with a gauzy ribbon the exact same color as her eyes, and it nearly killed him, knowing she had been thinking of him. Finally able to ease the vicious cramp in his throat, he reached out and picked it up, his future stretching out like a black hole in front of him. He wasn't sure how he was going to survive without her.

Not wanting any spectators around when he opened it, he placed the parcel on top of his clothes, then zipped the duffel. Making sure his face revealed nothing, he picked up his jacket and glanced at Malcolm. "You said there was another way out of here?"

Finn caught Malcolm watching him, his arms folded, a thoughtful, assessing expression in his eyes. He immediately smiled and nodded his head. "That's correct." He went to the door and opened it for Finn. "I'll escort you out."

It was a miserable night—cold and wet, with the kind of blackness that seemed to swallow any illumination. It was a helluva night to be going anywhere. Finn followed Malcolm's Range Rover down a barely discernible trail through what appeared to be some kind of orchard, then onto a narrow, winding road. About a hundred yards further on, the Range Rover's taillights flashed as the vehicle slowed and pulled over onto the grassy verge.

A heavy chained metal gate barred the way, and Finn pulled up beside the other vehicle and stopped. Feeling totally spent, he got out and started toward the gate, the freezing rain like needles against his face. Both vehicles had been traveling with the headlights and fog lights on, and the illumination cast the bodyguard in an eerie, diffused aura as he unlocked the heavy padlock on the gate. He glanced up as Finn approached, his face and leather coat already slick with rain. The familiar twinkle appeared in his eyes. "I think we can safely assume that you can make a clean getaway, Mr. Donovan. There isn't a media van in sight." He indicated the highway on the other side of the gate. "That road will take you to the main interchange. It's well marked."

He pulled the chain loose and had his hand on the gate to push it open when he stopped and took a cell phone out of his inside pocket. He flipped open the mouthpiece and turned away from Finn as he put the phone to his ear. He listened a moment, then looked at Finn. "Very good. I'll tell him."

He closed up the phone and stuffed it back in his inside pocket. "That was Mr. O'Brien. He just got word that the other two men are in custody. So Ms. Mallory is absolutely safe, and he has dismissed her security."

Finn looked away and nodded. That was all he cared about. That she was safe.

He heard the gate rattle and turned back, knowing he had to get through the next few minutes.

The gate open, Malcolm turned and looked at Finn, extending his hand. "It was a pleasure meeting you, Mr. Donovan. And thank you for taking such good care of Ms. Mallory. We're all very grateful."

Experiencing an unexpected weight in his chest, Finn grasped the other man's hand and spoke, his voice very husky. "Then I'll leave her in your very capable hands."

Malcolm held onto Finn's hand, looked at him with a solemn, steady gaze. "I think not, Mr. Donovan," he said, his tone kind. "Ms. Mallory has a mind of her own. And I have always had implicit faith in her excellent judgment. Ms. Mallory is seldom wrong."

Faced with making the final separation, Finn stepped back and abruptly stuffed his hands in his jacket pockets. His voice didn't even sound like his own when he spoke. "Tell her goodbye for me." Then he turned and went back to his vehicle, emptiness radiating through him.

Now it was really time.

He made it as far as the exchange—and that was as far as he could go. Driven by something he couldn't even define, he pulled onto the shoulder and stopped. The duffel was on the passenger seat beside him, and he stared at it, his heart suddenly jammed in his throat. He flexed his hands; then abruptly dragged the bag onto the console and located the gift. Touching that package was almost like touching her, and he held it for a moment, his chest getting tighter and tighter, emotion compressing his heart. Finally he undid the bow and slipped a black velvet box out of the wrapping paper. Braced for a whole lot of hurt, he opened the lid, his heart stopping altogether when he saw what was inside.

It was the pendant—the one he'd found, the one her father had given her mother. He still had a mental image of her clutching it to her heart, as if it was the most precious thing she possessed. His vision blurring, he carefully lifted it out, the metal cold to his touch. He couldn't believe she had given him something that meant so much to her— something with so much meaning attached to it. The necklace clasped in his hand, he clenched his eyes shut and tipped his head back, his throat cramping even worse.

He sat there for a long time, the lights from passing cars flashing behind his eyelids. He wasn't sure he could do this. He knew it was the right thing to do, but he wasn't sure he could walk away from her.

Finally he straightened, his face feeling leaden as he picked up the box. Certain he was incapable of feeling anything more than he was already feeling, he went to replace the necklace in the box, and it was then he noticed that the broken chain had been replaced—the new one longer and heavier. He fingered the new chain, a strange floating sensation overwhelming him. And he knew, as sure as he was sitting there, she meant for him to wear it. Wanted him to wear it.

Finn got another light-headed rush, and he stared at the

piece of jewelry, the heaviness in his chest breaking into a million little pieces. And he knew that there was no way he could leave without looking directly into her eyes, and telling her how he felt about her. He had to tell her that. If nothing else, he had to tell her.

His hands not quite steady and his heart pounding, he pulled the chain over his head; then he undid his seat belt and turned on the interior light. Twisting around in the confines of the cab, he tore the back seat apart, looking for the map Mallory had tossed back there. He didn't have a damned clue where he was, and he didn't have a clue how to get back to her place, but he was going. He didn't care what time of night it was. He was going.

The map located, he opened it up and quickly plotted his route, then tossed it on the passenger seat. Shutting off the interior light, he felt for her apartment key in his jacket pocket, then switched on the ignition. He couldn't get there fast enough.

It was just going on midnight when Finn arrived at her place. He spotted a media van parked up the street, and he swore under his breath. Wanting to avoid that circus if at all possible, he pulled onto the ramp leading into the underground garage, hoping like hell he could remember the security code he'd seen her punch in.

He got it on the second try. Certain his heart couldn't possibly beat any faster, Finn parked in the empty space beside her coupe. He didn't know he could feel so damned shaky—it was almost as if he'd scaled an entire mountain.

Using the exact same route as before, he took the stairs two at a time, his heart still thundering in his chest. He hoped like hell the security people had already left. And he didn't even want to think about what he would do if she weren't there.

Finn was breathing hard when he reached her landing.

He wasn't quite sure why he did it, but he avoided the security camera the same way she had, so much adrenaline in his system he could have floated a boat in it.

Expelling the air out of his lungs, Finn silently entered her apartment and closed the door, sticking her key back in his pocket. His heart gave a violent lurch when a loud crash came from the kitchen, and he heard Mallory swear.

Fear shot through him, and he headed for the kitchen, keeping to the shadows and not making a sound. If someone had her, he would tear them apart limb from limb.

He moved against the wall until he could see in. Another crash sounded, and he stopped dead in his tracks. There was no one with Mallory. She was making that racket all by herself.

He wouldn't have believed it unless he'd seen it with his own eyes. Dressed in a pair of his navy sweats, Mallory O'Brien was flinging things out of her cupboard, swearing and crying at the same time. "Damn it, damn it, damn it!" She threw a box on the floor, and spaghetti spilled out. "Damn it all to hell!"

The tension abruptly let go in Finn's chest, and something else expanded to fill the space. He felt almost weightless—and lighter than he had in days. Folding his arms, he propped his shoulder against the door frame, watching her temper tantrum. She looked like hell. Her bright copper hair was slipping from a large clasp on top of her head, her nose was red, her eyes were swollen, and her face was so puffy, it looked as if she'd been crying for days. But she was in top form. She flung several more boxes on the floor, and a crazy kind of lightness blossomed in Finn's chest. She was so splendid in her rage he couldn't believe it. How in hell did he ever think he could survive without this kind of passion in his life? Grinning, he watched her decimate another cupboard; then he spoke. "Is this some kind of make-work project for your housekeeper?"

Mallory whirled, her expression fixated by shock, then she snatched up a box of crackers and threw it at him, narrowly missing his head. Finn held his position, not even moving his head as he continued to grin at her.

"You can wipe that damned smirk off your face," she yelled, picking up another box. "If you think you can just walk out of my life without so much as a word, you can go to hell."

Holding his pose, Finn continued to watch her, emotion softening his expression. "I came to thank you for the present," he said, his voice very husky.

She tried to stop crying, but she couldn't. That set her off again, and she furiously swept a stack of packaged soups off the island. "Well, I've changed my mind! I want it back!"

Straightening, Finn started sauntering toward her. His gaze fixed on her, he smiled—a soft, for-her-only smile. "Too bad, Red. You can't have it back. I'm wearing it."

Her freckles standing out on her blotchy face, she went very still, almost as if she'd been transformed. Taking a deep, shuddering breath, she looked at his neck. The top three buttons were undone, and he knew she could see the pendant. He made damned sure she could see the pendant. He smiled again. "I think we need to talk, Red," his said softly, moving closer.

Her gaze immediately riveted on his face, and she took two steps back, trying to dredge up some more temper. "Not a chance, Donovan. I have nothing to say to you."

Finn kept on moving toward her until he had her back up against the built-in ovens; then he reached out and ran his fingers across her swollen mouth. "Well, I have something to say to you."

She tried to move away, but he placed his hands on either side of her, trapping her. Looking directly into her eyes, he said what he'd come to say. "I tried to do what I thought was right for you," he said, a thousand feelings suddenly loose in his chest. "And yeah, I was going to walk away."

She stared up at him, as if transfixed by doubt. He didn't want her to have a single doubt about him. Not one. Holding her gaze, he cupped the side of her puffy face, caressing her cheek with his thumb. "But I can't walk away, Red. Not until I tell you how damned much I love you."

For an instant she didn't move, and Finn thought he'd lost the game. Then another sob was wrenched from her and she launched herself into his arms, holding on to him as if he'd just rescued her all over again. Clenching his jaw against the painful cramp in his throat, Finn closed his eyes and crushed her against him, a crazy kind of hope breaking loose inside him. Maybe there were second chances after all.

Dawn was beginning to blossom when Mallory stirred, pulling the bedding up over both of them. She snuggled deeper into his arms and repositioned her head on his shoulder; then Finn felt her trace the path of the chain around his neck. Finn smiled into the darkness and let his eyes drift shut as he tightened his hold. He spoke, his voice gruff with sleep. "If you keep this up, you're going to kill me, Red."

He felt her smile against him. "Come on. Admit it. You like it."

He rubbed his hand up her naked arm, grinning again. "Yes, I do."

Lifting up on one elbow, she looked down at him, then brushed a soft kiss against his mouth. "I love you," she whispered, and Finn clenched his jaw and roughly clasped her head against him, emotion swamping him. The words still got to him, in spite of how many times they'd been uttered throughout the night. But somehow the words never seemed to be enough when he said them to her—what he felt for her was simply too big, too eternal, too significant for just words. Easing in a deep breath, he kissed her back. "Are you still going to marry me?"

Folding her arms on his chest, she lifted her head and looked down at him, cocking one eyebrow. "Are you still asking me?"

He laughed and pulled her on top of him. "Don't give me a hard time, Red. I'm too damned exhausted for a hard time."

She grinned and kissed him again. "You're going to have to live with my money, Donovan."

He smoothed both his hands up her naked back. "I can live with your money. But I'm not taking any of the damned stuff."

"Fine. And I've decided I want a slug of kids. I hated being an only child. I never want to have just one."

He gave her an uneasy look. "How many is a slug? I thought we agreed on two or three."

Mallory pinched his shoulder, mischief dancing in her eyes. "*You* said two or three. But we'll negotiate that." She placed her hand on his jaw and gave him another long, slow kiss, then sighed and dropped her head back on his shoulder. "I want to go home," she whispered, sounding forlorn. "I want to wear your shirts and make biscuits, and I want to walk up to the tree stump and watch the northern lights."

Touched to the core by her wistful admission, Finn wrapped his arms around her and hugged her hard, his own voice gruff. "We can't go home, Red. Not until this business is finished."

"Yes, we can," she whispered. "We can throw our stuff in your truck and we can just take off." She tightened her arms around him. "I don't want to be here—let's go home, Finn."

Capturing her face, he lifted her head and looked at her, loving her so damned much he could hardly hold it all. "Is that what you really want?"

She nodded, touching his mouth. "Yes."

He stared up at her. "I won't leave without telling your father."

Sensing a win, she gave him a beguiling smile. "We can phone on our illegal cell phone when we get on the road."

Amused by her, he narrowed his eyes at her. "And there's a hell of a mess to clean up in the kitchen."

Mallory turned on all the charm, tracing small, tormenting circles around his ear. "It's all dry stuff—it'll keep. I'll leave a note for the housekeeper." She shifted on top of him, trying to get loose. "Come on." When he didn't move, she tried another angle. "I've got my driver's license and my passport, and I'll even drive."

Knowing he was eventually going to give in to her, Finn continued to watch her, trying not to smile. "You're ready to run that gauntlet of reporters camped out front?"

She grinned at him. "If we go before it gets really light, they won't even see us."

He grasped her head and gave her a firm kiss. "God, but you're a nuisance. And you're pretty damned good at getting your own way."

She let out a triumphant "Yes!" and hugged him hard. Finn hugged her back, a kind of lightness radiating through him. It was nuts. He knew it was nuts. Her father would not be pleased. And the FBI would go ballistic when they found she was gone. But he really didn't care. Mallory

O'Brien wanted to go home, and he was damned well going to take her. Like a miracle, she had turned up in his life.

But the real miracle was that she was going to stay.

*   *   *   *   *

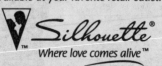

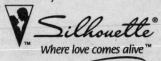